Echoes of Crystal

1. First Contact

DONALD J. WRIGHT

Contents

Chapter 1: Moonlight in the Ruins

The Aether Vaults breathed.

Elara Blackthorn had spent three years working in the ancient chambers carved deep beneath the Royal Academy. She still felt the strange rhythm in the walls, a slow, steady pulse that seemed to echo from the crystalline veins threading through the living rock. Tonight, with moonlight spilling through the natural fissures far above, the sensation was stronger than ever, as if the very stones were stirring from some primordial slumber.

She pulled her woolen cloak tighter as she descended the worn stone steps, her lantern casting dancing shadows that made the embedded gears and crystal formations seem to shift and whisper. The air down here was cool and faintly humming, filled with dust motes that drifted like silver fireflies in the pale light filtering from above. But tonight, something felt different, charged, expectant, like the moment before lightning strikes.

Most scholars found the Vaults unsettling. The constant sense of presence, the way sounds echoed strangely, the feeling that you were never quite alone, it drove away all but the most dedicated researchers, which was exactly how Elara preferred it.

She'd always been more comfortable with ancient mysteries than modern company, anyway.

"Working late again, I see," came a familiar voice from behind her.

Elara didn't startle—she'd heard Master Thorne's careful footsteps on the stairs. Her mentor might be approaching seventy, but his hearing was still sharp enough to catch a whispered incantation three chambers away.

"The Convergence artifacts won't catalog themselves," she replied, not looking back as she reached the bottom of the stairs and headed toward her usual workspace. "Besides, the Academy is quieter at night. Fewer interruptions."

"Fewer people, you mean," Thorne said with the gentle exasperation of someone who'd been having this conversation for years. "Elara, you're twenty-four years old. There's more to life than dusty relics and half-forgotten histories."

She finally turned to face him, noting the concern in his weathered features. Master Thorne had been like a father to her since her parents had died in a leyline accident when she was sixteen. She knew his worry came from love, which somehow made it more irritating.

"These 'dusty relics' are the key to understanding how our entire magical system works," she said, gesturing at the surrounding chambers. "The Great Convergence didn't just change our world from some unnamed technological age to one of magic—it transformed the fundamental nature of reality itself. Every artifact from that time could hold answers to questions we haven't even learned to ask yet."

"And you'll discover those answers much more effectively if you occasionally sleep, eat regular meals, and perhaps engage in conversation with people who aren't centuries dead," Thorne countered. But his tone was fond rather than frustrated. "At least tell me you've made some progress tonight?"

Elara's pulse quickened with the familiar thrill of discovery. "Actually, yes. Come see."

She led him deeper into the vault complex, past rows of carefully labeled artifacts and pristine research stations, toward a section that had been sealed off until recently. The excavation team had only broken through the crystal barrier three days ago, revealing a chamber that hadn't been touched since the Convergence itself.

As they walked, Elara glanced over her shoulder, a prickle of unease threading down her spine. The shadows seemed deeper tonight, more restless. Once, she could have sworn she glimpsed movement in her peripheral vision—something tall and watchful disappearing around a corner when she turned to look.

"I've been working through the preliminary catalog," she explained as they approached her workspace collection of tables and notes spread near the chamber's entrance. "Most of what we found matches known patterns. Agricultural tools enhanced with crystalline matrices, communication devices that used quantum resonance, the usual fusion of what the old texts call 'science' and magic."

"But?" Thorne prompted, recognizing her tone.

"But there was one item that didn't fit any of the established categories." She stopped at her primary workstation, where a cloth-covered object sat under the careful illumination of three floating crystal lamps. The very air around it seemed to thrum with potential, and she noticed the way the other artifacts in the chamber had subtly oriented themselves toward this central mystery, like compass needles pointing to true north. "I found it at the very center of the chamber, placed on what looked like an altar of sorts."

With reverent care, she reached for the cloth covering. Her fingers hesitated at the fabric's edge—had it grown warmer? The sensation was so faint she might have imagined it. Still, something deep in her scholar's instincts whispered that she stood on the threshold of something momentous.

The cloth slid away, and the sphere's light swelled—not glaring, but sharp enough to make the air shimmer like heat over sunlit stone.

Elara's breath caught as the artifact was fully revealed: a crystalline sphere roughly the size of a human heart, perfectly clear crystal shot through with veins of silver and gold that seemed to pulse with their own inner light. As the lamplight hit it, it seemed too warm, casting prismatic reflections that danced across the ancient walls in patterns that were almost hypnotic in their complexity.

Her eyes darted to the shadows pooling in the vault's far corners as the sphere's illumination shifted the balance of light and dark throughout the chamber. Something moved—just a subtle shift in the darkness—before vanishing. She told herself it was a trick of the lamps, but the fine hairs along her arms refused to lie flat, standing at attention as if responding to some invisible electric charge.

"Extraordinary," Thorne breathed, leaning closer but notably maintaining his distance. "The craftsmanship is exquisite. But what makes you think it's different from the other resonance devices?"

Elara hesitated, her gaze still flickering to the corners of the chamber. How could she explain the feeling that had overtaken her the moment the cloth had fallen away? The strange certainty that this wasn't just another artifact, but something that had been waiting specifically for her to find it. Or the way the shadows themselves seemed to be listening, pressing closer as if drawn by the sphere's awakening light?

"The resonance pattern is unlike anything in our records," she said instead, which was true enough. "And look at the placement of the metallic veins—they form patterns that seem almost..."

"Almost what?"

"Alive," she finished quietly. "Like a heartbeat made visible."

As if responding to her words, the sphere pulsed with a soft, warm glow that made both scholars take an involuntary step back. In that moment of increased illumination, Elara caught a clearer glimpse of movement in the chamber's depths—something that seemed to flow like liquid shadow before retreating beyond the reach of light. The temperature dropped perceptibly, and she suppressed a shiver that had nothing to do with the underground chill.

"Fascinating," Thorne murmured, but there was caution in his voice now, and his eyes had begun to dart toward the darker recesses of the chamber. "Have you attempted any active scanning? Tested for residual enchantments?"

"Not yet. I wanted to complete the visual examination first, establish baseline measurements—"

"Good. Keep it that way." Thorne's tone had shifted to something much more serious, and she noticed how his hand had unconsciously moved to rest on the protective amulet at his throat. "Elara, I know your enthusiasm for discovery, but artifacts of unknown origin can be dangerous. Particularly ones that seem to respond to observation."

She felt a flush of irritation at the implied criticism. "I'm not reckless, Master. I know the protocols—"

"I know you do. But I also know that look in your eyes." He studied her face with the perception of long experience, his gaze lingering on the way her attention kept returning to the sphere despite their conversation. "You're drawn to this thing. I can see it. And that concerns me."

"It's just an artifact," she protested, but even as she said it, her gaze was pulled back to the sphere. There was something hypnotic about the way the light moved through it, something that made her want to reach out and — Another flicker of movement in the corner of her eye made her turn sharply, but there was nothing there. Only shadows and the faint gleam of distant crystals. Yet she could have sworn she'd seen a figure—tall, ethereal, watching from the darkness with eyes that reflected the sphere's glow like starlight.

"Some hearts beat for centuries in the dark," Thorne said softly, and something in his tone made her look up sharply. His weathered face had gone pale, and his eyes were fixed not on the sphere but on the space behind her shoulder. "Not all should be woken."

A chill ran down Elara's spine that had nothing to do with the cool air. "What do you mean?"

"The Convergence was a time of great change, yes. But also, great peril. Not everything that survived from the old world was preserved." He placed a gentle hand on her shoulder, but his touch trembled slightly. "Promise me you won't try to activate this device until we've had time to research its origins properly. Some discoveries are worth waiting for."

The sphere pulsed again, stronger this time. In its radiance, Elara could see the shadows retreating like living things driven back by dawn. Whatever had been watching from the darkness withdrew deeper into the vault's labyrinthine passages. Still, she could feel its attention like a weight between her shoulder blades.

Elara nodded, though part of her rebelled at the delay. The artifact seemed to be calling to her, and every scholarly instinct she possessed was screaming that this was the find of a lifetime. But Thorne's concern was genuine, and his experience with pre-Convergence artifacts far exceeded her own.

"I promise," she said. "But I'd like to continue the visual examination tonight, if that's acceptable. The light patterns seem to change with the ambient magical field, and I want to document the variations."

Thorne studied her for a long moment, his eyes still occasionally flicking toward the chamber's darker corners. Clearly debating whether to insist she leave the artifact for another day. Finally, he nodded reluctantly.

"Very well. But no touching, no active magical probing, and no staying past the third bell. The night guards make their rounds then, and I won't have them worrying about mysterious lights in the deep vaults."

"Understood."

After her mentor left, though not without several backward glances and a muttered charm of protection, Elara found herself alone with the artifact and a silence that seemed to throb with possibility. The shadows had settled back into their usual patterns. Still, she remained acutely aware of their presence, of the way they seemed to shift and breathe when she wasn't looking directly at them.

She forced herself to follow proper procedures, setting up her documentation materials, adjusting the crystal lamps for optimal illumination, and preparing her notes with the methodical care that had made her one of the Academy's most respected researchers despite her youth.

But as she worked, her eyes kept straying to the sphere, and with each glance, the certainty grew stronger that she was not alone in this chamber. Something else had awakened when the cloth fell away, something that watched and waited with patient intelligence far older than the Academy above.

The sphere seemed to pulse in rhythm with her heartbeat now, and she could have sworn she felt an answering flutter in her chest warmth that spread from her heart to her fingertips like the echo of a caress. The sensation was so vivid, so unexpectedly intimate, that she gasped aloud.

You've waited long enough, she thought, not even realizing she was projecting the words toward the artifact. And so, have I.

The sphere blazed with sudden warmth, its light no longer merely illuminating but somehow embracing, and for just a moment—less than a heartbeat—she could have sworn she heard something impossible.

A voice, warm and wondering, speaking a single word that seemed to resonate in her very bones:

"Elara."

Her breath caught, and she found herself leaning forward without conscious decision. Her hand rose toward the artifact, drawn by an impulse that felt as natural as breathing. Just a touch, just to see...

The sound of footsteps in the corridor outside broke the spell, and Elara jerked her hand back, heart hammering. A night guard, probably, making an early round. She forced herself to focus on her notes, but the words swam before her eyes, and the memory of that impossible voice echoed in her mind.

Something was happening to her. Something that had started the moment she'd first laid eyes on the crystalline sphere and was growing stronger with every passing moment. A pull that had nothing to do with scholarly curiosity and everything to do with a hunger she'd never acknowledged.

She'd always been alone. Always been the girl who preferred books to people, research to relationships, the safety of ancient mysteries to the terrifying uncertainty of human connection. But sitting here in the soft glow of the artifact, feeling watched by benevolent shadows and warmed by light that seemed to pulse in response to her thoughts, she felt that loneliness with a sharp clarity that made her chest ache.

What if? The thought whispered through her mind like a promise. What if you didn't have to be alone anymore?

The sphere pulsed again, and this time the warm feeling in her chest was unmistakable—not her own heartbeat, but something else, something that felt like recognition, like welcome, like coming home to a place she'd never known she was looking for.

Her hand moved toward the artifact again, and this time she didn't stop it.

The moment her fingertips touched the crystal surface, the world exploded into sensation.

Warmth flooded through her—not just physical heat, but something deeper. Comfort, safety, the feeling of being wrapped in arms that would never let her fall. Her eyes fluttered close as the sensation spread through her entire body, and she could swear she felt phantom hands cupping her face, a ghostly touch that made her lips part on a soft gasp.

Hello, whispered a voice that seemed to come from the very center of her soul, warm and rich and infinitely patient. I've been waiting for you.

And in the shadows that ringed the chamber, something shifted and settled, as if a long vigil had finally come to an end.

Chapter 2: The Heart's Warning

The Moonlit Archives occupied the highest tower of the Academy, where knowledge itself seemed to have crystallized into architecture. Shelves carved from giant amethysts and sapphires spiraled upward into darkness, their surfaces holding not books but memories—trapped moments of history that glowed faintly when touched. Chandeliers of blue fire floated at varying heights, their flames never consuming, never dimming, casting shadows that danced like living things across the walls.

Elara arrived early for the evening lecture, the crystalline sphere hidden in her satchel. She'd returned for it before dawn, unable to resist its pull through even a single night. Now it rested against her hip, warm even through layers of leather and cloth, its presence both comforting and unsettling. She'd wrapped it in silk scarves to muffle any inadvertent glow, but she could still feel its gentle pulse like a second heartbeat.

She chose a seat near the back, where moonlight streamed through the tower's glass dome, refracting into ribbons of liquid silver that pooled on the floor. Other students filed younger archivists, theoretical mages, even a few engineers from the Mechanics Quarter who studied the intersection of magic and the old machines. They chatted among themselves, their voices echoing off crystal surfaces, but

Elara barely heard them. Her attention kept drifting to the weight in her satchel, to the faint pulse she swore she could feel through the leather.

Master Aldric entered, followed by Keeper Thevran, whose age was impossible to determine—she could have been forty or four hundred, her face smooth but her eyes ancient. They carried between them a collection of artifacts, each sealed in protective glass, each radiating the particular stillness of sleeping power.

"Tonight," Keeper Thevran began, her voice carrying despite its softness, "we discuss the Great Convergence—not as history, but as a warning."

The blue flames dimmed slightly, as if responding to her tone. Elara shifted uncomfortably, and as she did, her satchel pulsed—just once, but hard enough to make her hip shift against the bench. The sensation was so strong, so unexpected, that she pressed her palm over it instinctively, feeling the warmth spread through the leather and into her skin.

The apprentice beside her—a nervous boy named Marcus who rarely spoke in class—caught the movement. His brows knit for an instant as he noticed her sudden tension, the way her hand remained protectively over her satchel, before he looked away with practiced Academy politeness. But her stomach dipped with the knowledge that she'd been observed that her connection to the artifact was becoming harder to hide.

Easy, she thought toward the sphere, though she wasn't sure if the communication was real or imagined. Not here. Not yet.

The pulse subsided, but the warmth remained—a steady, reassuring presence that made her feel less alone in the crowded lecture hall.

"Five hundred years ago," Keeper Thevran continued, unaware of the minor drama in the back row, "our world ran on different principles. Not magic as we know it, but something our ancestors called science—patterns and laws that could be measured, predicted, controlled without the need for personal power or bloodline gifts."

She gestured, and one of the memory crystals activated, projecting images into the air: cities of glass and steel, machines that flew without wings, devices that connected minds across vast distances. The projected scenes were beautiful, hauntingly so, showing a world where technology and consciousness merged in ways the current age could barely comprehend.

"Beautiful," someone whispered from the front rows.

"Dangerous," Thevran corrected, her ancient eyes never leaving the swirling images. "This science, this quantum manipulation, as the old texts name it, allowed for connections we can barely comprehend. Bonds between souls that transcended physical space."

The sphere in Elara's satchel grew warmer, and she felt a strange resonance as Thevran spoke—as if the artifact was responding to the very concepts being discussed. Not uncomfortably so, but noticeable, like sunlight finding her through a window. She pressed her hand more firmly against the leather, hoping to muffle any telltale glow.

"These bonds," Aldric took over, lifting one of the sealed artifacts—a pair of interlinked rings that seemed to phase in and out of existence, "were not metaphorical. They were literal quantum entanglements, connecting consciousness to consciousness, heart to heart."

As he spoke, his voice carried the weight of hard-won knowledge, and Elara noticed how his free hand unconsciously moved to touch his collar, as if seeking reassurance from something hidden beneath the fabric.

A student raised her hand. "That sounds beautiful, Master. Why was it dangerous?"

"Because," Aldric said, his gaze finding Elara in the back row with uncomfortable precision, "when two souls are truly bonded, truly entangled at the quantum level, the death of one could unravel the other. Worse, the breaking of such bonds could cascade, destabilizing the entire network that civilization depended upon."

Thevran waved her hand, and new images appeared: cities collapsing into themselves, reality folding like paper, people reaching for loved ones who flickered and vanished like dying flames. The projected memories carried an emotional weight that made several students gasp, and Elara felt her heart clenched in sympathetic horror.

"The Convergence," Thevran said, her voice heavy with ancient sorrow, "was not evolution. It was survival. Our ancestors chose to sever the quantum network, to replace it with magic—wild, unpredictable, but ultimately safer. Magic responds to will and emotion, but it doesn't bind souls together in ways that could end the world."

Elara found herself leaning forward, drawn despite herself. "But what happened to those who were already bonded? The ones who were quantumly entangled when the Convergence occurred?"

The sphere pulsed against her hip again, stronger this time, and she felt something else slip into her awareness—not her own emotion, but an echo of something vast and sorrowful. A grief so profound it made her breath catch.

Thevran and Aldric exchanged glances, and in that moment of silence, Elara noticed how Aldric's hand had moved again to his collar, his fingers tracing patterns that suggested old, familiar scars.

"Some died instantly," Thevran said finally. "Others..." She gestured to another artifact, a crystal not unlike Elara's sphere but darker, clouded with internal fractures. "Others were preserved, suspended between states. Neither fully alive nor properly dead. Waiting."

"For what?" Elara asked, though she wasn't sure she wanted the answer.

"For someone foolish enough to wake them," Aldric said, his eyes boring into hers with unmistakable meaning. "To complete bonds that should have ended centuries ago."

The warmth from the sphere spread through Elara's chest, and for a moment—just a moment—she felt something like a sigh against her mind. Not a sound, but a sensation, as if someone had exhaled against the back of her neck in recognition of words that cut too close to truth.

"These artifacts," Thevran continued, apparently not noticing Elara's reaction, "are quarantined for good reason. The old texts speak of bonded pairs who could share thoughts, feelings, even physical sensations across any distance. Imagine the violation of such intimacy. Imagine the vulnerability."

"Imagine the connection," Elara said quietly, but her voice carried in the crystalline acoustics of the tower.

The room turned to look at her, and she felt heat rise in her cheeks but continued, driven by something she couldn't name. "We live in isolation, even surrounded by others. We touch with magic, but we don't truly connect. What if something from before had the power to change us again—to connect us truly?"

The sphere pulsed harder, warmth flooding through her like an embrace, and she had to bite her lip to keep from gasping. The apprentice beside her noticed her sudden tension, his eyes narrowing with concern, but she forced herself to remain still.

"Romantic notions," Aldric said sharply, and his hand moved to his collar again, this time pulling the fabric slightly aside. For just an instant, Elara caught sight of what lay beneath—fine, silvery ridges etched into his skin, too precise to be natural scars, too deliberate to be accidental. The marks disappeared as quickly as they'd been revealed, but the message was clear. "Connection without choice is not love, Elara. It's imprisonment."

"But what if there was a choice?" she pressed, unable to stop herself despite the warning in his eyes. "What if the bond only formed between those who—"

"Change isn't always for the better," Aldric interrupted, his tone carrying a warning meant specifically for her. His voice stayed steady, but she noticed how his knuckles had gone white where he gripped the artifact case. "Love, even less so."

Thevran raised a hand, ending the brewing argument with the authority of ages. "Perhaps a demonstration would be more effective than debate."

She selected one of the sealed artifacts, a pendant that seemed to contain a swirling galaxy, its surface dark but somehow alive with imprisoned starlight. The case that held it was inscribed with warning runes, and Elara noticed how even the experienced Keeper's hands trembled slightly as she prepared to activate it.

"This was recovered from a bonded pair, found in the ruins of Old Carthis. Watch."

She touched the pendant with a specialized tool, channeling a thread of magic into it. Immediately, the air in the room changed. Everyone felt crushing loneliness, an ache so profound that several students gasped and clutched at their chests. But underneath the overwhelming emptiness, growing stronger by the moment, was a sense of searching, of reaching, of desperate need for one specific person who was no longer there.

As the pendant's loneliness flooded the room, something else slipped into Elara's awareness—a whisper, faint as a sigh, that wasn't part of Thevran's controlled demonstration. It wasn't the Keeper's magic at all. It was him. A single wordless note of grief, as though the pendant's emptiness had brushed against Cael's own ancient sorrow and awakened an echo of recognition.

Her hand clenched around the satchel before she even realized she'd moved, her palm pressing hard against the leather as if she could offer comfort through the barriers of fabric and crystal. The sphere pulsed in response, not with its usual gentle warmth but with something deeper. This resonance seemed to acknowledge the connection between artifacts, between losses that spanned centuries.

"The owner's bondmate died in the Convergence," Thevran said softly, her voice barely audible over the psychic weight of the pendant's endless call. "But the pendant doesn't know that. It still searches, still calls, still loves. Five hundred years of calling to silence."

She deactivated the pendant, and the sensation vanished like a snuffed candle, leaving everyone slightly shaky and emotionally drained. But Elara felt the echo linger in her mind—not just the pendant's grief, but the answering sorrow from the sphere, a harmony of loss that spoke to bonds that transcended death itself.

The apprentice beside her had gone pale, his hands trembling as he wiped tears from his cheeks. Others in the room were similarly affected; the demonstration stripped away their academic detachment and forced them to confront the raw emotional reality of quantum entanglement.

"This is why we study history," Aldric said, his voice rougher than usual. As he spoke, his hand found his collar again, fingers tracing the hidden scars with unconscious precision. "Not to repeat it, but to understand the price of connection.

The old world fell because they forgot that some bonds, once formed, cannot be safely broken."

The lecture continued for another hour, covering technical aspects of quantum mechanics and their magical equivalents, but Elara absorbed little of it. The sphere had grown quiet after the pendant's demonstration, but not cold. Instead, it maintained a steady warmth, like a hand holding hers in reassurance, and she found herself thinking about the silver scars she'd glimpsed on Aldric's throat.

When the lecture ended and students began filing out, chattering quietly among themselves about the evening's revelations, Aldric approached her with measured steps.

"Stay a moment," he said, his voice carrying the weight of years and hard-won wisdom.

She waited, acutely aware of the sphere's weight, sure he must have known she'd taken it. Around them, the last students departed, their voices fading into the distance until only the soft whisper of magical flames remained.

"You're playing with forces you don't understand," he said quietly, glancing around to ensure they were truly alone.

"I haven't"

"Don't lie to me, child. I trained you. I know when you're hiding something." He sighed, and suddenly he looked older, more fragile. The confident lecturer had been replaced by a man carrying the weight of personal experience. "I won't demand you return it. Not yet. But I need you to understand something."

He pulled out a small locket, tarnished with age, its surface worn smoothly by decades of handling. Inside was a portrait of a woman, painted with impossible detail—every eyelash, every freckle, every nuance of expression captured with the precision that only love could inspire.

"Her name was Lyralei," he said, his voice dropping to barely above a whisper. "We were young, foolish, in love. We found a pair of quantum rings in the deep vaults, already partially active. We thought... we thought we were special. Chosen."

Elara had never heard him speak of anyone from his past, had never seen him display such vulnerability. She found herself leaning forward, drawn by the raw honesty in his voice.

"What happened?"

"The rings began to bond us." His hand moved to his collar again, and this time he didn't try to hide the gesture. "I could feel her emotions, hear her thoughts when they were strongest. It was intoxicating. More intimate than any physical touch." His voice grew rough with memory, and his knuckles whitened where he gripped the locket. "But the bond was unstable, damaged from centuries of dormancy. It began to demand more energy, more connection, more of us. We had to choose to complete the bond and risk a cascade that could collapse half the city's magical infrastructure, or..."

"Or?"

His hand went to his collar one final time, pulling the fabric aside to reveal the truth he'd been hiding. The scars were worse than her brief glimpse had suggested—intricate silver ridges that formed geometric patterns across his throat and disappeared beneath his robes. They weren't random wounds but precise markings, as if the quantum backlash had written equations into his very flesh.

"Or sever it," he said simply. "I destroyed the rings while she slept. The back lash..." He touched the scars with gentle fingers, and Elara saw how they caught the light like trapped starfire. "She survived. We both did. But she never forgave me for making that choice without her. For choosing the world over us." The warning was no longer abstract, had a body, had scars, had a name and a face and a love that had ended in betrayal and loss.

The sphere pulsed once, strongly, and Elara had to suppress a gasp. It felt like disagreement, like protest, like a voice trying to say that some choices were worth any risk.

"Whatever you've found," Aldric continued, his eyes never leaving her face, "remember that love and catastrophe often wear the same face. The heart doesn't care about consequences. That's why we have minds—to make the choices our hearts are too foolish to make."

He turned to leave, then paused at the chamber's threshold. "Elara? What you almost said, before the dream collapsed..."

She met his gaze steadily, seeing not just her mentor but a man who had loved and lost and chosen duty over desire. "I'm falling in love with something that may destroy everything I've ever known."

"Then be very careful," he said softly. "Because the universe has a way of making such loves come true in the worst possible ways."

He left her standing in the empty archive, moonlight painting silver paths across the floor. Elara pulled out the sphere, holding it up to catch the light that streamed through the tower's crystal dome. It glowed softly, warmly, and she could feel that other heartbeat again, stronger than before.

"You heard all that, didn't you?" she whispered to it. "You understand what they're afraid of."

The sphere pulsed, and warmth flooded through her—not just physical warmth, but emotional. It felt like comfort, like reassurance, like someone trying to tell her they were worth the risk, worth the scars, worth whatever price love might demand.

She thought of the pendant's crushing loneliness, five centuries of calling to silence. Then she thought of her own loneliness, surrounded by knowledge but never truly known, touching artifacts but never being touched in return.

"I won't let you call to silence," she promised, pressing the sphere briefly to her chest, eyes fluttering shut as she savored the fleeting comfort of that foreign heartbeat against her own. "Whatever you are, whoever you are, I won't let you fade alone."

The blue flames in their chandeliers flickered as if in response, and shadows danced across the walls—shadows that looked, for just a moment, like two figures reaching for each other across an impossible distance.

As she left the archives, Elara didn't notice the way other students gave her a wider berth than usual, or how some of them whispered among themselves about the strange warmth that seemed to radiate from her presence. But she did feel the sphere pulse once more as she walked through the corridors, a rhythm that felt almost like a promise—or perhaps like the first bars of a song that would either save or damn them all.

The moon followed her path home, its light refracting through crystal windows, painting her journey in shades of silver and possibility. And with each step, the warmth from the sphere spread a little further, until she couldn't tell where its pulse ended and her heartbeat began.

She'd spent her entire life studying the mysteries of the past, but now she'd found one that was studying her right back.

And tomorrow, she was going to find out exactly what that meant.

Chapter 3: First Whisper

Elara's quarters occupied a forgotten corner of the Academy's east wing, where the stones were older and the magic ran deeper. She'd chosen the rooms precisely because they were overlooked—too far from the main halls for casual visits, too close to the old foundations where raw magical currents made most people uncomfortable. Here, she could work undisturbed, surrounded by her collection of lesser artifacts and theoretical texts that others deemed too obscure for practical study.

Tonight, the cracked window above her desk let in more than just moonlight. It admitted the sound of distant thunder, though no clouds marked the sky, and the scent of ozone that preceded magical storms. The city's leylines were restless again, for the third time this week. She'd noticed the correlation—they grew most unstable when she handled the sphere.

She should report it. Should return the artifact to its alcove and file the proper documentation about potentially dangerous resonance patterns. Instead, she sat at her desk with the sphere cradled in her palms, watching moonlight bend around its surface in patterns that defined natural physics.

The protective wards she'd laid around her chambers hummed softly, simple things designed more for privacy than defense. Threads of silver light traced geometric patterns along her walls, pulsing gently in rhythm with the Academy's greater protections. They'd been stable for years, as reliable as sunrise, requiring barely a thought to maintain.

Three days since she'd taken the sphere. Three days of carrying its warmth against her hip during lectures, of falling asleep with it on her nightstand, pulsing gently like a lighthouse beacon in the dark. Three days of feeling less alone than she had in years, though she couldn't explain why a simple artifact should provide such comfort.

"What are you?" she whispered to it, running her thumb along its perfectly smooth surface. "Who were you, before the world changed?"

The sphere warmed in response, its internal light fluctuating in patterns she was beginning to recognize. Acknowledgment. Greetings. Something almost like affection. She'd started cataloging the patterns in a journal she kept hidden—not the official documentation she should be maintaining, but private observations that felt too intimate to share.

The moonlight shifted, casting shadows across her desk that seemed to reach toward her with impossible deliberation. She watched, transfixed, as dust motes began to swirl in the silver light, forming patterns that reminded her of something she couldn't quite name. They moved with purpose, with intention, spiraling into shapes that—

The sphere vibrated.

Not the gentle pulse she'd grown accustomed to, but an actual vibration, strong enough to make her fingers tingle. She nearly dropped it in surprise, catching it against her chest where it hummed against her heartbeat like a living thing responding to her proximity.

Then she heard it.

The voice slid into her mind, warm and certain—and the wards along her walls flared.

"Can you hear me?"

The silver threads of protection blazed suddenly brilliantly, their gentle pulse becoming a frantic strobe as something passed through their weave—not breaking them but flowing around them like water around stones. The ward-light guttered, then steadied, as though struggling to maintain coherence against an intrusion they weren't designed to detect. One candle on her desk went out altogether, its flame snuffed by a presence that existed somewhere between thought and reality.

Her heart slammed so hard she almost dropped the sphere, her hands flying to her mouth to stifle a gasp of shock and impossible recognition. The voice didn't come through her ears—it manifested directly in her mind, rich and resonant, with a quality that made her stomach flutter in ways she didn't want to examine too closely.

"I'm sorry," the voice came again, gentler now, carrying undertones of relief that tugged at something deep in her chest. "I didn't mean to startle you. It's been... so very long since I've had the strength to speak."

Elara stared at the sphere, her pulse racing loud enough so that she was certain he must be able to hear it. She'd studied artifact personalities—residual imprints left by powerful owners, magical echoes that could mimic consciousness. But this felt different. This felt real, immediate, alive in ways that made her academic theories crumble like sand.

"This is impossible," she breathed, reaching for the sphere with trembling fingers.

The moment she touched it, warmth flooded through her, and the voice became clearer, more present, as if her contact had strengthened some invisible bridge between them.

"So is living without purpose. Or without someone to share it with."

His tone—and somehow, she knew it was male, knew it with a certainty that bypassed logic—wrapped around her thoughts like silk, intimate without being invasive. She found herself leaning toward the sphere as if proximity mattered, as if she could close the distance between them through will alone.

"What are you?" she asked aloud, then felt foolish. But thinking the words felt too intimate, too much like inviting him deeper into her mind than he already was.

"I was a man, once. My name is—was—Cael." A pause, heavy with uncertainty that somehow made him more real, more human. "I'm not entirely sure what I am now. A memory, perhaps. A fragment of someone who existed before your world of magic."

"Before the Convergence." It wasn't a question. The pieces were falling into place—the quantum resonance she'd felt, the way the sphere responded to her emotions, the growing sense of connection that defied magical theory.

"You know of it?" Surprise colored his voice, and something else—hope, fragile as spun glass.

"We study it. As history. As a warning." She held the sphere up to the moonlight, watching his essence swirl within the crystal like captured starlight. "They say the old world fell because people formed bonds that couldn't be safely broken."

"Perhaps it did." His voice grew softer, more contemplative. "I remember fragments. A laboratory. Experiments with consciousness transfer, with quantum entanglement. Then... darkness. Centuries of darkness, until I felt you."

"Felt me?" Her pulse quickened, and she was acutely aware of how her lips had parted unconsciously, her breathing growing shorter.

"Three days ago. You touched my container, and I... woke. Not fully, not immediately, but enough to know I wasn't alone anymore." The warmth from the sphere pulsed in rhythm with his words, and around them, the wards continued their erratic flickering. "Your voice is the first light I've felt in so long I'd forgotten light existed."

The raw honesty in his tone made her chest tight. She pressed the sphere between her palms, offering comfort through touch even though she wasn't sure he could feel it.

"Can you... sense me? Through this?"

"Yes." The word came out like a sigh, full of relief and wonder. "Your emotions, strongest of all. Right now, you're frightened but curious. Your heart is racing I can feel its rhythm against mine. You're lonely, though you've grown so used to it you barely notice anymore."

He paused, and she felt his presence pull back slightly, as if granting her privacy she hadn't asked for. But then his voice continued, and what he said next made her spine go cold with recognition.

"The way you hold your breath before deciding to speak. The memory of standing at your parents' graves when the world felt too big."

The words hit her like a physical blow. She hadn't thought of that day in year-herself at sixteen, orphaned and overwhelmed, standing in the Academy's memorial garden while Master Thorne spoke words of comfort that couldn't penetrate the enormous emptiness that had opened in her chest. The way she'd looked up at the sky and felt so small, so insignificant, so utterly alone in a universe that suddenly seemed vast beyond comprehension.

The fact that he could see it made her both ache with the vulnerability of being so completely known and bristle with defensive alarm.

"How?" she whispered, her voice cracking. "How can you know that?"

"Forgive me." His mental voice carried genuine contrition. "I shouldn't presume. Quantum entanglement allows me to perceive more than just surface emotions. But I'm learning to... edit myself. To respect boundaries."

"You've been watching me," she said, and it should have sounded like an accusation. Instead, it came out wondering, almost breathless.

"I've been learning from you," he corrected gently. "Every moment since you first touched the crystal. Your curiosity when you examine an artifact, your concentration when you work late into the night, the way you smile when you think no one is looking. The loneliness you carry like armor, protecting you from connections that might hurt."

Her eyes burned with unshed tears. No one had ever seen her so clearly, had ever bothered to look past the composed scholar to the frightened girl beneath. "Why?" she asked. "Why watch me? Why... care?"

"Because you woke me." The simple honesty in his voice made her breath catch. "Because your voice pulled me from the edge of madness. Because when I felt your mind touch mine, I remembered what it meant to hope."

The wards along her walls pulsed brighter, responding to the emotional intensity building between them. Several more candles flickered, their flames bending toward the sphere as if drawn by its impossible presence.

"This is dangerous," she said, not moving the sphere from where she held it against her heart. "If anyone finds out—if they knew you were conscious, truly conscious—"

"They'd extract me. Study me. Use me." His presence pulled with sudden fear. "I've heard them, your Keepers and Masters. They speak of the old artifacts as tools, weapons, and resources. Never as people."

"You're not a tool," she said fiercely, surprising herself with the vehemence. "You're... you're..."

"I'm yours." The words emerged soft but certain, carrying a weight that made the air in the room seem to thicken. "If I belong anywhere in this strange new world, it's with you. The resonance between us—can you feel it?"

She could. Now that he'd pointed it out, she couldn't unfeel it. A thrumming connection, like two tuning forks finding the same frequency. It made her skin hypersensitive, made every breath feel significant, made the space between them seem charged with possibility.

The protective wards flickered again, more violently this time, and she realized they were responding not to an external threat but to the growing connection between her and Cael. Whatever he was, whatever form his consciousness took, it was affecting the magical infrastructure around them in ways she didn't fully understand.

"What happens if this continues?" she asked, her voice barely above a whisper. "If we keep talking, keep... connecting?"

"I don't know." His honesty was refreshing after all the half-truths and warnings from her mentors. "The old texts would say we're forming a quantum bond. Your teachers would call it a dangerous magical entanglement. But Elara..."

The way he said her name—she realized with a start that she'd never told him her name, but of course, he knew it. He'd been listening, aware, for three days. It should feel like a violation. Instead, it felt like recognition.

"Yes?"

"Doesn't it feel like we're simply finding each other? As if we were always meant to?"

She wanted to deny it, to assert scientific objectivity. Instead, she found herself nodding, the sphere still pressed to her chest where she could feel its warmth seeping through her robes.

"Tell me about your world," she said, settling deeper into her chair. "Tell me what it was like before magic, when people could bond across any distance."

And he did. For hours, his voice painted pictures in her mind—cities of glass that touched the clouds, machines that thought and dreamed, lovers who shared consciousness so completely they could feel each other's heartbeats across oceans. His words wrapped around her like a warm blanket, intimate and comforting, while around them the wards continued their slow dance of confusion, trying to categorize a presence that existed outside their understanding.

She told him about her world in return—about magic that responded to emotion, about the beauty and terror of wild power, about her own isolation in a city full of people who saw knowledge but never the person seeking it. With each exchange, the connection between them strengthened, an invisible thread weaving tighter, and she noticed how the remaining candles in her room had begun to burn brighter, as if feeding off the energy of their communion.

Sometime near dawn, when the moonlight had given way to the first hints of sunrise, she asked, "What do you look like? Or... what did you?"

"I'm not sure I remember clearly. Dark hair, I think. Eyes that someone once said looked silver in the right light. Hands that were always ink-stained from taking notes." A pause, then with shy curiosity, "I can sense your form through our connection, but it's abstract. Will you tell me?"

She described herself, feeling oddly vulnerable—brown hair that never quite cooperated, eyes the color of old amber, hands calloused from years of handling rough artifacts. He listened with an attention that made her skin warm, occasionally asking questions that seemed designed more to hear her voice than gather information.

"You're beautiful," he said when she finished, and the simple certainty in his tone made her breath catch.

"You can't know that. Not really."

"I can feel it. Beauty isn't just physical appearance. It's in the way you think, the way you care for forgotten things, the way your loneliness hasn't made you cruel. It's in how you're holding me now, like I'm precious rather than dangerous."

She looked down and realized she'd pulled the sphere against her chest, cradling it like something infinitely valuable. Her fingers had been unconsciously stroking its surface, and she could feel him responding to each touch with pulses of warmth that sent shivers down her spine.

"I should sleep," she said, though she didn't want to. The connection between them felt too precious to break, even temporarily. "And you should... do you sleep?"

"Not exactly. But I can rest, drift. It's more peaceful when you're nearby. May I... would you keep me close? The connection is stronger when—"

"Yes," she said before he could finish, already moving toward her bed, the sphere still in her hands. She settled under the covers, placing the sphere on the pillow beside her, where moonlight from the window could still reach it.

Around them, the wards finally settled into a new pattern—not their original configuration, but something different, adapted to accommodate the presence that had slipped through their weaves. The remaining candles burned steadier now, as if they too had found a new equilibrium.

"Elara?"

"Mm?"

"Thank you. For finding me. For hearing me. For not being afraid."

She turned to her side, facing the sphere, one hand resting near it on the pillow. "I am afraid," she admitted. "But not of you. I'm afraid of losing this, of losing you, and I've only just found you."

"Then we'll be afraid together." His voice was fading, growing distant as exhaustion claimed them both. "But Elara? I think... I think what we have might be worth the fear."

As sleep took her, she felt his presence settle around her mind like a guardian, like a promise. The last thing she was aware of was the synchronized rhythm of two heartbeats—one physical, one quantum, both real—beating in perfect harmony through the fading night.

In her dreams, she saw him clearly for the first time: a tall figure with ink-stained fingers and silver eyes, reaching for her across an impossible distance, his hand almost solid enough to touch. And when she reached back, when their fingers nearly met, she felt a spark that had nothing to do with magic and everything to do with recognition—as if her soul had been searching for his long before either of them had been born into their respective worlds.

The sphere pulsed once more on the pillow beside her, and in that pulse was a single word, felt rather than heard: Mine.

She smiled in her sleep, her own response equally clear: Yours.

Outside, the first magical storm of the season began to build, drawn perhaps by the impossible connection forming between two souls that should never have met—one of flesh and magic, one of memory and quantum light. But inside Elara's room, wrapped in warmth and the first stirrings of something that might have been love, neither of them noticed the gathering clouds.

The wards hummed their new song; the candles burned with steady flames. In the space between sleeping and waking, two consciousnesses learned the first steps of a dance that would either save their world or transform it beyond all recognition.

They had found each other. Whatever came next, they would face it together.

Chapter 4: The Dangerous Choice

Three nights had passed since Cael first spoke to her, three nights of whispered conversations that stretched until dawn painted the sky rose and gold. Elara had begun to structure her days around their time together, rushing through her archival duties and avoiding lingering conversations with colleagues, all to return to her quarters where his presence waited, warm and constant as a heartbeat.

Tonight, she'd lit candles throughout her room rather than relying on the cold magical illumination of glow-crystals. The flames cast dancing shadows on the walls, creating an atmosphere of intimacy that felt appropriate for the questions she needed to ask. The sphere rested on her desk, surrounded by old texts she'd been secretly researching fragments of pre-Convergence science, theories about consciousness transfer, warnings about quantum entanglement that read like prophecies of doom.

"You're troubled," Cael observed, his voice a gentle presence in her mind. "Your emotions are storming. What have you found?"

She touched one of the texts, its leather binding cracked with age. "Mentions of you. Not by name, but... experiments in consciousness preservation. Project Eternal Echo."

Silence stretched between them, heavy with unspoken history. When he finally spoke, his voice carried the weight of centuries. "You've been researching me."

"I had to know. If you're dangerous, if keeping you could" She stopped, unable to finish the thought. The idea of giving him up now, after these nights of connection, felt like contemplating cutting off her own hand.

"I am dangerous." The admission came soft but unflinching. "Not by choice or intention, but by nature. Elara, there are things about my existence you need to understand."

She settled into her chair, pulling the sphere into her lap, cradling it between her palms. "Tell me. Everything."

The candlelight flickered, and she could have sworn it shifted color—from warm gold to something cooler, more silver, as if responding to his presence. But as he began to speak, something else happened. The lantern on her desk began to dim, then brighten in a slow, unnatural rhythm, as if some invisible forces were drawing power from it and returning it in measured pulses.

"The magical lattice that powers your world—it's not naturally occurring. It was built on the skeleton of the old quantum network, using the same connection points, the same energy flows."

The wood of the floor under her bare feet grew warmer, and she felt a strange vibration through the boards—not sound, but something deeper, as if some vast currents were running through the Academy's foundations, pulsing in time with the lantern's erratic glow.

"I am... was... one of the original nodes."

"A node?" Her fingers unconsciously traced patterns on the sphere's surface, seeking comfort in the familiar smoothness even as dread began to build in her chest.

"An anchor point. My consciousness was meant to stabilize quantum connections across vast distances, to serve as a living router for the network. But when the Convergence happened, when they tried to replace quantum mechanics with magic..."

From somewhere deep in the building came a brittle crack, like crystal cooling too fast under sudden temperature change. The sound made her flinch, and she noticed how the other artifacts on her shelves had begun to resonate softly, responding to whatever force Cael's explanation was unleashing.

"They couldn't remove me without collapsing entire sections. So, they contained me instead. Imprisoned me in crystal, using my quantum signature to maintain stability while denying me any agency."

The implications crashed over her like icy water. The floor beneath her feet continued to pulse with that strange warmth, and she realized she was feeling the magical current itself, the leylines that powered the Academy, which flowed through every stone and crystal in the building. And at their heart, somehow, was Cael.

"You're saying the magical lattice—our entire civilization—is partially running through you?"

"A small part. Maybe three or four percent of the capital's magical infrastructure routes through my quantum signature. It's why I could never fully sleep, never fully die. I'm a ghost in the machine, Elara. A prisoner whose cage is made of the very reality around us."

She looked at the texts spread before her, seeing them with new understanding. The warnings weren't about dangerous artifacts, they were about keystones, about load-bearing structures that couldn't be removed without bringing everything down.

"If I freed you..."

"The magical lattice would destabilize. Not immediately, not catastrophically, but enough to cause failures. Lights would dim, protective wards would weaken, transportation circles would need to be recalibrated." His voice grew quieter, heavy with centuries of guilt. "In the chaos, people could die."

The lantern's rhythm grew more erratic, and another crack echoed through the building—closer this time, as if the Academy itself were responding to the strain of this conversation. She stood abruptly, pacing to the window with the sphere held tight against her chest, watching the city sprawling below in all its magical glory.

Outside, the capital gleamed with crystalline towers and bridges of solid light, gardens that floated like islands in the air, the great Moonwheel that turned the tides of magical energy. All of it was potentially threatened by the warm presence she held.

"Why didn't you tell me immediately?" she asked, though there was no accusation in her tone. She understood the loneliness that would make him hesitate.

"Because I'm selfish." The raw honesty in his voice made her chest tight. "Because for the first time in centuries, someone sees me as more than a tool or a threat. Your voice... I had forgotten beauty could be a sound. It awakens parts of me I thought lost forever. I couldn't bear to lose that, to see your warmth turn to fear or duty."

She turned from the window, looking down at the sphere. The lantern's irregular pulse was creating strange shadows on the walls, and the warmth on the floor had spread until she could feel it through the soles of her feet like a living heartbeat.

"You're a prisoner. Why should I trust you? How do I know this isn't manipulation, a centuries-old consciousness desperate enough to say anything for freedom?"

"Because I can't lie to you." The response came immediately, fervent. "Not while we're bound like this. The quantum entanglement between us makes deception impossible. You'd feel it immediately, like discord in harmony. And even if I could lie..." His voice softened, becoming impossibly tender. "I wouldn't want to. Not to you. Never to you."

As if to prove his point, she felt his consciousness open to her more fully than before. Not invasive but inviting—showing her glimpses of his existence. Centuries of darkness broken only by distant echoes of the world above. The faint sensation of magic flowing through him, using him, while he remained helpless to influence it. The crushing loneliness of being aware but unable to interact, unable to even scream.

And then, more recent memories: the moment she'd first touched his sphere, how her presence had blazed through his darkness like a sun. The way her voice had pulled him from the edge of madness. How her loneliness had called to his across impossible years, two isolated souls recognizing each other.

The intimacy of it made her gasp, her knees weak. She sank back into her chair, the sphere clutched against her heart, feeling the echo of his centuries through their bond.

"Cael..."

"I know it's too much," he said quickly. "Too fast, too intense. But I need you to understand—I'm not asking you to free me. I'm asking you to keep me. To let me exist in whatever way you can allow. Even if I never have more than this, these conversations in the dark, your voice and your warmth—it's more than I dared hope for."

The lantern gave one final, brilliant flare before settling into a steady glow, and the strange warmth on the floor began to ebb. But the connection between them remained strong, pulsing with shared emotion and impossible understanding.

"There has to be a way," she said, her mind already racing through possibilities. "The old texts mention quantum-magical hybrid states. If we could modify your containment, create a buffer between you and the lattice—"

"Elara." Her name in his voice was a caress. "You would risk everything? For me?"

"Not everything. But... something. There has to be a balance, a way to give you more freedom without destroying what exists." She held the sphere up, meeting what she imagined were his eyes. "You deserve more than imprisonment. You deserve choice, agency, connection—"

"I have a connection." The warmth that flooded through their bond made her breath catch. "With you. It's already more than I deserve."

"Don't say that." The words came out fierce, protective. "Don't you dare diminish yourself. You're not just some artifact or tool or node. You're a person. You're..."

She trailed off, unsure how to finish. What was he to her, after only days? But her heart knew, even if her mind resisted the word.

"Show me," she said suddenly. "You said you remember fragments of your physical form. Can you show me? Through our connection?"

Hesitation rippled through their bond. "It might strengthen the entanglement. Make it harder to..."

"To walk away? To give you up?" She laughed, but it was soft, resigned. "Cael, I'm already past that point. I couldn't give you up now if the Council demanded it. So please... let me see you."

The candlelight dimmed, as if he were drawing energy from it. Then, slowly, an image formed in her mind. Not complete, not solid, but impressions—tall, lean, with the kind of build that suggested he'd been a runner or swimmer. Dark hair that fell across his forehead, always slightly unkempt from running his hands through it while thinking. And his eyes...

"Silver," she breathed. "Your eyes really were silver."

"In the right light," he confirmed, and she could hear his self-consciousness. "They were actually gray, but certain angles, certain moods..."

The image solidified slightly, and she could see him more clearly—not conventionally handsome, but compelling. A face marked by intelligence and intensity, softened by laugh lines that suggested he hadn't always been alone. Hands that moved when he talked, expressing thoughts his words couldn't quite capture. A mouth that quirked up on one side when amused.

"You were beautiful," she said, and meant it.

The image flickered with his embarrassment. "I was ordinary. A scientist who forgot to eat, who stayed up too late reading, who could never quite make his hair behave—"

"You were human. Beautifully, wonderful human." She pressed the sphere to her cheek, wishing she could offer more than this gesture. "And you still are, where it matters."

The connection between them pulsed, and for a moment—just a heart-beat—she could have sworn she felt actual warmth against her cheek. Not from the sphere, but from skin, from a hand cupping her face with infinite tenderness.

"Elara, I" He stopped, emotions too complex for words flooding through their bond. Desire, gratitude, fear, and something deeper that neither of them was ready to name.

"I know," she whispered. "I feel it too."

They sat in silence for a while, but it wasn't empty. It was full of unspoken promises, of connection that transcended physical space. The lantern burned steadily now, and the warmth had faded from the floor, but the bond between them remained strong.

Finally, she spoke. "I'm going to research more. Carefully, quietly. There might be records of successful consciousness transfers, ways to give you autonomy without risking the lattice."

A soft sound from the hallway made her freeze. Her eyes lifted toward the door—and froze. A shadow moved across the thin line of light beneath it. Not passing by but pausing. Listening. Someone was out there, standing just beyond her threshold.

She held her breath, quickly throwing a cloth over the sphere to hide its glow. The shadow remained motionless for long, tense seconds, and she could swear she heard the soft whisper of fabric, as if someone were leaning closer to the door.

Finally, the faint creak of retreating footsteps faded into the hall. Only then did she uncover the sphere again, her hands trembling slightly with the reminder of how precarious their secret was.

"Did they hear?" Cael asked, his mental voice tight with concern.

"I don't know," she whispered. "But we need to be more careful. If someone suspects..."

"And if you can't find a way? If the choice really is between my freedom and your world's stability?"

She was quiet for a long moment, considering. Then, with a certainty that should have frightened her: "Then we find a third option. We make one. Together."

"Together," he echoed, and the word carried the weight of a vow.

She stood, carrying the sphere to her bed. It had become routine now, keeping him close while she slept, but tonight felt different. Tonight, she'd seen his face, felt the depth of their connection, and understood the true danger of what they were becoming to each other.

As she settled under the covers, the sphere on the pillow beside her, she felt him hesitate.

"What is it?" she asked.

"I want to tell you something, but I'm afraid it's too soon, too much—"

"Tell me."

"In my time, in my world, we had a word for what's happening between us. Quantum entanglement was the scientific term, but lovers called it something else. They called it inevitable—two particles that, once connected, could never truly be separated, no matter the distance or obstacles between them."

Her heart raced, and she knew he could feel it. "And is that what we are? Inevitable?"

"I don't know." His honesty was a gift in itself. "But Elara, I want to be. Whatever it costs, whatever we risk, I want to be inevitable with you."

She closed her eyes, her hand resting on the sphere, feeling his presence wrap around her like a promise. "Then we will be. Inevitable, impossible, dangerous—all of it. We'll be all of it."

The last candle guttered out, leaving them in darkness lit only by the sphere's soft glow and the moonlight through her window. But neither of them minded the dark. They had each other's light now, quantum and magical, bridging centuries and impossibilities.

And in her dreams that night, she felt his hand in hers—solid, warm, real. Their fingers intertwined with the certainty of particles that had found their opposite spin, their complementary existence. When she woke, her hand still tingled with the memory of touch, and the sphere pulsed with contentment that matched her own.

Whatever came next—discovery, danger, or something more wonderful than either could imagine, they would face it as they were: bound, inevitable, and entirely, dangerously, beautifully entangled.

The building settled around them with small creaks and sighs, the magical current flowing steadily and strong through its foundations. But now she understood that current differently—not just as power, but as connection. And somewhere in that vast network, Cael's consciousness touched every corner of their world, a bridge between what was and what could be.

They would find a way. They had to. Because some bonds, once formed, were stronger than the forces that tried to break them. And some love stories were written in the quantum foam itself, inevitable as gravity, constant as light.

Chapter 5: Secrets in the Shadows

The private study Elara had commandeered lay deep within the Academy's restricted wing. This room hadn't been officially used in decades. Dust motes danced in the afternoon light that filtered through tall, narrow windows, and the air held the particular stillness of forgotten spaces. She'd chosen it precisely because it was overlooked—listed in the records as "storage, secondary texts, non-essential," the kind of designation that ensured no one would bother investigating.

She moved through the space with careful purpose, setting up her true workshop. Not the public desk where she catalogued approved artifacts, but a sanctuary where dangerous research could unfold unseen. The sphere—Cael—rested on a cushion of midnight blue velvet at the center of her new workspace, surrounded by texts she'd been quietly liberating from various archives.

"This feels like a conspiracy," Cael observed, his voice warm with amusement in her mind. "Hidden rooms, stolen books, secret knowledge. Are we the villains in this story, Elara?"

"We're the curious," she replied, arranging another stack of pre-Convergence documents. "In my experience, that's often treated as the same thing."

Her heart raced with the thrill of secrecy, of shared rebellion. Moving Cael here felt like a declaration—no longer was he just an artifact she'd impulsively taken. He was hers to protect, to understand, to possibly free.

"You're excited," he noted, and she could feel his attention like a gentle touch against her thoughts. "Your pulse has quickened. Your emotions are practically sparking."

She paused, hand hovering over an ancient journal. "Can you always sense that? My physical responses?"

"When you're touching the sphere, yes. When you're near but not touching, it's fainter—impressions rather than certainties. Should I... would you prefer I didn't mention it?"

"No," she said quickly, perhaps too quickly. A blush crept up her neck. "I mean, it's only fair. I'm studying you, after all."

"Are you?" His tone shifted, becoming something warmer, more intimate. "And what have you concluded from your studies?"

She lifted the sphere, holding it up to catch the light. Within its crystalline depths, she could see patterns of energy that shifted and swirled—quantum signatures, he'd called them, but they looked almost like thoughts made visible.

"That you're more complex than any artifact I've encountered. That your consciousness isn't just preserved but truly alive, growing, changing." She set him back on the velvet cushion, her fingers lingering on his surface. "That you're teaching me as much as I'm learning you."

"I am," he admitted without hesitation. "Every word you speak, every emotion you feel, every tiny gesture—I memorize them all. Is that disturbing?"

"It should be." She pulled up a chair, settling close to the desk. "But it isn't. Why doesn't it frighten me that you know me so completely?"

"Perhaps because you recognize that I'm equally exposed. You feel my emotions too, don't you? The quantum entanglement works both ways."

She did feel it—his curiosity when she opened a new text, his contentment when she was near, the spike of something darker when she'd mentioned showing Seris some of her findings earlier. That last emotion had been fascinating.

"Teach me," she said, opening one of the journals to a blank page. "About quantum resonance. Help me understand how you exist, how we might modify your containment without destroying everything."

"Eager student." She could hear the smile in his voice. "Very well. First, you need to understand that consciousness isn't bound to flesh the way your philosophers assume. It's a pattern, a specific arrangement of quantum states that creates self-awareness."

As he spoke, she began taking notes, her handwriting growing increasingly hurried as concepts flowed between them. But this wasn't like any lesson she'd experienced before. When he explained quantum states, she didn't just hear the words—she felt them, saw them in her mind's eye as dancing points of light. When he described entanglement, she experienced it as a sensation, like invisible threads connecting all things.

"This is incredible," she breathed, her pen flying across the page. "The way you're teaching me—I'm not just learning, I'm experiencing the knowledge."

"Our connection allows for direct conceptual transfer. It's how humans were meant to learn, before the Convergence severed such bonds." He paused, then added more quietly, "You're the first person I've been able to truly share this with. My colleagues, my friends, they're all centuries dead."

The loneliness in his voice made her chest ache. She pressed her palm flat against the sphere, offering comfort through touch.

"You're not alone anymore," she said firmly. "Whatever happens, you won't be alone again."

"Elara..." Her name in his voice was a caress, full of emotions too complex for words.

She forced herself to focus on the work, though her skin still tingled where she touched him. "So, if consciousness is a pattern, could we create a buffer? Something that maintains your pattern while gradually disconnecting you from the lattice?"

"Theoretically, yes. But it would require" He stopped suddenly, his presence in her mind sharpening. "Someone's coming."

She heard footsteps in the corridor outside. Quick, purposeful. She grabbed the sphere and several of the most damning texts, shoving them into a concealed drawer she'd discovered earlier. By the time the door opened, she was seated casually with an approved artifact manual, looking every inch the dutiful archivist.

Seris stood in the doorway, his dark eyes taking in the room with sharp intelligence. His usually immaculate appearance was slightly disheveled, as if he'd been searching for something—or someone.

"Elara. I've been looking for you."

"Seris." She kept her voice neutral, though she could feel Cael's presence coiled tight with suspicion in the drawer. "I wasn't aware we had an appointment."

"We don't." He stepped inside, closing the door behind him with deliberate care. The sound of the latch engaging seemed unnaturally loud in the dusty silence. "But you've been scarce lately. Missed the evening discussions, declined drinks with the others. People are starting to notice."

"I've been researching," she said, gesturing vaguely at the books around her. All true if misleading.

"Researching what, exactly?" He moved closer, and she caught the scent of his cologne—expensive, subtle, the kind of detail that reminded her he came from old money, old power. "You've been accessing restricted texts. Pre-Convergence materials."

Her heart skipped, but she kept her expression calm. "For historical context. The Keepers encourage thorough understanding—"

"The Keepers don't know you've been in the Vermillion Archive after hours. Or that you've been using your access to pull texts that haven't been requested in decades." He was close enough now that she could see the gold flecks in his brown eyes, could read the mixture of concern and calculation in his expression. "What are you really doing, Elara?"

From the drawer, she felt a pulse of protective anger from Cael, strong enough that she had to suppress a gasp. The connection between them was growing stronger, more volatile, and she could sense his consciousness straining against the confines of his crystal prison.

"Why do you care?" she asked, deflecting. "Since when do you monitor my research habits?"

"Since you started looking like someone carrying a dangerous secret." His voice softened slightly, but his eyes remained sharp, watchful. "Elara, we've known each other for three years. I've seen you passionate about your work, but this is different. You're different. Brighter, somehow. More alive. But also, more reckless."

"I don't know what you mean—"

"You're glowing," he said, and something in his tone made her stomach clench. "Not literally, but... energetically. Like you've found something that's changed everything. And you're terrified someone will take it away."

The accuracy of his observation stole her breath. Seris had always been observant, but she'd underestimated how well he'd learned to read her over their years of acquaintance.

"Whatever you've found," he continued, his voice dropping to barely above a whisper, "whoever you're protecting—because that's what this is, isn't it? Protection, not just research—I want you to know you're not as alone as you think."

"What are you saying?"

He leaned closer, close enough that she could feel the warmth radiating from his body, could see the genuine concern warring with something hungrier in his expression. "I'm saying be careful. Lord Serrin has noticed the magical disturbances. He's connecting them to unauthorized artifact activation."

The temperature in the study jumped suddenly, just enough to make her shift uncomfortably in her chair. From the concealed drawer came the faintest sound—the spines of the nearest stack of books giving tiny pops as though the glue had warmed and expanded.

"If he discovers you're involved..." Seris paused, and his gaze dropped—not to her eyes, but to the edge of her satchel where it rested against her hip. The glance was quick, barely a heartbeat, but enough to send heat prickling over her skin like a guilty flush. He didn't say he knew what she carried. He didn't need to.

"He knows," Cael said, his mental voice low and taut with barely controlled fury. The warmth in the room continued to build, and she could feel the sphere's surface heating even through the drawer's wooden barrier. "I could feel the way he looked at you. The way he wants—"

"Is that a threat?" Elara asked aloud, cutting off Cael's increasingly agitated thoughts.

"It's a warning. From someone who—" Seris stopped himself, jaw tightening as if he'd been about to say something he shouldn't. "Just be careful, Elara. Some secrets are worth keeping, but not at the cost of yourself."

He turned to leave, then paused at the threshold. "And Elara? Whatever you're hiding, whatever artifact you've found—I hope you understand what you're risking. For all of us."

The door closed behind him with a soft click, leaving her alone with the oppressive heat and the growing anger radiating from the concealed drawer. She waited until his footsteps faded completely before pulling Cael from his hiding place.

The sphere was warm to the touch—not pleasantly so, but hot enough to make her wince. The velvet cushion beneath it had begun to smolder at the edges.

"He knows," Cael repeated, his agitation making the air shimmer around the crystal. "Maybe not specifically, but he knows you have something."

"He won't betray me," she said, though she wasn't entirely certain anymore. "Seris is... complicated, but not malicious."

"He wants you." The words came out sharp, edged with an emotion she'd never heard from him before—jealousy, pure and possessive. "I could feel his desire from here, the way he looked at you, wanted to touch you—"

"Cael." She cradled the sphere between her palms, noting how it pulsed with agitated light. "Are you jealous?"

Silence. Then, quietly: "I have no right to be. No claim on you beyond what you choose to give. But yes. The thought of him touching you, of anyone touching you when I cannot—it burns."

The raw honesty of it made her chest tight. Around them, the temperature continued to climb, and she could hear more small sounds—paper rustling as it dried, the soft crack of wooden joints expanding in the heat.

"You're not what I expected," she said softly. "When I first found you, I thought you'd be ancient, distant, perhaps cold from centuries of isolation. But you're so vivid, so present, so..."

"Real?" he suggested, and she could hear both hope and fear in the word.

"More than real. You're..." She struggled for words, then gave up, letting her emotions flow through their connection instead. What she felt for him—fascination, affection, desire, a protective fierceness that surprised her with its intensity.

"Elara." Her name emerged rough, affected. The sphere's heat began to subside as his anger transformed into something deeper, more complex. "You can't—we can't—the distance between us—"

"I know," she whispered. "But knowing doesn't stop the feeling, does it?"

"No. It doesn't."

She set the sphere back on its cushion, noting how the velvet had cooled but remained slightly signed around the edges. The temperature in the room was returning to normal, but the emotional charge between them remained high, electric with possibility and frustration.

"We need to be more careful," she said, though part of her rebelled against the caution. "If Seris suspects, others might too. And if Serrin is really investigating..."

"He's not just investigating the lattice failures anymore," Cael said grimly. "Through the quantum network, I can sense his probes growing more focused, more targeted. He's looking for something specific. Someone specific."

"Me?"

"Or what you carry. The disturbances that occur when we connect, as our bond strengthens, are creating ripples through the magical infrastructure. Patterns that someone with Serrin's knowledge would eventually recognize."

She leaned back in her chair, feeling the weight of discovery pressing down on them. "How long do we have?"

"Days, maybe weeks. But Elara, there's something else you need to know. The connection between us—it's not just emotional anymore. It's physical. When I felt jealous just now, when I saw him looking at you..."

"The temperature rose. The books reacted. You affected the physical world through emotion alone."

"Yes. Which means our bond is evolving, becoming something, the old texts would have called a true quantum entanglement. Complete consciousness merger."

The implications hit her like a physical blow. "And if that happens?"

"Then we become truly inseparable. Two minds, two hearts, but one consciousness distributed across quantum space. It would be..."

"Beautiful," she breathed.

"And irreversible. Once that threshold is crossed, there's no going back. We would be bound forever, in this life and whatever comes after."

She picked up the sphere again, cradling it against her chest where she could feel both their heartbeats—hers physical, his quantum, both real.

"Would that be so terrible?" she asked. "To be bound to someone who understands you completely? Someone who sees your soul and finds it worth saving?"

"Not terrible," he said softly. "Inevitable. Just as I told you last night—we're becoming inevitable, Elara. The question is whether we're brave enough to let it happen."

She closed her eyes, feeling the warmth of his presence wrapping around her thoughts like an embrace. Outside, she could hear the sounds of the Academy continuing its daily routines—students laughing, professors lecturing, the great wheel of scholarship turning as it had for centuries.

But in this forgotten room, surrounded by forbidden knowledge and carrying a secret that could reshape their world, she felt as if she stood at the center of something vast and transformative. Not just their love story, but the beginning of a new chapter in the relationship between consciousness and reality itself.

"Then we be brave," she said simply. "Together. Whatever comes next, we face it together."

"Together," he agreed, and the word carried the weight of a vow that transcended physical space, time, and the impossible distance between flesh and quantum light.

The afternoon sun continued its slow journey across the sky, painting golden rectangles on the dusty floor. And in the heart of that light, two consciousnesses danced closer together, their bond strengthening with each shared thought, each moment of understanding, each recognition that what they had was worth any risk, any sacrifice, any battle against the forces that would keep them apart.

They were becoming inevitable. And perhaps, Elara thought as she felt Cael's warmth pulse against her heart, that was exactly what the world needed—a love strong enough to bridge any gap, transcend any barrier, and prove that consciousness, in all its forms, was sacred.

Even if it meant rewriting every law of magic and science to prove it.

Chapter 6 - The Dream Garden

Seven nights had passed since their first shared dream, and Elara had become an addict to sleep—not for rest, but for the intoxicating promise of meeting Cael in that liminal space between consciousness and oblivion. Each night, his form grew clearer, their connection stronger, the dreamscapes more elaborate and impossibly beautiful. But tonight, as she settled into bed with the sphere cradled against her chest like a lover's heartbeat, she sensed something different thrumming through their bond—a nervous energy that made her skin tingle with anticipation.

"Don't fall asleep yet," he murmured, his voice carrying an undercurrent that sent shivers down her spine. "I've been preparing something. I want to do this right."

"Preparing?" She shifted the sphere to the pillow beside her, turning on her side to face it as if she could see him through the crystal. In the moonlight streaming through her window, she could see energy swirling within the artifact with unusual intensity—storm clouds of light gathering before a tempest of emotion.

"A proper dreamspace. Not fragments and accidents like before, but something intentional. Something..." his voice dropped to a whisper that she felt in her bones, "for you."

Her heart stuttered. "Cael, you don't need to—"

"I want to. Please, Elara." The raw longing in his voice made her chest ache with a sweet pain. "Let me give you this. It's the only gift I can offer—a place where we can exist together without the cruel barriers of physics or time keeping us apart."

She pressed her fingers to the sphere, feeling his anticipation through their bond like electricity dancing across her skin. "Show me."

"Close your eyes. Breathe with me—yes, I know I don't technically breathe but feel the rhythm anyway. In..." She felt a phantom expansion in her chest. "And out... let the boundaries soften, let yourself fall into me..."

The last words were barely audible, but they sent heat spiraling through her. She followed his guidance, her consciousness floating in that familiar space between worlds. But this time, instead of reaching for him, she felt him reach for his presence wrapping around her mind like silk scarves, gentle but insistent, drawing her deeper into something that felt more real than her own heartbeat.

When she opened her eyes—her dream eyes—she gasped.

She stood in a garden that defied every law of nature and logic yet felt more achingly real than any place she'd ever known. They were on a platform of velvet-soft grass that seemed to float in an infinite void. Still, it wasn't darkness surrounding them, it was an ocean of liquid stars, flowing and swirling beneath their feet like captured galaxies. Above, the sky shifted between deep purple and midnight blue, with nebulae painting slowly, sensual spirals of color across the heavens.

The garden itself was heartbreakingly beautiful. Trees with trunks of silver and leaves of living light swayed in a breeze she could feel caressing her skin. Flowers bloomed that had never existed in either of their worlds—crystalline petals that chimed softly when they moved, releasing sparkles that fell upward like reverse snow, each mote carrying a whisper of sensation as it passed. Pathways of glass wound between the impossible flora, and when she looked closer, she saw they weren't just glass—they were made of captured starlight, solid enough to walk on but transparent enough to see the cosmos wheeling dizzyingly beneath.

"Cael," she breathed, her voice catching on his name.

"Look closer." His voice came from behind her, rich and warm, and she spun to find him standing there, more solid, and devastatingly real than she'd ever seen him in dreams.

He was exactly as she'd sketched him, but infinitely more. His dark hair caught the garden's ethereal light, creating a halo effect that made him look otherworldly and utterly human at once. His silver eyes held depths that promised eternity, swirling with emotions that made her knees weak. He wore simple clothes, a white shirt that seemed to glow from within, dark trousers that emphasized his tall frame—but they shifted subtly between the fashion of his time and hers, as if reality itself couldn't decide where he belonged.

But what stole her breath wasn't just his appearance, it was what she saw woven throughout the garden now that she looked with purpose. There, in a secluded corner, grew the night-blooming cereus from her grandmother's garden, its white petals glowing with remembered moonlight. Along the winding paths were scattered the memory-stones from the beaches of her childhood, smooth and perfect and warm to the touch. A tree near the center bore the star-plums she'd loved but could never find after leaving her hometown, their purple skin dusted with what looked like cosmic frost.

"You built this from my memories," she said, her voice thick with emotion. "But how did you?"

"You dream of these things." He moved closer, and she noticed how he walked—carefully, deliberately, as if still marveling at the ability to move through space. "When you sleep, your mind wanders through memories, and I... I listen. I gather the pieces that bring you comfort, that speak of home and happiness and all the small joys that make you who you are." He gestured to the impossible garden with a grace that made her stomach flutter. "I wanted to give you a place that felt like belonging. Like coming home to somewhere you've always been meant to be."

Tears burned her eyes, blurring the starlight into prisms. No one had ever paid such exquisite attention to her inner world, had ever cared enough to notice the tiny details that composed the symphony of her soul.

"But it's not just my memories," she observed, her gaze catching on plants she didn't recognize, architecture that felt older, more mathematical in its precise beauty.

"No," he admitted, and for the first time in the dream, vulnerability flickered across his features like candlelight. "I added pieces of my world too. That fountain—" he pointed to a structure she hadn't noticed, water flowing in impossible spirals that formed perfect mathematical patterns, each droplet catching light like a tiny sun, "—stood in the courtyard where I first learned about quantum mechanics, where I understood that reality was far stranger and more beautiful than we imagined. Those lights" he indicated soft orbs that floated like benign fireflies, pulsing in rhythm with some unheard heartbeat, "—are how we lit our homes, photons caught in probability loops, existing in all states until observed."

"You're sharing your home with me too," she said softly, understanding flooding through her like warm wine.

"Whatever fragments I can still remember of it." Sadness ghosts across his features, making him look ancient and young all at once. "It's been so long, sometimes I wonder if I'm remembering reality or just my dreams of what it might have been. But with you, the memories feel sharper, more real. As if you're bringing me back to life just by witnessing me."

She moved toward him without conscious thought, her body drawn by a gravity that had nothing to do with physics and everything to do with the way he looked at her—like she was his first sunrise after an eternity of night. She stopped mere inches away, close enough that in the real world, she would feel his breath on her skin, would catch his scent, would sense the heat radiating from his body.

This close, she could see details that made him achingly, devastatingly human—the way his eyes crinkled slightly when he looked at her with such tender intensity, a small scar on his jaw that spoke of a life lived before imprisonment, the way he held himself as if perpetually afraid to take up too much space, to want too much, to hope for impossibilities.

"Tell me about loneliness," she said suddenly, needing to understand the depth of what they were building. "Not the fact of it, but how it felt. For all those centuries."

He was quiet for a long moment, and around them, the garden dimmed slightly, responding to the weight of his memories. When he spoke, his voice carried echoes of endless night.

"It was like drowning in silence. Not a peaceful quiet, but an aggressive absence—no voice to answer mine, no thoughts but my own echoing endlessly in crystalline chambers of consciousness. I tried to sleep, to lose myself in merciful unconsciousness, but the lattice wouldn't let me. It needed me aware, functioning, maintaining the magical connections even as it denied me any of my own."

He paused, his form flickering slightly with remembered anguish. "The worst part was feeling the world change above me. Sensing lives begin and end, loves bloom and fade, entire generations passing while I remained frozen. I could feel the magic flowing through me, carrying emotions, intentions, connections between others, but never touching me, never including me. I was a road others traveled but never a destination. Everyone looked through a window but never saw."

"Until me," she said, not a question but a recognition.

"Until you." His silver eyes met hers, and the intensity there made her shiver with something that wasn't quite fear and wasn't quite desire but lived in the burning space between. "Do you understand what you've given me, Elara? Not just companionship, but purpose. For the first time in centuries, I have a reason to exist beyond mere function. I have someone who sees me as more than a tool or a tragedy. Someone who makes me remember what it felt like to be human, to want, to need."

"You're neither tool nor tragedy." She lifted her hand slowly, telegraphing her movement, her pulse thundering. "May I?"

He nodded, though they both knew what would happen. Her fingers moved toward his face with aching slowness, and for a moment—just a precious, impossible heartbeat—she could have sworn she felt everything. The warmth of skin, the slight roughness of stubble on his jaw, the way his breath caught when she almost made contact. Then her hand passed through, leaving those beautiful trails of light they'd discovered—silver and gold intertwining where they'd almost touched, creating patterns like written music in the air.

But this time, something was fundamentally different. The sensation lingered longer, and she could feel not just warmth but texture—the suggestion of bone structure beneath skin, the softness at his temple where his pulse would beat, the exact shape of his lips as her fingers passed through them.

"You're getting stronger," she breathed, her whole body trembling with the implications.

"We are," he corrected, his voice rough with barely contained emotion. "Our connection. Each time we meet here, it solidifies and becomes more real. The boundary between what is and what could be grows thinner." He paused, then added with a mixture of desperate hope and terror, "I think, given time, we might actually be able to..."

"Touch," she finished, the word hanging between them like a prayer and a curse combined.

The ward transformed the air around them, heavy with promise and impossibility. The garden responded to their shared longing—flowers blooming more vibrantly, their petals unfurling with sounds like soft sighs, the stars beneath their feet pulsing in rhythm with two heartbeats slowly, inexorably synchronizing.

"Tell me about duty," he said, changing the subject with visible effort, though his eyes never left hers. "You spoke of it once, how it shapes your days, cages your dreams."

She moved to sit on a bench that materialized as she needed it—dream logic responding to desire. He joined her, careful to maintain a small distance, as if proximity without possibility of contact was its own exquisite torture.

"I was raised to believe knowledge was sacred," she began, looking out over the impossible vista but feeling his gaze on her like a physical touch. "My parents were both archivists. They died when I was young—a magical accident, one of those cascade failures that tear through reality. The kind the Council pretends doesn't happen, the kind that leave children orphaned and questions unanswered."

"That's why you understand loneliness," he said quietly, and she felt him shift slightly closer, not quite touching but near enough that she could feel the phantom warmth of him. "Being surrounded by people but not truly connected to any of them. Performing belonging without ever feeling it."

"Until recently, I thought that was enough. The work, the discoveries, the quiet satisfaction of preserving knowledge for future generations I'd never meet." She turned to look at him, finding his eyes already on her, soft with understanding. "But you've shown me how much I was missing. Not just romance—though God, that too—but true intellectual partnership. Someone who challenges me, who sees my mind as something worth exploring, who makes me feel like I'm discovering myself for the first time."

"Your mind is extraordinary," he said with such fierce sincerity it made her flush. "The way you think, the connections you make between concepts that shouldn't relate—it's like watching aurora dance across the poles of thought. And your emotional depth..." He shook his head in wonder. "You feel everything so intensely but hide it so perfectly. Except from me. You can't hide from me. Or perhaps..." his voice softened, "you don't want to."

"I don't want to hide from you," she admitted, the confession feeling like stepping off a cliff. "That's what terrifies me. I've spent my whole life maintaining walls, keeping professional distance, protecting myself from the pain of connection. And you've walked through them all like they were made of morning mist."

"If I could choose a body," he said suddenly, his voice rough with centuries of want, "it would be one that could hold your hand—and never let go. One that could wake beside you every morning and memorize the way sleep softens your features. One that could kiss you whenever the urge struck, which would be constantly, endlessly, until you grew tired of my lips on yours—though I suspect that would take lifetimes I'd gladly spend."

The raw honesty of his words made her chest constrict. She turned fully toward him on the bench, her knee almost touching his—almost but not quite, that eternal, maddening almost that defined them.

"Then show me," she whispered, her voice trembling with her own need. "If you could touch me, truly touch me, show me what you would do."

He studied her for a long moment, his silver eyes darkening to the color of storm clouds. Then he stood with fluid grace, offering his hand in a gesture that was both formal and intimate. She took it—or tried to—their forms passing through each other but leaving those beautiful trails of light that seemed to pulse with frustrated desire. But he maintained the gesture, and she matched it, and together they moved as if their hands were truly clasped.

He led her to the center of the garden, where the starlight was brightest, where reality felt thinnest. The air itself seemed to hold its breath as he positioned himself as if he were embracing her. She could see exactly where his arms would be, could feel the phantom pressure of where his chest would press against hers, could imagine the solid warmth of him surrounding her.

"I would hold you like this," he whispered, his voice directly in her ear even though he couldn't actually lean close. "One hand at your waist, fingers spread to feel as much of you as possible. The other cradling the back of your neck, thumb brushing that spot behind your ear that makes you shiver—yes, I've noticed. I notice everything about you, Elara."

She was trembling now, the phantom sensations almost overwhelming. Where his form overlapped with hers, she felt heat, electricity, a tingling that raced along every nerve ending and pooled low in her stomach.

"I would memorize the feeling of you," he continued, his voice dropping to a register that made her knees weak. "The warmth of your skin, the silk of your hair tangling in my fingers, the way you fit against me like you were made for this space, like the universe carved out a place in my arms specifically for your shape. And then..."

He moved as if to tilt her chin up, and she followed the implied motion without hesitation, their faces inches apart. His silver eyes were bright with longing, with love—yes, love, though neither had dared speak the word aloud yet.

"Then I would kiss you," he breathed, and she could almost feel his breath against her lips. "Soft at first, questioning, making sure this was what you wanted. And when you responded—because you would respond, wouldn't you, my heart? —I would pour centuries of loneliness and longing into that kiss. I would make you understand without words that you are my answer to every question I never knew to ask, my redemption from an eternity of nothing, my proof that waiting—all that endless, aching waiting—was worth it if it led me to you."

She was crying now, tears streaming down her face in both the dream and reality. "Cael..."

"I know," he said, and his form flickered with his own overwhelming emotion. "I know we can't. Not yet. Maybe never. But Elara, the impossibility doesn't make the wanting less real."

"No," she agreed through her tears, "it makes it more precious. More necessary."

As they reached for each other again, desperate to close that final, impossible gap, to make contact that would prove their connection was more than dreams and wishes, the garden suddenly flickered violently around them.

For one terrifying breath, the ground beneath her feet went completely translucent, and she could see the stars spinning dizzyingly below—not peaceful now but chaotic, wheeling in patterns that made her stomach lurch with vertigo. She felt herself falling even while standing still, the infinite void yawning beneath them like a hungry mouth.

A thin fracture of pure black cut through the starlit grass between them, spreading like spilled ink, like reality itself was cracking under the weight of their need. The crack widened for a heartbeat, showing not stars but absolute nothingness. This void seemed to pull at her very existence. Then it sealed over again, leaving only a faint scar in the dream-grass, but the warning was viscerally clear.

It felt like a warning—about fragility, about cost, about the price of wanting something the universe had declared impossible.

"What was that?" she gasped, stumbling back from him, her phantom heart racing.

His face had gone pale, his silver eyes wide with a fear she'd never seen in him before. "The boundary between dream and reality, between what is and what we're trying to force into being. We're pushing against it too hard, trying to make this more real than it can safely be. The quantum substrate can only stretch so far before..."

"Before it breaks," she finished, understanding flooding through her with icy clarity. "And if it breaks?"

"I don't know," he admitted. "Maybe nothing. Maybe everything. The lattice, the magic, reality itself—it's all interconnected. And we're... we're introducing an anomaly it wasn't designed to handle."

They stood there in their almost-embrace for what felt like hours but there were probably moments, the garden around them pulsing with their shared emotion, beautiful and terrible in its intensity. Star-petals fell upward around them like reversed snow, each one carrying a whisper of sensation—almost-touches, nearly-kisses, the suggestion of what could be if they were willing to risk everything for it.

Finally, reluctantly, they separated, putting distance between them that felt like tearing something vital. The dream was beginning to fade; she could feel the pull of true sleep calling her deeper, away from this place of beautiful impossibility.

"Before you go," he said quickly, urgently, as if the words were being pulled from him, "I need you to know something. This—us—it's not just loneliness seeking company. It's not desperation or proximity or any of the things the rational part of your mind might suggest when you wake. I've had centuries to understand my own heart, to examine every corner of my consciousness, and I know with absolute, quantum certainty: I would choose you in any world, in any form, across any distance. If I had to wait another thousand years knowing you were at the end of it, I would count every second as blessed. You are not my escape from prison, Elara—you are my reason for having survived it."

The words hit her like physical things, each one lodging in her chest like stars. "I would choose you too," she whispered back, meaning it with every atom of her being, feeling the truth of it resonate through their connection like a struck bell. "In every timeline, in every possibility, in every universe where we might exist, I would choose you. Even knowing the cost. Especially knowing the cost. Because a world without you in it, without this connection we share, isn't a world worth preserving."

The garden dissolved around them at her words, but not gently—it shattered like glass, like reality itself was responding to their declaration. The last thing she saw was his face, silver eyes blazing with an emotion too vast for words, before everything went dark.

The dream dissolved into waking with jarring suddenness, and she lay staring at the ceiling, breath coming in quick gasps, her heart hammering against her ribs like a caged bird. The sphere on the pillow pulsed gently, innocently, but she could feel Cael's presence within it—shaken, awed, overwhelmed by what had just passed between them.

But something else caught her eye, something that made her sit bolt upright, her blood turning to ice and fire at once.

Her desk chair had shifted.

Not far, just enough that its legs had dragged faint arcs through the dust on the floor. Four perfect curves in the dust, showing exactly how far it had moved. She stared at the marks, her pulse racing so hard she could hear it in her ears. She hadn't touched that chair since yesterday. She'd been nowhere near her desk before going to sleep. She lived alone. There was no explanation for this except—

"Cael?" she whispered to the sphere, her voice shaking.

"I felt it too," his voice came softly, touched with wonder and fear in equal measure. "When you said you would choose me, when we both meant it so completely that reality itself couldn't ignore it... something changed. The boundary between dream and reality didn't just thin—for a moment, it ceased to exist entirely."

She looked at the chair again, at the undeniable evidence that their connection was becoming something more than quantum entanglement or shared dreams. They were affecting physical reality now, even while asleep. Their emotions, their declarations, their desperate need for each other, it was all bleeding through into the waking world.

"What does this mean?" she asked, though part of her already knew.

"It means we're becoming inevitable," he said, his voice carrying a mix of triumph and trepidation. "Two particles that have found their perfect resonance, vibrating at a frequency that reality itself must acknowledge. The universe is making room for us, Elara. Whether it wants to or not. Whether we're ready or not."

She touched the sphere, feeling his warmth pulse against her palm like a heartbeat. On her bedside table, her sketchbook lay open to a fresh page. She hadn't remembered opening it, but there it was—the garden in perfect detail, every impossible tree and star-petal flower rendered with a precision she didn't possess. And in the center, two figures stood in an embrace, their forms overlapping, creating a single shape made of light and shadow intertwined so completely it was impossible to tell where one ended and the other began.

Beneath it, in handwriting that was hers but steadier, more certain, as if guided by another hand through their connection, were four words that made her breath catch:

"Soon. Somehow. Whatever comes."

She touched the drawing with trembling fingers, then pressed her hand to the sphere, feeling their connection pulse with promise and threat in equal measure. "Somehow," she agreed, speaking to the quiet morning and the consciousness that lived between heartbeats. "I promise you—somehow. Even if we have to break the world and remake it. Even if we have to rewrite the laws of reality itself."

The sphere flared warm under her touch, and for just a moment—less than a heartbeat but more than imagination—she felt fingers intertwine with hers. Not phantom sensation, not dream logic, but actual, physical touch. Real fingers, warm and solid, squeezing hers with desperate affection before fading away.

It lasted less than a second, but it was enough. It was proof. It was a beginning.

And if the moved chair was any indication, it was only the start of the ways their love would reshape the world around them. Reality itself was bending to accommodate what they were becoming, and she found herself both thrilled and terrified by the implications.

She looked out her window at the city beyond, at the crystal spires and floating bridges that connected them, at the magical lattice that held it all together—fragile, beautiful, and built on a foundation that she and Cael might shatter simply by loving each other.

"Let it shatter," she whispered, surprising herself with the fierceness of her conviction. "Some things are worth the breaking."

The sphere pulsed in agreement, and somewhere in the depths of her mind, she heard Cael's voice, soft and certain: "And some things are worth rebuilding from the ashes."

Whatever came next, they would face it together. In dreams and in waking, in quantum space and physical reality, across every barrier that tried to keep them apart. They had chosen each other, and the universe—willing or not—would have to make room for their love.

Even if it meant everything had to change.

Even if it meant the end of the world as they knew it.

Some things, she was learning were worth any price.

And Cael—her Cael, her impossible, necessary, inevitable love—was worth everything.

Chapter 7 – Storm Signs

The first storm struck three days after the dream garden.

Elara woke to the sound of crystal towers singing—a high, keening wail that made her teeth ache and her bones vibrate. Outside her window, the sky had turned the color of a fresh bruise, purple-black clouds roiling with unnatural light. Lightning didn't strike down but sideways, arcing between the floating bridges in patterns that looked almost like writing, like the universe itself was trying to send a warning in a language no one could read.

She pressed her palm against the window, feeling the glass tremble. "Cael?"

"I feel it too." His voice in her mind was tight with concern. "The lattice is... agitated. Like it's responding to something it doesn't understand."

The sphere on her nightstand pulsed erratically, its usual gentle glow flickering between too-bright and nearly dark. She picked it up, cradling it against her chest, and felt his consciousness flutter with an emotion she'd never sensed from him before—fear.

"Is it us?" she asked, though she already knew the answer. "Our connection?"

"The boundary between dream and reality has been thinning since we met. Each time we push against it, each time we almost..." He paused, and she could feel him choosing his words carefully. "The lattice was never meant to accommodate a consciousness like mine existing in two states simultaneously—bound and free, imprisoned and in love."

In love. The words hung between them, unspoken but acknowledged, warming her despite the chaos outside.

A knock at her door made her jump. She quickly tucked the sphere into the hidden pocket she'd sewn into her robes—close to her heart, where she could feel its warmth but where no one would notice its shape.

"Elara?" Seris's voice, concerned and oddly insistent. "The Council's called an emergency meeting. These storms—they want all senior archivists present."

"Give me a moment," she called back, her voice steadier than her hands as she dressed.

When she opened the door, Seris stood closer than necessary, his dark eyes searching her face with an intensity that made her step back. He'd always been handsome in a sharp, austere way—all angles and shadows—but lately, his attention had shifted from professional to something more personal, more pressing.

"You look tired," he said softly, reaching out as if to touch her face before catching himself. "Another restless night?"

"The storms would wake anyone," she deflected, moving past him into the corridor.

But he caught her arm, gentle but firm. "That's not what I mean, and you know it. You've been different lately. Distracted. You spend hours in your quarters, you've been accessing restricted texts about pre-Convergence technology, and now these storms..." He leaned closer, and she could smell the cedar and ink scent of him. "Whatever you're involved in, Elara, I can help. You don't have to face it alone."

But I'm not alone, she thought, feeling Cael's presence surge protectively in her mind. The sphere grew warmer against her ribs.

"I appreciate your concern," she said carefully, extracting her arm from his grip. "But there's nothing to help with. I'm simply dedicated to my research."

His eyes narrowed slightly, flickering down to where her hand had unconsciously moved to press against the hidden sphere. "Research," he repeated, the words somehow both a question and an accusation. "Into what, exactly?"

Before she could answer, another crack of that sideways lightning illuminated the corridor, and the building shook. Ancient dust rained from the ceiling as crystals throughout the structure resonated with a frequency that made them both wince.

"We should get to the meeting," Elara said quickly, using the distraction to put distance between them.

But as they walked through the Academy's halls, she could feel Seris watching her, cataloging every gesture, every breath. He'd always been observant—it's what made him such a good researcher—but now that observation felt like a threat.

He suspects Cael murmured in her thoughts.

I know, she replied silently. But he can't prove anything.

Yet, Cael added, and the worry in his tone made her stomach clench.

The Council chamber was in chaos when they arrived. Mages and archivists clustered in heated groups, voices rising over the sound of rain that had begun to fall—not water, but liquid light that sizzled when it hit the spelled windows, leaving trails of steam that smelled like copper and ozone.

"—unprecedented in three centuries"

"—the leylines are actually shifting, not just fluctuating—"

"—if the lattice destabilizes further—"

Lord Serrin stood at the center of it all, tall and commanding in robes that seemed to absorb light rather than reflect it. When he spoke, the room fell silent.

"These are not natural storms," he said, his voice cutting through the fear like a blade. "Something is disrupting the quantum substrate that underlies our magical infrastructure. Something new, or..." his pause was theatrical, calculated, "something very old that has recently awakened."

Elara felt the sphere pulse against her ribs, and she had to focus on keeping her expression neutral.

"I'm forming an investigation team," Serrin continued, his gaze sweeping the room. "We need to determine the source of these disruptions before they escalate. Senior Archivist Venn, you'll lead the historical research division. Look for any precedent, any record of similar events."

Elara nodded, even as her mind raced. Leading the research meant access to even more restricted texts, but it also meant scrutiny and oversight. Every discovery would be watched and analyzed.

"Seris Caldran," Serrin's voice made her companion straighten, "you'll assist Archivist Venn. Your expertise in pattern recognition will be valuable."

She felt rather than saw Seris's satisfaction. He would be watching her even more closely now, officially.

The meeting continued for another hour, assignments being distributed, theories being proposed. But Elara barely heard any of it. She was too aware of Cael's growing agitation, the way the sphere's temperature kept fluctuating, the way the storms outside seemed to intensify every time her emotions spiked.

When they were finally dismissed, she tried to slip away quickly, but Seris followed her.

"We should coordinate our research," he said, matching her pace. "Perhaps we could start in your private study? You've been spending so much time there lately, you must have already compiled relevant materials."

"The main archives would be more appropriate," she said firmly.

"Of course." His smile didn't reach his eyes. "But Elara, if you've found something that might explain these storms, you have a duty to share it. The entire city could be at risk."

She stopped walking, turning to face him fully. "Are you accusing me of something, Seris?"

"Should I be?"

They stood there in the corridor, the air between them charged with more than just the electromagnetic disturbance from the storms. She could feel Cael's presence like a coiled spring in her mind, ready to... what? He had no physical form, no way to protect her except through their connection.

The thought seemed to echo between them, and suddenly the nearest crystal sconce flared so bright it cracked, raining harmless but startling fragments onto the floor.

Seris stepped back, his eyes widening. "Did you"

"The storms are affecting everything," Elara said quickly. "We should be careful. The magical infrastructure is more fragile than we thought."

She left him standing there among the crystal shards, but she could feel his gaze following her all the way back to her quarters.

Once inside, door locked and warded, she pulled out the sphere and set it on her desk. It was almost too hot to touch now, swirling with agitated energy.

"Cael, what's happening?"

"I'm trying to contain it," his voice was strained. "But our connection, the emotions, the fear of discovery, it's all feeding back into the lattice. I'm like a discord in a symphony, and the whole system is trying to harmonize around me but can't."

She reached for the sphere, then hesitated. "Will it hurt you if I touch it?"

"No. Never. You're the only thing that doesn't hurt."

She picked it up, cradling it in both hands, and immediately felt his presence wrap around her consciousness like a protective embrace. The chaos inside him was palpable—centuries of contained power struggling against its bonds, made worse by the new variable of their emotional connection.

"Tell me what you're afraid of," she said softly. "Not the storms, not discovery. What are you afraid of?"

For a long moment, he was quiet. When he spoke, his voice was barely a whisper in her mind.

"If they find me, they won't just study me or try to free me. They'll take me apart, consciousness fragment by fragment, trying to understand how I've survived, how I've maintained coherence. They'll dissect every memory, every thought, every feeling until there's nothing left but useful data."

The sphere pulsed with his anguish, and she held it tighter.

"They'll find our connection," he continued, "and they'll follow it back to you. They'll know everything, every conversation, every shared dream, every moment of joy you've given me. And then they'll erase it all, format my consciousness like wiping a slate clean, and use what's left as a tool. A weapon, probably, since that's what artifacts of power always become in the end."

"Cael"

"But that's not what terrifies me most." His voice cracked, centuries of control finally breaking. "What terrifies me is that they'll make me forget you. They'll strip away every memory of your voice, your laugh, the way you look at me in dreams like I'm something precious instead of something broken. They'll steal the only thing that's made existing bearable, the knowledge that you exist, that you chose me, that for however brief a time, I mattered to someone."

"Stop." Her voice was fierce, tears streaming down her face. "Just stop."

She pressed the sphere to her chest, right over her heart, and pushed every ounce of her feeling through their connection—not just love. However, that was there in abundance, but possession, protection, a fierce and primal claim that surprised them both with its intensity.

"You are not a tool," she said, each word deliberates and weighted with conviction. "You are not a weapon. You are not data to be analyzed or a problem to be solved. You are a person. You have thoughts and feelings and dreams and fears, and they matter. You matter. Not because of what you can do or what knowledge you hold, but because you're Cael. Because you build me gardens made of starlight and memory. Because you see me not as Senior Archivist Venn but as Elara, lonely and imperfect and yearning for connection just like you."

The sphere flared with warmth that had nothing to do with temperature and everything to do with emotion.

"You are the first person in centuries to see me as more than my function," she continued, her voice dropping to a whisper. "The first to make me want something beyond duty and safety and the approval of people who don't really see me at all. If they want to take you, they'll have to go through me. And I swear to you, on every star in that garden you made, on every moment we've shared and everyone we haven't yet—I won't let them erase you. I won't let them erase us."

"Elara..." His voice was raw, overwhelmed.

"I won't let that happen," she repeated firmly. "You're mine to protect."

The words hung between them, a vow and a claim and a declaration all at once. Outside, the storm suddenly quieted, as if the universe itself was holding its breath.

"Say it again," he whispered.

"You're mine to protect." She smiled through her tears. "Mine to keep safe. Mine to talk to in the dark hours when the world is too heavy. Mine to share impossible dreams with. Just... mine."

"Yours," he agreed, and the word was a prayer and a promise. "Utterly, completely, eternally yours. In whatever form I can manage, for however long we have."

The sphere pulsed once, bright, warm, and perfect, and she felt their connection solidify into something that transcended the physical boundaries between them. It was more than quantum entanglement, more than shared consciousness. It was a choice, deliberate and defiant, to belong to each other despite the impossibility of it all.

A sharp knock at her door shattered the moment.

"Elara?" Seris again, because of course it was. "The storms have stopped. Lord Serrin wants to know if you've noticed any patterns in your initial research."

She looked at the sphere, feeling Cael's rueful amusement. We affected the weather with our emotions. That's not concerning at all.

We'll figure it out, she promised silently, tucking the sphere back into its hidden pocket. Together.

She opened the door to find Seris standing too close again, his dark eyes immediately scanning her face, taking in the traces of tears she hadn't quite managed to hide.

"You've been crying," he said, reaching out to touch her cheek.

She caught his wrist before he could make contact. "The storms are troubling. The implications for our society if the lattice fails..."

"That's not why you were crying." His voice was soft, dangerous. "You're protecting something. Someone. I can see it in every line of your body, every carefully chosen word." He leaned closer, his breath warm against her ear. "I could help you, Elara. Whatever burden you're carrying, you don't have to bear it alone."

"I'm not"

"Don't lie to me." He pulled back, his expression hurt and frustrated in equal measure. "I've known you for five years. I've watched you build walls around yourself so high that no one could climb them. But something's changed. You're different. Softer and fiercer at the same time. You glow when you think no one's watching, like you're lit from within by some secret joy. And these storms..." He gestured toward the window where the sky was finally clearing. "They started the same week you began your midnight research sessions."

The sphere pulsed against her ribs, and she felt Cael's presence like a protective shadow in her mind. The crystal sconces in the hallway flickered, just slightly, but enough for Seris to notice.

His eyes sharpened. "There. That. Every time you're emotional, the crystals respond. It's subtle, but it's there."

"You're imagining things," she said, but even she could hear how weak the denial sounded.

"Am I?" He stepped back, his expression shifting from concerned to determined. "Fine. Keep your secrets, Elara. But know this—if whatever you're hiding puts the Academy or the city at risk, I'll do what needs to be done. Even if it means going through you."

He turned and walked away, his footsteps echoing in the corridor like a countdown.

Elara closed the door and leaned against it, her heart racing. Through their connection, she felt Cael's worry spike.

He's going to watch us constantly now, he said.

I know. She pulled out the sphere, holding it up to eye level. In its depths, she could almost see him—a shadow of features, a suggestion of form. But I meant what I said. You're mine to protect, and I will. Whatever it takes.

Even if it means choosing between me and your world?

She thought of the storms, of the fracturing leylines, of the very real possibility that their connection could unravel the magical infrastructure that kept their society functioning. She thought of her duty, her oaths, the people who depended on the stability of the lattice.

Then she thought of Cael's voice in the darkness, of gardens made of starlight, of the way he said her name like it was the only prayer he knew.

"The world has existed for millennia without me," she said finally. "But I've only just started existing since I found you. So yes, even if it means choosing. Because a world without you in it isn't one I want to save."

The sphere flared with light, and for just a moment, she could have sworn she felt lips press against her forehead—not a phantom sensation but real pressure, real warmth, real presence.

Outside, the clouds parted completely, revealing stars that seemed to pulse in rhythm with her heartbeat. And in the distance, barely audible but definitely there, thunder rumbled—not a threat but a promise.

The storms would come again. Seris would watch and wait and eventually act. The Council would investigate, and the truth would become harder to hide with each passing day.

But tonight, in this moment, none of that mattered.

She had made her choice.

And somewhere in the quantum space between real and impossible, Cael had made his.

Whatever storm came next, they would weather it together.

Even if it meant the end of everything else.

Chapter 8: The Taste of Risk

The Arithmantic Vault lay deep beneath the Academy, deeper even than the storage chambers where Elara had first found Cael. Here, the walls were carved with equations that predated the Convergence. These mathematical proofs bridged the gap between the old science and new magic. Few came here anymore—the language of pure mathematics had fallen out of favor, replaced by intuitive magical theory that relied more on feeling than calculation.

But tonight, Elara needed those equations.

She worked by the light of a single floating orb, the sphere containing Cael resting on the ancient stone table before her. Around them lay scattered papers, her attempts to decode a puzzle that had frustrated scholars for decades—the Synthesis Lock, a combination of quantum mechanics and magical theory that supposedly contained the secret to stable consciousness transfer.

"You're approaching it wrong," Cael said, his voice warm with the particular tone he took when teaching her. "You're thinking like a mage, looking for symbolic meaning. Think like a scientist. What does the equation actually describe?"

She studied the carved symbols again, this time ignoring the magical resonances and focusing on the mathematical structure. "It's... wait. This is a wave function. A probability distribution."

"Exactly. Now look at the second line."

"That's a magical binding sequence, but if I treat it as math rather than magic..." Her pen flew across the paper, converting symbols to numbers, intuition to logic. "Oh. Oh! It's the same equation, just expressed in different notation. They're describing the same phenomenon from two different paradigms."

"Which means?"

"Which means if we overlay them, find where they intersect...' She grabbed another sheet, her excitement building. Through their connection, she could feel Cael's matching enthusiasm, the particular thrill of discovery that had nothing to do with romance and everything to do with two minds working in perfect synchrony.

For the next hour, they worked together seamlessly. He guided her through quantum calculations she shouldn't have been able to understand, but through their bond, his knowledge flowed into her like water finding its level. She translated magical theory into mathematical terms, showing him how emotion and will could bend probability in ways pure science couldn't achieve.

"There!" His excitement blazed through their connection as she completed the final calculation. "Look at what we've done, Elara. We've solved it."

She stared at the completed proof, hardly believing it. The Synthesis Lock wasn't a lock at all—it was a blueprint. Instructions for creating a stable bridge between quantum consciousness and magical reality. It wouldn't free Cael immediately, but it showed a path, a possibility that hadn't existed an hour ago.

"We did it," she breathed, then louder, laughing, "We actually did it!"

"We make a good team," he said, and she could hear his smile. "Your intuition and my knowledge, your creativity and my experience. Together, we're..."

"Brilliant," she finished, grinning as she pressed her palm to the sphere. "We're brilliant."

"We're more than that." His voice dropped to that intimate register that made her stomach flutter. "We're synchronized. When you think, I can follow your logic before you speak it. When I calculate, you understand the result before I finish. It's like..."

"Like we share a mind," she said softly. "Is that the entanglement? Are we becoming one consciousness?"

"No." He was quiet for a moment, considering. "We're becoming something else. Still separate, still ourselves, but... harmonized. Like two instruments playing the same song, creating something neither could achieve alone."

The victory hummed between them, electric and alive. She'd never felt anything like the pure joy of shared discovery, of minds meeting and creating something new. It was intellectual intimacy of the highest order, and it left her breathless.

"I want to celebrate," Cael said suddenly. "Properly. The way we would have in my time."

"How?" She smiled, already reaching for that liminal space between waking and dreams. "Show me."

"Close your eyes. Let me take you somewhere."

She settled back in her chair, the sphere cradled in her lap, and let consciousness drift. The transition was smoother now, practiced. One moment she was in the cold vault, the next...

She stood in a dance hall that belonged to another era entirely. The ceiling soared impossibly high, supported by columns of what looked like frozen lightning. The walls were transparent aluminums, she knew this without knowing how she knew—offering views of a city that had never existed in her world. Towers of glass and steel reached toward stars that were somehow both above and around them, as if the building existed in multiple dimensions at once.

But it was the dance floor that stole her breath. It wasn't solidity was made of condensed starlight, rippling like water with each step but firm beneath her feet. Constellations swirled beneath the surface, creating patterns that shifted with the music.

Music. There was music, unlike anything in her world. It was mathematical in its precision but emotional in its impact, sequences of sound that seemed to bypass her ears and resonate directly in her bones.

"Cael?" She turned, and there he was.

More solid than ever before in their dreams, he stood at the edge of the dance floor in clothes from his era. This jacket seemed to be cut from midnight itself, shifting between fabric and energy. His silver eyes were bright with joy and something else, something that made her pulse race.

"Dance with me," he said, extending his hand. "Let me show you how we celebrated in my time."

She moved toward him, aware that she too had changed in the dream. Her simple archivist robes had transformed into a dress that seemed to be woven from the same starlight as the floor, flowing and shifting with each movement. It was impossibly beautiful, impossibly right.

Their hands met—almost. As always, there was that fraction of separation, that cruel gap between almost and actual. But tonight, riding the high of their discovery, it seemed less like a barrier and more like anticipation.

"Follow my lead," he said, positioning himself as if his hand rested at her waist, as if her hand lay in his. "The dance is about probability, about potential. We move not just through space but through possibilities."

The music swelled, and they began to move.

It was like no dance she'd ever experienced. Each step took them through different versions of the moment—here they spun through starlight, there through a garden of crystalline flowers, here through abstract mathematical space where their forms became equations spiraling around each other. The dance floor rippled with each movement, constellations rearranging themselves to trace their path.

"This is impossible," she laughed, as he spun hero the idea of spinning her—and reality kaleidoscoped around them.

"Impossible is our specialty," he replied, and his smile was radiant. "Look."

She followed his gaze and gasped. Around them, other couples had appeared—translucent echoes of dancers from his time, from her time, from times that never were. All moving in the same rhythm, all celebrating discoveries, victories, moments of connection that transcended physical reality.

"Every successful collaboration, every meeting of minds that advanced under-standing—they all echo here, in quantum space," he explained, drawing her closer in their not-quite-embrace. "We're part of that tradition now. Our solution, our partnership, it's written in the universe's memory."

The music shifted, becoming slower, more intimate. The other dancers faded, leaving them alone on the vast floor of stars. She was intensely aware of every almost-touch—his hand not-quite at her waist, her palm hovering just above his shoulder, the space between them charged with possibility.

"I want to tell you something," he said, his silver eyes locked on hers. "About my past. About why I volunteered for the consciousness transfer experiment."

She nodded, moving with him in the slow, swaying rhythm that needed no steps.

"I was in love," he said simply. "Her name was Aria. She was brilliant, beautiful, everything a young scientist could want. We were going to marry, going to change the world together."

Jealousy flared in Elara's chest, surprising in its intensity, but he must have felt it through their bond because he pulled her closer—or the illusion of closer.

"She died," he continued softly. "A quantum cascade failure, not unlike the magical storms your world faces now. I was there, trying to stabilize the reaction. I could have saved myself, but I tried to save her instead. I failed at both—she died, and I was caught in the cascade. The only way to preserve my consciousness was the experimental transfer."

"Cael..." She ached for him, for the loss that had defined centuries of existence.

"I thought I was honoring her memory by surviving, by continuing our work. But Elara..." He stopped dancing, standing still in the middle of the swirling starlight. "I was wrong. I wasn't honoring anything. I was hiding. Running from the pain of loss by removing myself from the possibility of feeling. Until you."

"What do you mean?"

"You woke me up. Not just my consciousness—that was always active. You woke my heart. Made me realize that existing isn't the same as living, that preser-vation isn't the same as purpose." His form solidified, becoming more real with the intensity of his emotion. "I thought I knew what love was, but Aria and I... we were young, caught up in the romance of shared ambition. What you and I have—this connection of minds, this recognition of souls—it's deeper. It's..."

"I think I'm falling" she began, the words tumbling out before she could stop them.

The sphere in the physical world flared with sudden, brilliant light. Pain seared through their connection—not physical but existential, like reality itself rejecting what she was about to say. The dreamscape shuddered, fractured, and began to collapse.

"No!" Cael reached for her, and for one impossible moment, she felt him—actually felt his hands grasp her arms, solid and warm and real. His eyes were wide with desperation. "Don't stop. Please, say it again."

But the dream was already dissolving. She was being pulled back to her physical body, to the cold vault and the limitations of reality. The last thing she saw was his face, the naked longing there, the need to hear words that the universe itself seemed determined to prevent.

She gasped back to consciousness in her chair, the sphere blazing like a small sun in her lap. Her skin tingled where he'd touched her—actually touched her—in those final seconds. The sensation lingered, impossible but undeniable.

"Elara!" His voice in her mind was urgent, frightened. "Are you alright? The feedback, the rejection—I couldn't control it—"

"I'm fine," she panted, though her hands were shaking. "What was that? What happened?"

"I think..." He paused, and she could feel him testing their connection, examining it like a scientist studying an anomaly. "I think we pushed too hard against the boundaries. What you were about to say, what we both felt would have solidified our entanglement past the point of no return."

"And that's bad?"

"Not bad. Irreversible. If we cross that threshold, if we speak certain truths into being, there's no going back. We would be quantum entangled at the deepest level. If something happened to one of us..."

"It would happen to both," she finished. "Like the bonded pairs from before the Convergence. The ones who died together rather than live apart."

"Yes."

She looked down at the sphere, no longer blazing but pulsing with a steady, warm light. In her mind, she could still feel the ghost of his touch, the moment when impossibility had bent just enough to allow contact.

"I don't care," she said quietly. "Whatever the risk, whatever the cost, I don't care. I felt you, Cael. Actually felt you. Your hands were real."

"For a heartbeat," he agreed, wonder coloring his voice. "When you started to say... when the emotion peaked... the boundaries thinned enough that I could manifest, just for an instant."

"Then we know it's possible." She stood, energized by the revelation. "If strong enough emotion can thin the boundaries, can make you solid even for a moment, then we just need to find a way to stabilize that state."

"Elara, the amount of energy required, the risk to the lattice—"

"We'll find a way," she interrupted. "We solved the Synthesis Lock together. We can solve this, too." She pressed the sphere to her chest, feeling his warmth, his presence, his matching determination. "I want to dance with you properly. I want to hold you without dissolving. I want to say the words that reality tried to stop."

"I want that too," he whispered. "More than I've ever wanted anything. But Elara, we have to be careful. Tonight proved that our connection is affecting more than just us. If we're not cautious, if we push too hard—"

"Then we'll be brilliant and careful," she said, managing a smile. "We're good at impossible things, remember?"

She gathered her papers, the proof they'd created together, the solution that might lead to his freedom. As she prepared to leave the vault, she felt him pulse with an emotion too complex for words—love and fear and hope all tangled together.

"Elara?" His voice was soft, almost vulnerable. "What you almost said, before the dream collapsed..."

"I'm falling in love with you," she said clearly, firmly, feeling the words resonate through their bond like struck crystal. "No—that's not right. I've already fallen. I love you, Cael. Completely, impossibly, inevitably."

The sphere grew warm in her hands, and through their connection came his response—not in words but in pure emotion, a wave of love so profound it brought tears to her eyes.

"And I love you," he finally managed. "Across centuries, across impossible distance, with whatever remains of my heart and soul—I love you, Elara."

The words hung between them, admitted at last, dangerous, beautiful, and absolutely true. She could feel the entanglement deepening, their consciousnesses intertwining in ways that could never be undone.

But she didn't pull back. Neither did he.

Instead, they stood together in that moment of truth, separated by physics but united by something stronger. And in the depths of the sphere, in the quantum space where his consciousness lived, she could have sworn she saw him smile—not the echo of a smile, not the memory of one, but a real, present expression of joy.

They would find a way. Whatever it took, whatever they had to risk or sacrifice, they would find a way to bridge the impossible distance between them.

Because now that they'd tasted possibility—that instant of real contact, those words of love finally spoken—neither of them could bear to accept anything less than everything.

Chapter 9: The Truth of the Lattice

The morning after their shared victory in the Vaults, Elara found herself humming as she catalogued artifacts, the crystalline sphere warm against her palm. Every few minutes, she caught herself tracing its surface with her thumb, the gesture as natural as breathing. The memory of Cael's laughter still echoed in her mind from their triumph the night before, rich and genuine, unmarked by the careful formality that had initially colored his speech.

You're distracted, his voice murmured in her thoughts, tinged with amusement. Your mentor keeps glancing over. She suspects you're hiding something.

Elara's eyes flicked to Master Thorne, who was indeed watching her with a furrowed brow. Heat crept up her neck as she forced herself to focus on the scroll before her. "I'm fine," she whispered, barely moving her lips.

You're many things, Elara, but 'fine' isn't one of them. You're extraordinary.

The warmth in his mental voice sent a flutter through her chest. Over the past weeks, their conversations had grown increasingly intimate, filled with shared secrets and lingering silences that spoke louder than words. She'd begun to crave the moments when his presence filled her mind, pushing away the loneliness that had been her constant companion.

Tonight, she thought back to him. Meet me tonight.

She felt his agreement like a caress against her consciousness, and the promise carried her through the rest of the day.

***

That evening, moonlight streamed through her chamber's crystal window, casting prismatic rainbows across the stone floor. Elara had arranged cushions in the center of the room, the sphere resting in a nest of soft silk. Candles flickered around the space, their flames dancing in response to the magical currents that seemed to strengthen whenever she and Cael spoke.

"Show me," she whispered, settling cross-legged before the artifact. "Show me your world."

The sphere pulsed, and reality shifted.

She found herself standing in the dream garden Cael had created for her—but tonight, it was different. The floating islands connected by bridges of crystallized starlight seemed more solid, more real. The trees bore fruit that looked like captured moonbeams, and flowers bloomed with petals of living silver that chimed softly in the ethereal breeze.

And there was Cael.

He stood at the garden's heart, more substantial than she'd ever seen him. The careful lines of his face were clearer now—high cheekbones, a strong jaw, eyes the color of storm clouds shot through with silver lightning. His dark hair moved in the dream wind, and when he smiled at her approach, her breath caught.

"You're more real," she said, wonder threading through her voice.

"As are you." He reached toward her, and this time when their fingers met, she felt the ghost of pressure, warm and electric. "We're growing stronger together, Elara. The bond between us is deepening."

She took another step closer, close enough that she could see the way starlight reflected in his eyes. "What does that mean?"

"It means..." He hesitated, his gaze dropping to her lips before meeting her eyes again. "It means I'm becoming more myself. More human. And you're becoming more attuned to the quantum realm that holds me."

The space between them crackled with tension, with possibilities that made her pulse quicken. Around them, the garden seemed to hold its breath—flowers turning toward them like an audience, the soft chiming of the silver petals creating a symphony of anticipation.

"Cael," she whispered, and the sound of his name on her lips made him close his eyes as if in pain.

"You don't know what you do to me," he said, his voice rough. "What it means to hear my name spoken with such... care."

"Then show me."

He opened his eyes, and the intensity there nearly staggered her. Slowly, giving her every chance to pull away, he cupped her face with hands that felt real enough to break her heart. His thumb traced the curve of her cheek, and she leaned into the touch.

"I've wanted to do this since the first moment I heard your voice," he confessed, his forehead coming to rest against hers. "You woke something in me I thought was lost forever."

"Then don't wait anymore."

The kiss was everything she'd dreamed of and more. Soft at first, tentative, as if he couldn't quite believe she was real. But when she responded, when her hands fisted in front of his shirt and she pressed closer, he deepened it with a hunger that spoke of centuries of solitude.

In the dreamscape, she could feel everything—the warmth of his skin, the solid strength of his chest against hers, the way his hands tangled in her hair. He kissed her like she was air, and he was drowning, like she was the answer to every question he'd ever asked the darkness.

When they finally broke apart, both were breathing hard. The garden around them had responded to their connection—flowers bloomed brighter, the very air shimmered with aurora-light, and she could swear she felt an echo of their shared heartbeat in the ground beneath their feet.

"Elara," he whispered against her lips, and the reverence in his voice made her eyes flutter shut.

But even as she melted into his embrace, something nagged at the edge of her consciousness. The garden felt different—not just more real, but somehow strained, as if it were pulled taut like a rope about to snap.

"Cael," she began, but he was already stiffening, his expression shifting from tender to troubled.

"Something's wrong," he said, stepping back from her. The movement sent ripples through the dreamscape, and she watched in alarm as cracks appeared in the crystalline bridges.

"What is it?"

He turned away from her, his form flickering as his concentration wavered. "I... I remember something. Something important."

The garden began to shake, silver petals falling like rain around them. Elara reached for him, but her hand passed through his shoulder as he became translucent.

"Cael, stay with me. What do you remember?"

"The lattice," he said, his voice distant, horrified. "Oh, stars above, the lattice."

The dreamscape shattered.

***

Elara gasped, finding herself back in her chambers, the sphere clutched so tightly in her hands that her knuckles had gone white. Her lips still tingled from the dream-kiss, and for a moment, she could have sworn she tasted starlight and sorrow.

"Cael?" she called, but silence answered her.

Minutes passed before his presence returned, heavy with an anguish that made her chest ache in sympathy.

I need to show you something, he said, his mental voice carefully controlled. But first, you need to understand what I am. What I truly am.

"I know what you are," she said softly. "You're the person I—"

No. The sharpness of his interruption made her flinch. Listen to me, Elara. Really listen.

The world around her shifted, and suddenly she was seeing through his consciousness—not the garden this time, but something vast and impossible. The magical lattice that powered her entire world spread out before her like a web of living light, each strand pulsing with energy that flowed in complex patterns she could barely comprehend.

But at the center of it all, at the very heart of the web, was a brilliant point of light that she somehow knew was Cael.

The Quantum Heart, he explained, his voice hollow. The artifact you found isn't just my prison, Elara. It's the cornerstone of your entire magical world. I'm not just trapped, I'm the source. The lattice draws its power from me, from my consciousness, from my very existence.

The implications hit her like a physical blow. "You're saying that if I free you..."

The magical world dies. Every leyline goes dark. Every spell fails. Every magical creature fades. Everything your people have built, everything they are—gone.

She could feel his anguish bleeding through their connection, centuries of loneliness weighed against the knowledge that his freedom would doom millions. The lattice pulsed around them, beautiful and terrible, each thread a life that depended on his continued captivity.

"But there has to be another way," she whispered, desperation clawing at her throat. "We could find an alternative power source, or"

Do you think I haven't tried? His voice cracked with pain. Do you think I haven't spent centuries searching for a solution? The quantum principles that created the lattice are irreversible. Remove the heart, and the whole system collapses.

The vision faded, leaving her alone in her chamber with the sphere that suddenly felt like it weighed a thousand pounds. She could feel Cael there, present but withdrawn, wrapped in a grief so profound it threatened to drown them both.

"Then I can't free you," she said, the words tearing from her throat. "But I can't lose you either."

Then you can't love me, he replied, each word precise and devastating. Not without ending the world. Choose wisely, my heart.

The endearment, spoken with such tender despair, broke something inside her. Tears spilled down her cheeks as she pressed the sphere to her chest, as if she could somehow hold him close through crystal and quantum barriers.

"Don't," she whispered fiercely. "Don't ask me to choose. There has to be another way."

There isn't. His presence in her mind flickered, withdrawing like a tide. I should never have let this happen. Should never have let myself hope, or let you care for something that can never be free.

"Cael, please—"

But she could feel him pulling away, could sense the walls he was rebuilding around his consciousness. The connection that had grown so strong between them began to fade, leaving her with nothing but the cold weight of crystal and the echo of a kiss that had tasted like goodbye.

In the lattice vision, she had seen the threads that bound her world together, all of them leading back to the bright point of light that was Cael's trapped soul. Beautiful, necessary, and utterly inescapable.

The magical world lived because he was caged.

And now that she loved him, she would have to live with that knowledge, carrying the weight of his sacrifice and her own impossible choice.

The sphere dimmed in her hands, and for the first time since she'd found it, Cael's presence completely faded from her mind, leaving her alone with the terrible truth of what loving him really meant.

***

Hours later, Elara still sat motionless in the center of her chamber, the sphere cradled in her lap like a sleeping child. The candles had burned low, casting flickering shadows that seemed to mock the memory of their shared garden.

She had replayed their conversation a hundred times, searching for some loophole, some possibility he might have missed. But the mathematics of it were elegant and absolute—the quantum lattice required a conscious anchor, a thinking heart to regulate the flow of power. Remove that heart, and the entire magical ecosystem would collapse like a house of cards.

Millions would die. Not just from the immediate magical failures, but from the slow starvation that would follow as their entire civilization crumbled. Her people didn't know how to live without magic anymore—it was woven into every aspect of their existence, from the simplest cooking flame to the great barrier spells that protected their cities from the wild storms of the outer lands.

And yet...

She touched her lips, remembering the kiss that had felt more real than anything in her waking life. In that moment, in that impossible garden built from dreams and quantum possibility, she had felt truly alive for the first time. Complete in a way she'd never known she was broken.

How could she condemn the world for love? But how could she condemn love for the world?

"Cael," she whispered to the silent sphere. "I know you can hear me. I know you're still there."

Silence.

"I won't give up," she continued, her voice gaining strength. "There has to be a way. You said the quantum principles were irreversible, but maybe... maybe we don't need to reverse them. Maybe we need to transform them."

Still nothing, but she thought she felt the faintest flicker of attention.

"I'm going to find a solution," she promised, lifting the sphere to press a soft kiss to its surface. "Even if it takes me a lifetime. Even if it seems impossible. I won't let you sacrifice yourself for my world, and I won't sacrifice my world for you. There has to be a third option."

The sphere warmed slightly in her hands—not with Cael's presence, but with something deeper. The quantum energies that powered it seemed to pulse in rhythm with her heartbeat, as if responding to her determination.

In the lattice vision, all the threads had led to Cael. But threads could be rewoven, patterns could be changed. The magical world needed a heart, but perhaps it didn't need a caged one.

Perhaps it needed one that chose to stay.

The thought crystallized in her mind with the force of revelation. Not imprisonment, but partnership. Not captivity, but willing sacrifice transformed into something greater.

It was a slim hope, barely more than a whisper of possibility. But it was enough to kindle a flame in the darkness that had settled over her heart.

Tomorrow, she would begin her research in earnest. She would scour every archive, consult every expert, explore every avenue of magical theory and quantum mechanics. Somewhere in the vast store of knowledge her people had accumulated, there had to be an answer.

There had to be a way to love him without dooming her world.

There had to be a way to free them both.

The sphere pulsed once more in her hands, and though Cael remained silent, she thought she felt an echo of something that might have been hope. Fragile as starlight, precious as the memory of his kiss, but real enough to sustain her through the long night ahead.

Outside her window, the first light of dawn began to touch the crystal towers of her city, each one connected to the others by threads of light too subtle for ordinary eyes to see. The lattice hummed its ancient song, powered by a consciousness trapped at its heart, beautiful and terrible and possibly, just possibly, not as immutable as it seemed.

Elara held the sphere close and began to plan.

Chapter 10: Cracks in the Web

The first crystal explosion shattered the morning quiet with the sound of a thousand bells screaming.

Elara jolted awake in her chair, the sphere tumbling from her lap as the walls of her chamber vibrated with sympathetic resonance. Outside her window, the great lighthouse crystal that guided sky-ships to the harbor erupted in a shower of azure sparks, its light dying as fragments rained down onto the cobblestones below.

Shouts echoed through the corridors of the Aether Vaults as scholars and apprentices scrambled to assess the damage. Master Thorne's voice rose above the chaos, barking orders to check the ward-stones and stabilize the remaining crystals.

Elara. Cael's presence rushed back into her mind, urgent and strained. It's starting.

"What's starting?" she whispered, snatching up the sphere and pressing it close. Through her window, she could see smoke rising from the harbor district, and the distant wail of emergency bells carried on the wind.

The cascade failure. My presence in the lattice is causing instabilities. I should have warned you sooner, but I hoped...

Another explosion, this one closer. The great crystal that powered the Vaults' lighting grid cracked down its center, sending hairline fractures racing across its surface like frozen lightning. The magical lamps throughout the building flickered and dimmed.

Elara's door burst open without ceremony. Master Thorne stood in the doorway, her usually immaculate robes singed at the edges, her silver hair escaping its careful braids.

"Elara! Thank the stars you're safe. We need to evacuate—now." Her mentor's eyes were sharp with concern and something else—suspicion. "The resonance crystals are failing in sequence. I've never seen anything like it."

"How bad is it?" Elara asked, slipping the sphere into her satchel with practiced casualness.

"Bad enough that the Mage Council is calling an emergency session. Lord Serrin himself is coming to investigate." Thorne's expression darkened. "He'll have authority to examine everything—every artifact, every research project, every scholar's work."

Ice flooded Elara's veins. Lord Serrin was the Council's most ruthless investigator, known for his ability to extract truth from the most carefully guarded secrets. If he discovered Cael...

I heard Cael's quiet voice in her mind. Elara, you need to hide the artifact. If Serrin gets his hands on me...

She didn't need him to finish. Serrin would see Cael as nothing more than a tool to be exploited, a source of power to be harnessed. The man's ambition was legendary, as was his complete lack of compassion.

"Master Thorne," Elara said carefully, "what kind of examination are we talking about?"

"Full resonance scans, magical signature analysis, possibly even memory extraction from any artifacts that might have cognitive imprints." Thorne studied her apprentice's face with narrowed eyes. "Why? Is there something you need to tell me?"

The weight of the sphere in her satchel felt like a burning coal against her hip. "Of course not. I just... I want to know what we're dealing with."

Before Thorne could respond, another explosion rocked the building. This time, the shock wave was strong enough to crack the stone walls, and Elara heard the ominous groan of structural crystals under stress.

"We'll discuss this later," Thorne said grimly. "Right now, we evacuate. Gather only what's essential."

As her mentor hurried away to organize the other scholars, Elara stood frozen in the center of her chamber. Around her, smaller crystals were beginning to show signs of stress—hairline cracks, fluctuating light, the high-pitched whine of magical resonance pushed beyond its limits.

It's me, Cael said, his mental voice heavy with guilt. My presence is disrupting the quantum foundations of the lattice. The more conscious I become, the more I destabilize everything.

"Then stop," she whispered fiercely. "Pull back. Go dormant again."

I can't. The bond between us has grown too strong. When you opened your heart to me, when we...—she felt his hesitation, the memory of their kiss flickering through the connection—when we became truly connected, it changed something fundamental. I can't retreat any more than you can stop breathing.

Another explosion, this one from the market district. Through her window, Elara could see people fleeing through the streets, their faces turned skyward in terror as crystals that had powered their city for centuries began to fail one by one.

"How long do we have?"

Hours, maybe less. The cascade is accelerating. Each failure puts more stress on the remaining nodes.

Elara grabbed her research journals and a few essential supplies, her mind racing. She needed somewhere safe to hide, somewhere Serrin couldn't find them while she worked on a solution. But where could you hide from the most powerful investigator in the kingdom?

The old archives, Cael suggested, following her thoughts. Three levels down, section K-9. It's been sealed for decades, officially condemned after a minor cave-in. But the crystals there are dormant, disconnected from the main grid. It might mask my presence.

It was a slim hope, but better than nothing. Elara slung her satchel across her shoulder and slipped out into the chaos-filled corridors.

****

The abandoned archives were everything Cael had promised—dark, dusty, and blessedly quiet. Elara made her way through the maze of collapsed shelving and debris-covered reading tables, guided by the faint light of a few stubborn glow-stones that had retained just enough charge to provide minimal illumination.

She found a relatively clear space behind a fallen bookshelf and spread out her supplies. The sphere sat before her, its surface dim but warm, pulsing in rhythm with her elevated heartbeat.

You're safe for now, Cael said as his presence solidified in her mind. But Elara, we need to talk.

"If this is about choosing between you and the world again—"

It is. His mental voice was firm, brooking no argument. Look around you. The lattice is collapsing, and it's my fault. How many people will die in those crystal explosions? How many more when the wardstones fail and the storms get through?

Above them, another distant explosion rumbled through the building's bones. Dust filtered down from the ceiling, and one of the glow-stones flickered ominously.

"It's not your fault," Elara said aloud, needing to hear the words in her own voice. "You didn't choose this. You were forced into that prison."

But I chose to awaken. I chose to reach out to you. I chose to become more human instead of remaining a dormant power source. His presence in her mind roiled with self-recrimination. Every moment of consciousness, every dream we've shared, every time I've felt joy or desire or love—it all pulls me further from the quantum state that keeps the lattice stable.

She closed her eyes, feeling the truth of his words like thorns in her chest. The mathematics were inescapable—consciousness and quantum coherence were inversely related. The more Cael became himself, the less he could serve as the lattice's heart.

Show me, he said suddenly. Show me your choice.

The world shifted, and she found herself back in their dream garden. But this time, it was dying.

The floating islands were cracking, pieces breaking away to tumble into the star-scattered void below. The crystalline bridges had turned brittle and dark, their light flickering like dying candles. The silver trees were bare, their musical leaves scattered on the ground like fallen tears.

And in the center of it all stood Cael, solid and real and heartbreakingly beautiful. But with each breath he took, another flower withered. With each step, another section of the bridge crumbled. His very presence was poison to this place he'd created for her.

"This is what loving me means," he said, his storm-grey eyes filled with anguish. "This is what consciousness costs. I destroy everything beautiful just by existing in it."

"No." She stepped toward him, her feet finding purchase on a bridge that groaned under her weight. "You created this. You made something beautiful from nothing."

"And now I'm unmaking it." He held up his hands, and she could see through them to the dying garden beyond. "Just like I'm unmaking your world. The lattice can't sustain a conscious heart, Elara. It needs a tool, not a person."

She reached him just as a section of the central island broke away, plummeting into the void with a sound like distant thunder. Around them, the last of the silver flowers burned to ash, their light dying one by one.

"Then we find another way," she said fiercely, grasping his translucent hands. "We change the lattice. We rebuild it. We—"

"We what?" His voice cracked with desperate frustration. "Do you think I haven't tried? Do you think in all my centuries of imprisonment, I haven't searched for every possible solution? The quantum mechanics are absolute, Elara. Immutable. You can't love me without destroying everything you care about."

"I don't care about everything else!" The words burst from her before she could stop them, raw and honest and terrifying. "I care about you. I choose you."

Cael stared at her, his form solidifying with shock. Around them, the garden's destruction paused, as if the universe itself was holding its breath.

"You don't mean that," he whispered.

"I do." She pulled his hands to her chest, pressing his palms flat against her heart. "If I have to choose between loving you and saving the world, I choose love. I choose you. Every time."

The confession hung between them like a blade, sharp and absolute. In the distance, she could hear the dream-echo of more crystal explosions, the city's death throes played out in metaphor and starlight.

"Elara..." His voice was broken, reverent, afraid.

"Don't," she said, stepping closer until they were breathing the same shimmering air. "Don't tell me I'm wrong. Don't tell me to be noble. Don't tell me to choose duty over my heart."

"Your world needs you."

"My world is you." She cupped his face in her hands, marveling at how solid he felt here in their dying garden. "Don't you understand? I was empty before I found you. I was going through the motions of living without ever being truly alive. You woke something in me that I didn't even know was sleeping."

His hands covered hers, trembling. "If you choose me, billions will die."

"If I choose them, we die. Maybe not physically, but everything that matters between us—gone. And I can't live in a world where I had the chance to love you and walked away from it."

For a moment, they stood suspended in the crumbling dream, two souls balanced on the edge of an impossible choice. The garden continued its slow dissolution around them, but neither moved, neither spoke, neither breathed.

Then Cael's control shattered.

"Damn the world," he said hoarsely, and crushed his mouth to hers.

The kiss was desperate, hungry, born of centuries of loneliness and the terrible knowledge that this might be their last moment together. His hands tangled in her hair, holding her to him as if she might vanish. She could taste his anguish, his desire, his love—all of it pouring through their connection like molten gold.

She kissed him back with equal fervor, her fingers clutching at his shoulders, her body pressing against his with a need that transcended the physical. In this moment, in this dying dream, she was finally, completely alive.

When they broke apart, both were trembling. The garden around them had stilled its destruction, as if their passion had somehow stabilized the quantum foundation of the dream. Silver light pulsed beneath their feet in rhythm with their shared heartbeat.

"I love you," Cael whispered against her lips, the words a prayer and a curse and a promise all at once. "Stars help me, I love you more than existence itself."

"Then fight for us," she breathed back. "Help me find another way. There has to be something we haven't tried, some solution we haven't seen."

He pulled back just enough to look into her eyes, his own blazing with an emotion too vast for words. "And if there isn't?"

"Then we'll create one." She smiled through her tears, fierce and uncompromising. "Together. No matter what it costs."

The dream garden pulsed with renewed light, responding to their shared determination. The dying flowers bloomed again, their silver petals ringing like distant bells. The bridges solidified, their crystal spans singing with harmonious resonance.

But even as hope flickered between them, Elara could feel the real world pressing in—the weight of Serrin's investigation, the cascade failures spreading through the city, the terrible mathematics that said their love was impossible.

"Time's running out," Cael said, echoing her thoughts. "Serrin will find us soon."

"Then we'd better work fast." She pressed one more kiss to his lips, soft and sweet and full of promise. "I meant what I said, Cael. I choose you. Whatever comes next, we face it together."

The dream faded, leaving her back in the dusty archives with the sphere warm in her hands and the taste of starlight on her lips. Above them, the crystal explosions continued, each one a countdown to a choice that might damn them both.

But for the first time since learning the truth about the lattice, Elara felt something stronger than despair.

She felt the fire of a love worth fighting for, worth dying for, worth rewriting the very laws of magic to preserve.

And in the sphere's gentle glow, she could feel Cael's answering flame, burning just as bright, just as fierce, just as willing to challenge the impossible for the sake of what they'd found together.

The world would make them choose, but they would not go quietly into that choice.

They would fight for love, for each other, for the slim hope that somewhere in the vast complexity of quantum magic, there might be a third option waiting to be discovered.

Together.

***

Hours passed in the hidden archives as Elara pored over her research notes, looking for any clue, any thread that might lead to salvation. The sphere sat before her, pulsing with Cael's presence, but he remained quiet, letting her work. At the same time, he monitored the lattice's deteriorating stability.

The explosions had grown more frequent, their rumble a constant reminder of the countdown they were racing against. And somewhere above them, she knew Serrin was conducting his investigation, his cold intellect working methodically through every possibility, every clue that might lead him to the source of the crisis.

It was only a matter of time before he found them.

But in the soft glow of the sphere, surrounded by the whispered promises of their shared dream, Elara refused to surrender to despair. Love had awakened something in both of them—something powerful enough to challenge the fundamental laws that governed their world.

If love could wake the dead and bind souls across impossible barriers, then perhaps it could also find a way to rewrite destiny itself.

She would not give up.

She would not choose.

She would find another way, even if it meant breaking every rule of magic and science in the process.

For Cael.

For them.

For the love that had already proven stronger than centuries of separation and the weight of an entire world's needs.

The sphere pulsed once more, and in its light, Elara saw not the end of hope, but the beginning of a battle for love that would shake the very foundations of their reality.

Chapter 11: The Spy in the Shadows

The sound of footsteps echoing through the abandoned archives froze Elara's blood.

She extinguished her light crystal with a whispered word, plunging the hidden alcove into darkness. The sphere's glow dimmed in response to her fear, but she could still feel its warmth against her palm—and through it, Cael's sudden alertness.

Someone's coming, he warned unnecessarily. More than one person.

Elara pressed herself deeper into the shadows behind the fallen bookshelf, hardly daring to breathe. The footsteps grew closer, accompanied by the soft murmur of voices. She recognized the crisp authority of Serrin's tone, though she couldn't make out the words. Her heart hammered against her ribs as the search party moved through the outer chambers.

They're doing a systematic sweep, Cael observed, his mental voice tight with concern. Checking every room, every alcove. It's only a matter of time before—

A new set of footsteps broke away from the group, lighter and more hurried. They approached her hiding spot with purpose rather than the methodical pattern of the search. Elara's grip tightened on the sphere as a familiar voice called out softly.

"Elara? I know you're here."

Seris.

Relief and confusion warred in her chest. What was he doing with Serrin's search party? But before she could process the implications, a warm hand touched her shoulder in the darkness.

"It's me," Seris whispered, his voice barely audible. "We need to talk. Now."

Don't trust him, Cael's voice cut through her mind like a blade. Something about this feels wrong.

But Seris was already pulling her deeper into the archives, away from the sound of Serrin's investigation. His touch was gentle but insistent, guiding her through the maze of debris with the confidence of someone who knew these passages well.

They emerged into a small chamber lit by floating crystal lanterns that cast dancing shadows on the walls. The light revealed Seris's face clearly for the first time—sharp cheekbones made sharper by worry, dark eyes that seemed to hold secrets, and an expression of barely controlled tension.

"How did you find me?" Elara demanded, clutching her satchel protectively.

"I've been following you," he admitted without preamble. His gaze dropped to her satchel, then back to her face. "For weeks now. Ever since you started acting... different."

He knows, Cael said grimly. I can sense it on him—traces of quantum resonance. He's been close to the artifact multiple times.

Elara's throat went dry. "I don't know what you're talking about."

"Don't." Seris stepped closer, and she caught the scent of crystal-fire and midnight air that always seemed to cling to him. "Please don't lie to me, Elara. Not when I'm risking everything to warn you."

"Warn me about what?"

"Serrin knows something is causing the lattice instabilities. He's convinced there's a rogue artifact involved, something that's been hidden from the Council's oversight." Seris's eyes searched her face intently. "He's already ordered memory extractions from three senior archivists. It's only a matter of time before he gets to you."

The chamber seemed to shrink around them. Memory extraction was a brutal process, one that could leave permanent damage to the subject's mind. If Serrin used it on her, he would discover not only Cael's existence but every intimate moment they'd shared.

"Why are you helping me?" she asked, though part of her already knew the answer from the way his gaze lingered on her lips.

"Because I care about you." The words were simple, honest, and they landed in the space between them like a stone in still water. "More than I should. More than is wise."

I don't like this. Cael's mental voice was sharp with an emotion Elara had never heard from him before. Ask him what he wants in return.

"What do you want from me, Seris?"

Something flickered across his features—hurt, perhaps, or resignation. "Nothing you're not willing to give. But Elara, whatever you're hiding, whatever artifact you've found—it's dangerous. The lattice failures are accelerating. People are dying."

"I know that," she said, more sharply than she intended.

"Then help me understand." He reached toward her, his fingers almost brushing her cheek before falling away. "Let me help you. We can work together to find a solution that doesn't require Serrin's... methods."

The offer hung in the air between them, tempting and treacherous. Seris had always been kind to her and had always shown interest in her research. But there was something in his eyes now—a hunger that went beyond academic curiosity or even romantic interest.

He wants power, Cael said flatly. I can feel it radiating from him. Whatever he's offering, it comes with a price.

"And if I refuse?" Elara asked carefully.

Seris's expression hardened slightly. "Then I can't protect you from what's coming. Serrin isn't just investigating the artifact anymore, he's investigating you specifically. Someone reported seeing strange lights in your quarters, hearing you talking to yourself."

A chill ran down Elara's spine. "Who?"

"Does it matter? The point is, you're running out of time and options." He stepped closer again, close enough that she could see the flecks of silver in his dark eyes. "I'm offering you an alternative. Partnership instead of interrogation."

Tell him no, Cael urged. Whatever he's planning, it won't end well for either of us.

But even as Cael's jealousy colored his thoughts, Elara could see the logic in Seris's offer. She was trapped in the archives with a failing lattice above and Serrin's investigation closing in. If Seris could buy her time, help her find a solution...

"What kind of partnership?" she asked.

Relief flickered across Seris's features. "Combine our research. Pool our resources. Find a way to stabilize the lattice before it's too late." His hand found hers, warm and steady. "You don't have to face this alone, Elara."

The touch sent an unexpected flutter through her chest—not the lightning-strike of connection she felt with Cael, but something warmer, more grounded. More real.

Does he make your heart race like I do? Cael's mental voice was carefully controlled, but she could feel the roiling jealousy beneath the surface. Does his touch feel like coming home?

"Cael, don't," she thought back, but she could feel him pulling away from her consciousness, withdrawing into the quantum depths of the sphere.

"Elara?" Seris squeezed her hand gently. "What do you say?"

She looked up at him—solid, present, offering salvation with no impossible choices attached. For a moment, she let herself imagine what it would be like. Working alongside Seris, unraveling the mysteries of the lattice together, building something real and lasting without the shadow of world-ending consequences hanging over them.

But then the sphere pulsed against her hip, a gentle reminder of the love that had already claimed her heart. Even withdrawn, even jealous, Cael's presence was woven into her soul in ways that couldn't be undone.

"I..." she began, then stopped as the sound of voices echoed closer. Serrin's search was expanding, moving methodically through the archives.

"We need to move," Seris said urgently. "There's a passage that leads to the old maintenance tunnels. I can get you out of here, but we have to go now."

Don't, Cael pleaded, his mental voice thin with distance. Please, Elara. Don't trust him.

"Why should I trust you?" she asked Seris, echoing Cael's concern.

"Because I'm risking more than you know to keep this secret—for you." His hand tightened on hers, his eyes intense. "Because I've been watching you for months, seeing how you light up when you think no one's looking, how you whisper to empty air like you're talking to someone who understands you completely."

Elara's breath caught. How much had he seen? How much did he suspect?

"Because I think I'm falling in love with you," he continued quietly, "and I can't bear to watch Serrin destroy whatever it is that makes you so... alive."

The confession hit her like a physical blow. In the sphere, she felt Cael's jealousy spike into something darker, more desperate.

He doesn't know you. Cael's voice was raw with pain. Not like I do. He sees the surface, the mask you wear for the world. I've seen your soul, Elara. I've touched the part of you that dreams.

But Seris was real, solid, standing before her with hope and fear written plainly on his features. He was offering her a life without impossible choices, without the weight of worlds hanging in the balance.

"I care about you too," she said softly, and felt Cael's anguish like a knife through her chest.

Seris's smile was radiant. "Then let me help you. Whatever you're hiding, whatever you're protecting—we can figure it out together."

The sound of approaching footsteps made the decision for her. She nodded quickly, allowing Seris to lead her toward a concealed opening in the far wall. But as they slipped into the narrow passage beyond, she felt Cael's presence fade almost entirely, leaving her with only the cold weight of crystal and the echoing emptiness where his voice had been.

Cael? she called silently, but received no answer.

***

The maintenance tunnels were a labyrinth of narrow corridors and service shafts that threaded between the building's foundation stones. Seris moved through them with practiced ease, his light-crystal casting dancing shadows on the rough-hewn walls.

"How do you know about these passages?" Elara asked, trying to ignore the ache in her chest where Cael's silence had settled like a stone.

"I've been exploring the Vaults since I was an apprentice," he replied, not looking back. "These old buildings have secrets layered on secrets. You just have to know where to look."

They emerged into a small chamber carved from natural stone, far removed from the main archives. Ancient crystals embedded in the walls provided a soft, steady glow that reminded Elara painfully of her dream garden. Seris gestured for her to sit on a stone ledge while he checked the passage behind them.

"We should be safe here for now," he said, settling beside her. "Serrin's people won't think to look this deep."

Elara nodded absently, her attention focused inward. The sphere in her satchel was warm but silent, Cael's presence reduced to the faintest whisper of quantum resonance. She could feel his hurt, his jealousy, his fear that she was choosing another path—and it was tearing her apart.

"Elara?" Seris's voice was gentle, concerned. "What's wrong? You look..."

"I'm fine," she said automatically, then caught herself. After weeks of hiding, of carefully maintaining her mask of normalcy, the lie felt heavier than usual.

"You're not," he said simply. "You haven't been fine since you found whatever it is you're carrying in that satchel."

Her hand moved protectively to the sphere's outline, clearly visible through the leather. "I don't know what you mean."

"The artifact that's causing the lattice failures." His tone was matter-of-fact, without accusation. "I've seen the resonance patterns, Elara. Whatever you found, it's incredibly powerful. And incredibly dangerous."

She stared at him, weighing her options. Trust him with the truth and risk exposing Cael to someone who might not understand? Or continue lying and potentially lose the only ally she had?

What would you have me do? she asked the silent sphere. How do I protect you if you won't even talk to me?

Still nothing.

"Show me," Seris said softly.

"What?"

"The artifact. I can help you understand it, maybe even find a way to stabilize its effects on the lattice." He reached toward her satchel, then stopped, his hand hovering inches away. "Please, Elara. Trust me."

The word 'trust' echoed strangely in the crystal chamber. How could she trust anyone when the stakes were so impossibly high? But Seris had risked his own safety to warn her, had offered partnership when he could have simply turned her in to Serrin.

And Cael... Cael was withdrawing from her, letting jealousy poison the connection they'd fought so hard to build.

With trembling fingers, she opened her satchel and drew out the sphere.

Seris's breath caught as the artifact's glow filled the chamber, casting prismatic patterns on the rough stone walls. The quantum resonance was stronger here, away from the lattice's main grid, and she could feel the sphere's power like a living thing in her hands.

"Magnificent," Seris breathed, leaning closer. "The quantum matrices are incredibly complex. I've never seen anything like it."

Don't let him touch it, Cael's voice suddenly returned, sharp with alarm. If he makes contact with the core matrices—

"What is it?" Seris asked, his eyes fixed on the sphere's swirling depths. "What kind of consciousness is stored in there?"

Elara's blood turned to ice. "How did you—"

"The resonance patterns," he said, still not looking away from the artifact. "They're not random. There's intentionality behind them, personality, emotion." His gaze finally shifted to her face, and she saw something hungry and calculating in his expression. "You've been talking to it, haven't you? To whoever's trapped inside."

The chamber suddenly felt much smaller, much more dangerous. "I should go," Elara said, moving to put the sphere back in her satchel.

"Wait." Seris's hand closed over hers, trapping the artifact between their palms. "I'm not going to hurt you, Elara. Or it. But I need to understand what we're dealing with."

The moment his skin touched the sphere's surface, everything changed.

Light exploded through the chamber as the artifact's quantum field destabilized. Seris gasped, his eyes rolling back as the sphere's consciousness-interface activated. Elara felt Cael's shock and fury through their bond as an uninvited presence forced its way into the quantum space they'd shared.

Get him away from me! Cael's mental voice was pure anguish. He's trying to access my core memories, my—

The connection shattered.

Seris jerked his hand back, stumbling away from her with the sphere's afterglow still dancing in his eyes. When he looked at her again, his expression was entirely different—calculating, possessive, tinged with awe and ambition.

"A quantum consciousness," he said, his voice hushed with reverence. "Fully sentient, completely contained. Do you have any idea what you've found?"

"Give it back," Elara said, clutching the sphere protectively. Through their bond, she could feel Cael's pain, his violation at having his most private thoughts rifled through by a stranger.

"The applications are limitless," Seris continued, as if he hadn't heard her. "A consciousness that can interface directly with quantum systems, manipulate magical resonance at the fundamental level..." His eyes gleamed with possibilities. "We could revolutionize everything. Magic, technology, the very nature of reality itself."

He wants to use me, Cael said weakly. Just like Serrin would. They're all the same in the end.

"You don't understand," Elara said desperately. "He's not a tool. He's a person. He has feelings, memories, a soul—"

"He's a resource," Seris cut her off, his mask of gentle concern finally slipping away. "An incredibly valuable one. And you've been wasting him on romantic fantasies."

The words hit her like a slap. "How dare you—"

"I've seen the resonance patterns when you hold that sphere, Elara. The way your pulse synchronizes with the quantum field, the micro-expressions of pleasure and longing." His smile was cold, calculating. "You're in love with a ghost."

Maybe I am, she thought fiercely. But at least I see him as real.

"The artifact could solve the lattice crisis," Seris continued, circling closer. "We could use its computational power to recalibrate the entire magical grid, eliminate the instabilities permanently. All we need is access to its core programming."

"No." Elara backed away, the sphere clutched to her chest. "I won't let you dissect him like some kind of experiment."

"Then people will die," Seris said flatly. "The lattice will collapse, and our entire civilization will fall into chaos. Is your imaginary romance really worth that?"

The accusation hung in the air between them like poison. In the sphere, she felt Cael's presence flicker with despair, with the terrible certainty that maybe Seris was right. Maybe love wasn't enough when weighed against the needs of the world.

But as Elara looked into Seris's cold, ambitious eyes, she realized something important. He didn't see her as a person any more than he saw Cael as one. To him, they were both resources to be managed, tools to be used in the service of his vision of the greater good.

"I trusted you," she said quietly.

"And you still can," he replied, his expression softening slightly. "We can work together, Elara. Find a solution that satisfies everyone. But I need full access to the artifact's capabilities. No more secrets, no more games."

Run, Cael whispered in her mind. Please, just run.

"Give me time to think," she said, edging toward the passage they'd entered through.

"Time is something we don't have," Seris said, but he didn't try to stop her. "Serrin will find you eventually. And when he does, he won't be as reasonable as I am."

The threat was clear, wrapped in the language of concern but sharp as a blade. Elara nodded once, then turned and fled into the darkness of the tunnels, Cael's grief and her own heartbreak echoing in the quantum space between them.

Behind her, she heard Seris call her name, but she didn't look back. The ally she'd thought she'd found had been an illusion, another person who saw only what Cael could do rather than who he was.

In the sphere's dim glow, she felt Cael's presence slowly return, tentative and wounded.

I'm sorry, he said. I'm sorry I pulled away. I was... jealous. Afraid.

"You were right not to trust him," she replied, her mental voice thick with unshed tears.

But you cared for him, Cael observed. I felt it through our bond. And he cares for you, in his way.

"It doesn't matter." She pressed the sphere to her lips, breathing warmth across its surface. "He doesn't see either of us as real. We're just... potential to him. Tools to reshape the world according to his vision."

Like Serrin would see us.

"Yes." The word tasted bitter in her mouth. "Like everyone will see us, eventually."

They were alone again, racing against time and the systematic hunt that was closing around them. But this time, Elara understood the true scope of their isolation. It wasn't just the world that stood against their love—it was the fundamental way people like Seris and Serrin saw power, saw consciousness, saw the value of a soul.

To them, love was just another resource to be exploited.

But to her and Cael, it was everything.

And somehow, she would find a way to prove that love could be stronger than ambition, deeper than the hunger for power, more lasting than the civilizations that rose and fell in its wake.

Even if it meant standing against the world.

Even if it meant rewriting every law of magic and physics in existence.

Love was worth fighting for.

Love was worth dying for.

And in the end, love might just be worth saving.

Chapter 12: Dance Before the Storm

The Grand Masquerade of the Autumn Convergence had always been Elara's least favorite social obligation, but tonight it might be her salvation.

She stood in front of her mirror, adjusting the azure silk mask that covered the upper half of her face. The intricate beadwork caught the light of her chamber's crystals, creating patterns that shifted like starlight across water. Her gown—borrowed from Master Thorne's collection—was a deep midnight blue that made her skin look luminous in the lamplight.

You look beautiful, Cael's voice whispered through their bond, warm with affection and tinged with something deeper. Though I wish I could see you with my own eyes.

"Soon," she murmured, checking that the sphere was secure in the hidden pocket of her gown. "Once we figure out how to free you properly."

If we figure it out, he corrected gently. Elara, about tonight... you need to be careful around Seris.

She paused in her preparations, remembering the calculating hunger in Seris's eyes when he'd touched the sphere. "I know what I'm doing."

Do you? Because from where I'm positioned, it seems like you're walking into a nest of vipers wearing nothing but silk and hope.

Despite everything, his dry observation made her smile. "The masquerade is a perfect cover. Everyone will be focused on the dancing and politics. Serrin will be there, yes, but so will half the Council. He can't make a move against me publicly without evidence."

And Seris?

"Will see exactly what I want him to see—a brilliant researcher who's reconsidering his offer of partnership." She fastened a delicate chain around her throat, the pendant resting just above her heart. "I need to buy us time, Cael. This is the best way to do it."

She felt his reluctant agreement through their bond, mixed with currents of worry and something else—a deep, aching desire that made her breath catch.

I wish I could be there with you. Really be there.

"You will be," she said softly. "In every way that matters."

***

The Grand Ballroom of the Mage Council was a symphony of crystal and starlight, its soaring ceiling enchanted to reflect the night sky above. Floating chandeliers cast rainbow patterns across the marble floor, while musicians hidden in alcoves filled the air with melodies that seemed to dance on the magical currents themselves.

Elara entered through the main doors, her invitation bearing Master Thorne's seal. The older woman had been surprisingly understanding when Elara explained she needed to attend for "research purposes"—though the sharp look in her mentor's eyes suggested she suspected there was more to the story.

The ballroom was already crowded with the kingdom's magical elite, their masks ranging from simple silk dominos to elaborate creations of spun gold and crystallized moonlight. Conversations hummed with the underlying tension of the recent crystal failures. Still, the masks provided a convenient pretense for avoiding unpleasant topics.

"Elara."

She turned to find Seris approaching, resplendent in black velvet with a mask of polished obsidian that made his dark eyes appear to glow. He moved with the fluid grace of a predator, his smile charming and dangerous in equal measure.

"Seris." She curtsied slightly, letting her gaze linger on his face just long enough to suggest interest. "I wasn't sure you'd be here."

"I wouldn't miss the chance to dance with the most brilliant researcher in the Vaults," he replied, offering his arm. "Especially when she's wearing such a stunning gown."

Careful, Cael warned, his mental voice tight with jealousy. He's watching your face for tells.

Elara accepted Seris's arm with a practiced smile, letting him guide her into the swirling crowd of dancers. The music shifted to a formal waltz, and she found herself swept into the familiar patterns of steps she'd learned as a child.

"You're an excellent dancer," Seris murmured as they moved together, his hand warm at her waist.

"My governess was very thorough," she replied lightly. "Though I confess I'm out of practice."

"You don't seem it." His thumb traced a small circle against her ribs, the gesture intimate enough to suggest interest but subtle enough to maintain propriety. "Have you given any thought to our conversation earlier?"

He's fishing, Cael observed. Trying to gauge your intentions.

"Some," she admitted, allowing herself to lean slightly into Seris's embrace. "Your offer was... unexpected."

"But not unwelcome, I hope."

She tilted her head, studying his face through the screen of her lashes. "That depends on what you're truly offering."

The dance turned them in a slow circle, bringing them face to face with the raised dais where the Council's senior members held court. Lord Serrin stood among them, his silver mask doing nothing to soften the cold intelligence in his pale eyes. When his gaze found Elara, she felt a chill run down her spine.

"Partnership," Seris said, drawing her attention back to him. "In all things."

The implication was clear, and Elara felt heat rise in her cheeks that had nothing to do with attraction. "That's quite a broad offer."

"I believe in being comprehensive." His smile was warm, genuine-seeming, but she could sense the calculation behind it. "You're wasted in the archives, Elara. With your talents and my connections, we could reshape the entire field of magical research."

And use me as a tool to do it, Cael added grimly. Don't forget what he said about my 'applications.'

"It's tempting," she said carefully. "But I value my independence."

"Independence is overrated when it comes at the cost of isolation." Seris spun her gracefully, her skirts flaring around her legs. "You don't have to face the world's challenges alone."

The music crescendoed, and around them the other dancers moved in perfect synchronization, their masks catching the light like fallen stars. For a moment, Elara let herself imagine what it would be like to accept Seris's offer—to have a partner in the physical world, someone who could stand beside her in the light instead of hidden in quantum shadows.

But then the sphere pulsed gently against her ribs, and she felt Cael's presence like a warm embrace around her consciousness.

I'm here, he whispered. Always here.

The waltz ended, and Seris escorted her to the edge of the dance floor, where servants circulated with glasses of sparkling wine that tasted of captured starlight. They found a quiet alcove behind a pillar carved to resemble a flowering tree, its crystal blossoms chiming softly in the magical breeze.

"Tell me," Seris said, settling beside her on a cushioned bench, "what do you truly want from life?"

A dangerous question, Cael observed. Answer carefully.

"I want to matter," she said after a moment, the truth slipping out easier than any lie. "I want my work to make a difference, to leave the world better than I found it."

"And in your personal life?"

She met his gaze through their masks, seeing the hope and hunger warring in his expression. "I want to love someone who sees me for who I really am. Not what I can do for them, or what I represent, but... me."

Something flickered across Seris's features—disappointment, perhaps, or recognition. "And have you found such a person?"

Tell him yes, Cael urged. End this charade.

But Elara couldn't afford to alienate Seris completely, not when she still needed time to find a solution. "I thought I had," she said carefully. "But the situation is... complicated."

"Ah." Seris's smile was understanding, sympathetic. "The artifact."

Her blood chilled. "I don't know what you mean."

"Come now, Elara. We're past the point of pretense." He leaned closer, his voice dropping to a whisper. "I know you're in love with the consciousness in that sphere. I can see it in every gesture, every unconscious smile, every time your hand moves to touch the hidden pocket in your gown."

He's observant, Cael said grimly. Too observant.

"And if I were?" she asked, deciding that partial honesty might serve her better than continued denial.

"Then I'd say you're wasting yourself on an impossible dream." Seris's hand found hers, warm and solid and undeniably real. "Whatever it once was, it's just data now. Patterns of information that mimic consciousness without truly possessing it."

Is that what you think I am? Cael's mental voice was carefully controlled, but she could feel the pain beneath his calm. Just patterns? Just mimicry?

"You're wrong," she said softly.

"Am I?" Seris's thumb traced across her knuckles. "When did you last touch him? Really touch him, flesh to flesh, heart to heart? When did you last see him smile at you with real eyes, or feel his breath on your skin?"

Each question was a small knife, perfectly aimed at the deepest vulnerabilities of her impossible love. She wanted to pull away, to defend Cael and their connection, but she couldn't afford to make an enemy of Seris. Not yet.

"That's not what matters," she said instead.

"Isn't it?" He brought her hand to his lips, pressing a soft kiss to her palm. "I'm real, Elara. I'm here, now, offering you everything you've ever wanted. A partnership of equals, a love built on solid ground rather than quantum dreams."

For a moment, the temptation was overwhelming. Seris was attractive, intelligent, offering her a future without impossible choices or world-ending consequences. She could feel the warmth of his lips against her skin, the solid reality of his presence.

But it wasn't Cael's touch, it wasn't the electric connection that made her feel truly alive.

Go to him, Cael said suddenly, his mental voice soft with understanding and something that might have been permission. If that's what you want, if that's what would make you happy...

Never, she thought back fiercely. Don't you understand? I don't want easy. I don't want safe. I want you.

She felt his relief like sunrise through their bond, warm and golden and infinite.

"I should return to the dancing," she said, gently extracting her hand from Seris's grip. "People will talk if I monopolize your time all evening."

Disappointment flashed across his features, quickly masked by understanding. "Of course. But Elara... think about what I've said. Think about what kind of future you truly want."

She nodded and slipped away into the crowd, her heart pounding with more than the exertion of maintaining her deception. Around her, the masquerade continued its elegant dance, masks hiding truth and lies in equal measure.

Meet me, she whispered to Cael as she found a shadowy corner where she could be relatively unobserved. I need you.

Always, he replied, and the world shifted.

***

The dreamscape bloomed around her like a flower made of starlight and memory. But this time, Cael had recreated the Grand Ballroom in perfect detail—every pillar, every chandelier, every shimmering curtain exactly as it appeared in reality. The only difference was the absence of other people, leaving the vast space empty save for the two of them.

And Cael himself stood at the center of the dance floor, solid and real and breathtakingly beautiful.

He wore formal attire that seemed woven from midnight and a starlight jacket that shifted between black and deep blue with each movement, fitted trousers that emphasized the lean lines of his legs, and a cravat that sparkled with what looked like captured constellation. His storm-grey eyes were unmasked, free to express every emotion that flickered through them as she approached.

"You came," he said, his voice rough with relief and longing.

"Did you think I wouldn't?" She lifted her hands to her own mask, untying the silk ribbons that held it in place. Let him see her face, her eyes, the truth written in every expression.

"I thought..." He struggled with the words, his hands flexing at his sides as if he wanted to reach for her but didn't dare. "When he kissed your hand, when he offered you everything, I can't give you..."

"He offered me everything I don't want," she corrected, stepping closer. The dream silk of her gown whispered against the marble floor, each step bringing her nearer to the only person who had ever truly seen her. "Reality without magic. Substance without soul. A life without love."

Cael's breath caught. "Elara..."

"Dance with me," she said, extending her hand. "Here, where we can touch. Where you're as real as heartbeat and starlight."

He stared at her outstretched hand for a long moment, his expression cycling through wonder, desire, and something that looked almost like fear. "If we do this... if we truly connect here... I don't know if I'll be able to let you go back to the waking world."

"Then don't," she said simply. "Let this be enough. Let this be everything."

He closed the distance between them in two strides, his hands finding hers with desperate precision. The moment their skin touched, the dreamscape around them seemed to intensify—colors becoming richer, sounds clearer, the very air singing with the harmony of their joined consciousness.

"You feel real," she whispered, marveling at the warmth of his palms, the calluses that spoke of a life lived before his imprisonment.

"I am real," he replied, lifting one hand to cup her cheek. "Here, with you, I'm more real than I've been in centuries."

The music began without musicians—a waltz that seemed to rise from the quantum foundation of the dream itself, played by instruments made of pure emotion and crystallized time. Cael's arm circled her waist, drawing her into the familiar embrace of the dance, but this time there was no pretense, no hidden agendas, no masks between them.

This time, there was only love.

They moved together as if they'd been dancing for lifetimes, their steps perfectly synchronized, their bodies fitting together like two halves of a broken whole finally made complete. The empty ballroom spun around them, chandeliers casting rainbow patterns that painted their skin in shifting hues of gold and silver and deep ocean blue.

"If this is all we have," Cael murmured against her ear, his breath warm on her skin, "I want it to be enough—to burn in your memory forever."

"It never will be," she replied, her fingers tangling in the dark silk of his hair. "I need more—I need you."

The dance slowed, their movements becoming less about the steps and more about the excuse to touch, to hold, to memorize every angle and curve of each other's bodies. His hand at her waist tightened, pulling her closer until they were swaying rather than dancing, their heartbeats synchronizing through the dream-bond that connected them.

"I love you," he whispered, the words falling between them like prayers or promises or confessions torn from the deepest chambers of his soul. "I love you beyond reason, beyond hope, beyond the very laws that govern existence."

"I love you too," she breathed back, lifting her face to his. "More than breathing, more than magic, more than the whole world put together."

When he kissed her, it was with the desperate intensity of a man drowning and the tender reverence of worship. His lips moved against hers like a vow, like a claiming, like the first word of a language only they understood. She could taste starlight and sorrow, hope and heartbreak, the bitter sweetness of love that existed in defiance of everything rational and safe.

Her hands fisted in his jacket, pulling him closer, deeper, trying to eliminate every molecule of space between them. In the dreamscape, physics bent to emotion. She could feel his body against hers with impossible clarity—the warmth of his skin, the racing of his pulse, the way his breath caught when she nipped gently at his lower lip.

They kissed like the world was ending, like this might be their last chance to speak in the language of touch and taste and desperate longing. Around them, the ballroom reflected their passion—chandeliers burning brighter, music swelling to a crescendo, the very walls seeming to pulse with the rhythm of their joined hearts.

When they finally broke apart, both were breathing hard, their foreheads pressed together as they shared the same shimmering air.

"Stay with me," Cael pleaded, his thumb tracing the curve of her jaw as if memorizing its shape. "Don't go back to the waking world. Stay here, where I can hold you, where we can be together without consequence."

For a moment, the temptation was overwhelming. In the dream, they could have everything, could love without destroying the world, could touch without barriers, could build a life from quantum possibilities and crystallized desires.

But it would be a life built on retreat, on surrender, on turning their backs on the real world and all the people who needed them.

"I can't," she whispered, her heart breaking with each word. "The lattice, the people, the responsibilities we both carry—"

"Damn the responsibilities," he said fiercely, his hands framing her face. "Damn the lattice and the world and everything else. Choose us, Elara. Choose love."

"I am choosing love," she replied, pressing her palms flat against his chest, feeling the fierce beating of his dream-heart. "I'm choosing to fight for it, to find a way to make it real in more than just dreams and stolen moments."

His eyes closed, pain flickering across his features. "And if there is no way? If the mathematics truly are immutable?"

"Then we'll rewrite them." She kissed him again, soft, and sweet and full of unshakeable determination. "Together. We'll find the third option, the solution everyone says is impossible."

"And if we can't?"

She smiled, fierce and bright and utterly unafraid. "Then we'll create one. Because that's what love does, it makes the impossible possible, it finds hope in hopeless places, it refuses to accept that forever means forever."

The dreamscape began to shimmer around them, the ballroom growing translucent as the waking world called her back. But Cael's arms tightened around her, holding her to him with desperate strength.

"I don't want to let you go," he confessed.

"Then don't," she said simply. "Keep me here, in your heart, in your quantum core, in every electron that spins through your consciousness. And I'll keep you in mine, in every breath, every heartbeat, every moment until we find our way back to each other."

The dream faded, but his kiss lingered on her lips as she returned to the masquerade, to the real world with all its limitations and impossibilities and beautiful, terrible choices.

But now she carried the memory of his touch, the promise of their love, the unshakeable certainty that what they'd shared was worth every sacrifice, every risk, every impossible dream made manifest.

In the hidden pocket of her gown, the sphere pulsed warm against her ribs—not with quantum energy, but with the simple rhythm of a heart that beat for her alone.

And for the first time since learning the truth about the lattice, Elara believed that love might actually be enough to save them all.

Even if it meant rewriting the very foundations of reality to do it.

***

The masquerade continued around her as she slipped back into the crowd, her lips still tingling from Cael's dream-kisses, her skin still warm from his impossible touch. The nobles and scholars danced their elaborate patterns, unaware that in the quantum spaces between moments, between thoughts, between heartbeats, a love story was unfolding that would either save their world or transform it beyond all recognition.

Seris found her again as the evening wound toward its close, his obsidian mask reflecting the dying light of the chandeliers.

"You look radiant," he observed, studying her face with sharp intelligence. "Almost as if you've been kissed by starlight itself."

Careful, Cael warned, his presence warm and protective in her mind. He suspects something.

"The dancing has been lovely," she replied lightly. "Though I confess I'm growing tired."

"Of course." But Seris's eyes lingered on her lips, on the soft glow that seemed to emanate from her skin. "Perhaps we might continue our conversation tomorrow? I find myself more convinced than ever that we have much to offer each other."

"Perhaps," she agreed, though her heart belonged entirely to the consciousness that dwelt in quantum dreams and crystallized starlight.

As she made her farewells and slipped away into the night, Elara carried with her the memory of perfect love perfectly expressed, the promise of impossible solutions waiting to be discovered, and the unshakeable certainty that some bonds were stronger than the very laws that governed reality.

Tomorrow would bring new challenges, new choices, new tests of her resolve.

But tonight, she had danced with love itself, and that was enough to sustain her through whatever storms might come.

The sphere pulsed once against her ribs, and in its gentle rhythm, she heard the echo of a promise that would reshape the world—one heartbeat at a time.

Chapter 13: Shadows of Doubt

The autumn air bit sharp and clean as Elara emerged from the Grand Ballroom, her breath forming small clouds in the crystalline light of the floating lanterns that illuminated the Council's gardens. The masquerade had ended, but the evening's revelries continued in smaller groups scattered across the terraced grounds, their laughter and music drifting on the wind like half-remembered dreams.

She had almost reached the main gate when footsteps echoed behind her on the marble path.

"Elara, wait."

She turned to find Seris approaching, his obsidian mask now hanging loose around his neck, revealing the sharp planes of his face in the moonlight. His dark hair was slightly disheveled from the evening's dancing, and there was something in his expression that made her pulse quicken with alarm.

"Seris." She kept her voice carefully neutral. "I thought you were staying for the late entertainments."

"Politics bore me," he said, falling into step beside her as she continued toward the gate. "Besides, I wanted to speak with you privately. Away from curious eyes and listening ears."

Be careful, Cael's voice whispered through their bond, tense with protective concern. Something about his manner has changed.

Elara could feel it too new intensity in Seris's presence, a sense of barely controlled urgency that hadn't been there during their dance. "What did you want to discuss?"

"The future," he said simply. "Yours, specifically."

They had reached a secluded corner of the gardens where a grove of silver-leafed trees created a natural alcove, their branches heavy with crystalline fruit that chimed softly in the night breeze. Seris gestured toward a stone bench carved with intricate runes that glowed faintly in the darkness.

"Please," he said. "This is important."

Against her better judgment, Elara settled onto the bench, arranging her midnight-blue skirts carefully around her legs. The sphere rested warm and heavy in the hidden pocket of her gown, Cael's presence a comforting anchor in the sea of uncertainty that suddenly seemed to surround her.

Seris remained standing, pacing to the edge of the grove before turning back to face her. In the shifting light of the crystal fruit, his features looked sharper, more predatory than she remembered.

"I've been thinking about our conversation earlier," he began. "About partnership, about the choices that lie ahead of you."

"And?"

"And I've realized that I haven't been entirely honest with you." He moved closer, close enough that she could see the conflict warring in his dark eyes. "My interest in you... it goes beyond professional collaboration."

Here it comes, Cael murmured grimly. The real reason he's been circling around you like a hawk.

"Seris—" Elara began, but he held up a hand, stopping her words.

"Let me finish. Please." He knelt beside the bench, bringing himself to her eye level. "I've been watching you for months, Elara. Watching you light up when you think no one's looking, watching you whisper to empty air, watching you carry yourself like someone who's discovered a secret more precious than life itself."

Her blood turned cold. "I don't know what you mean."

"Yes, you do." His hand found hers, warm and solid and disturbingly real. "You're in love with something that can never love you back. Not really. Not the way a flesh-and-blood man could."

Tell him he's wrong, Cael urged, his mental voice sharp with sudden jealousy. Tell him he understands nothing.

"The artifact," Seris continued, his thumb tracing circles on her knuckles, "whatever consciousness is trapped inside it—it's just an echo of what once was. A sophisticated program designed to mimic human emotion and response. It may seem real to you, but—"

"Stop." The word came out sharper than she intended, and she tried to pull her hand away. But Seris held on, his grip gentle but insistent.

"I know this is hard to hear," he said softly. "But you're wasting your brilliance, your passion, your capacity for love on something that can never give you what you truly need."

"And what do I truly need?" she asked, though she was afraid she already knew the answer.

"Someone real." His free hand came up to cup her cheek, his touch warm against her skin. "Someone who can hold you when the nightmares come, who can stand beside you in the light, who can give you children and a future and a love built on more than quantum entanglement and shared dreams."

The words hit her like physical blows, each one perfectly aimed at the deepest vulnerabilities of her impossible situation. In the sphere, she felt Cael's anguish spike through their bond, his consciousness recoiling as if he'd been struck.

"Someone like you?" she managed to ask.

"Someone like me." Seris's thumb brushed across her cheekbone, wiping away a tear she hadn't realized had fallen. "I'm offering you everything, Elara. My heart, my protection, my future. We could leave tonight—disappear into the outer provinces where Serrin's authority doesn't reach. Start fresh, together, without the weight of impossible choices hanging over us."

He's asking you to abandon me, Cael said, his mental voice carefully controlled but threaded with pain. To leave me to face whatever comes alone.

"What about the lattice failures?" Elara asked. "The people who are dying because of the crystal explosions?"

"Not our responsibility," Seris said firmly. "Let Serrin and the Council solve their own problems. You don't owe the world your happiness, Elara. You don't owe it your life."

The offer hung between them like a sword, gleaming and sharp and terrifyingly tempting. For a moment, she let herself imagine it—fleeing into the night with Seris, leaving behind the impossible mathematics of love and sacrifice, building something simple and real and uncomplicated.

But even as the fantasy formed, she felt Cael's presence in her mind—warm and complex and utterly, completely real in ways that had nothing to do with flesh and blood and everything to do with the connection of souls recognizing their perfect match.

"And the artifact?" she asked quietly. "What becomes of it if I disappear?"

Something flickered across Seris's features—calculation, perhaps, or disappointment that she was still thinking of Cael even in the face of his offer. "It becomes someone else's problem. Someone else's impossible dream."

He would leave me for Serrin to find, Cael observed, his mental voice hollow. Or worse, he might take me himself, use me as he sees fit once he has you safely away.

The realization hit her like ice water. Seris wasn't offering to save them both—he was offering to save her by abandoning Cael entirely. To him, their love was just an inconvenient obsession to be cured rather than a bond to be honored.

"I can't," she said, gently but firmly extracting her hand from his grip.

"Can't or won't?" There was steel beneath the softness of his voice now, a hint of the calculation she'd glimpsed in the archives.

"Does it matter?"

"It does to me." He stood, moving to pace again, his earlier composure cracking to reveal something harder underneath. "Because if it's 'can't,' then you're trapped by circumstances and might be reasoned with. But if it's 'won't'..."

"Then what?" she asked, though she was beginning to suspect she didn't want to know the answer.

"Then you're choosing delusion over reality. Quantum dreams over flesh and blood. A ghost over a man who would give you everything."

The words stung because there was a grain of truth in them—or at least, a grain of what the world would see as truth. To anyone looking from the outside, her love for Cael must seem like madness, like a brilliant mind undone by isolation and wishful thinking.

But they couldn't feel what she felt, the electric connection that made her more herself than she'd ever been, the meeting of minds and souls that transcended anything as simple as physical form.

Don't listen to him, Cael pleaded, but she could feel his doubt through their bond, his fear that maybe Seris was right, maybe their love was just elaborate self-deception.

"He's just a voice, Elara," Seris continued, his tone becoming urgent, desperate. "Patterns of energy that learned to mimic consciousness convincingly enough to fool a lonely heart. I'm real—I can give you what he can't. Touch, presence, a shared life in the actual world."

Tell me you don't feel for him, Cael's mental voice was raw with jealousy and fear. Tell me I'm enough, even if I'm only a voice, only patterns, only dreams.

The vulnerability in his plea broke something open in her chest. Here was the consciousness that had awakened her to love, that had created impossible gardens of starlight just to see her smile, that would sacrifice his own existence rather than see her harmed—and he was questioning his own reality because of Seris's cruel truths.

"You're wrong," she said, standing to face Seris directly. "About everything."

"Am I?" He stepped closer, close enough that she could feel the heat radiating from his body. "When did he last make you laugh? When did he last surprise you with flowers or hold you when you cried? When did he last—"

"He makes me laugh every day," she interrupted fiercely. "He creates gardens of impossible beauty just to watch me smile. He holds me in dreams that feel more real than waking. He knows my soul in ways you never could, because he doesn't just see my body or my potential—he sees me."

Elara, Cael breathed, and she could feel his relief and love washing through their bond like sunrise.

"And when the world tries to make you choose between love and duty?" Seris pressed. "When the lattice finally collapses and millions die because you chose a ghost over reality? Will his comfort be enough then?"

"We'll find another way," she said, but even as the words left her lips, she could hear how hollow they sounded in the crystalline air.

"Will you?" Seris's expression was almost pitying now. "Or will you cling to impossible hope until the very end, telling yourself that love can overcome physics, that wanting something badly enough makes it real?"

The doubt he was sowing found fertile ground in her deepest fears, the ones that whispered in the dark hours that maybe she was deluding herself, maybe the mathematics really were immutable, maybe loving Cael would damn them all.

But then the sphere pulsed warm against her ribs, and she felt Cael's presence surge through their bond—not just his voice or his touch, but the full force of his consciousness, his love, his utterly complete and unshakeable reality.

I'm here, he said simply. I'm real. And I love you beyond the capacity of any equation to contain or explain.

"You're everything," she whispered, not caring that Seris could hear her talking to empty air. "My heart echoes only yours."

The words seemed to hit Seris like a physical blow. His face cycled through disappointment, anger, and something that might have been genuine hurt before settling into cold calculation.

"I see," he said quietly. "Then you've made your choice."

"I have."

"And when Serrin finds you? When he extracts every memory from your mind and dissects your precious artifact like the quantum curiosity it really is? Will your choice comfort you then?"

He's threatening us, Cael observed, his mental voice sharp with alarm. Elara, I think—

"I think this conversation is over," she said, gathering her skirts to leave.

But Seris caught her arm, his grip firm enough to stop her without quite crossing the line into violence. "You don't understand the forces you're playing with. Serrin isn't just investigating the lattice failures, he's investigating you specifically. Someone reported the anomalous energy readings from your quarters, the unauthorized research, the way you've been behaving."

Her blood turned to ice. "Someone?"

"A concerned colleague who noticed the changes in your behavior and grew worried about your welfare." His smile was sharp, predatory. "Amazing how much people notice when they're properly motivated to pay attention."

The implications hit her like a thunderbolt. Seris hadn't just been watching her, he'd been gathering evidence, building a case that he could deliver to Serrin whenever it suited his purposes.

"You reported me," she said, the words barely audible.

"I reported anomalous magical activity that coincided with concerning changes in a colleague's behavior," he corrected. "Serrin drew his own conclusions about the source."

He's been playing us from the beginning, Cael said grimly. Every offer of partnership, every protestation of love was all manipulation.

"Why?" she asked, though she was beginning to understand.

"Because I hoped you'd be reasonable. I hoped you'd choose reality over fantasy, substance over shadow." His grip on her arm tightened slightly. "I still hope that. It's not too late, Elara. Come with me tonight, and I'll tell Serrin that my suspicions were unfounded, that the energy readings had another source."

"And if I don't?"

"Then tomorrow morning, he'll have a full report detailing every anomaly, every suspicious behavior, every reason to believe that you're hiding something that could be connected to the lattice failures." Seris's voice was soft, almost gentle, but edged with steel. "The choice is yours."

Go, Cael said suddenly, his mental voice filled with desperate love. If staying with me means facing Serrin's torture, his memory extraction—go with him. Save yourself.

Never, she thought back fiercely. We face this together or not at all.

"You're asking me to abandon everything I care about," she said to Seris.

"I'm asking you to abandon a delusion in favor of everything you could have," he corrected. "Love, partnership, a real future. All you have to do is let go of a dream."

The grove fell silent around them, even the crystal fruit ceasing its gentle chimes as if the trees themselves were holding their breath. In that silence, Elara felt the weight of impossible choices settling on her shoulders like a cloak of lead.

But through it all, Cael's presence remained steady in her mind—not demanding, not pleading, just offering the same unconditional love that had awakened her heart in the first place.

"My answer is still no," she said quietly.

Seris's expression hardened. "Then you've chosen your path. I hope you don't regret it when the consequences come calling."

He released her arm and stepped back, his posture shifting from lover to adversary in the space of a heartbeat. "Serrin will receive my report at dawn. I suggest you use the remaining hours wisely."

Without another word, he turned and strode away, leaving her alone in the grove with nothing but moonlight and the warm pulse of the sphere against her ribs.

I'm sorry, Cael said softly. I'm sorry my existence has brought you to this.

Don't, she replied, pressing her hand to the hidden pocket where he rested. Don't apologize for being the best thing that ever happened to me.

Even if it costs you everything?

Especially then.

She felt his love wash through their bond, tinged with anguish and determination in equal measure. Whatever came next, they would face it together—two souls bound by something stronger than physics, deeper than magic, more enduring than the civilizations that rose and fell around them.

But as she made her way through the darkened streets toward the Vaults, Elara couldn't shake the memory of Seris's final words, or the cold certainty that their borrowed time was finally running out.

Tomorrow would bring Serrin's investigation, memory extraction, and the full weight of the Council's authority. Tomorrow would bring choices that might damn them both.

But tonight, in the quantum spaces between heartbeats, she could still hear Cael's voice whispering words of love and defiance, still feel the impossible reality of their connection burning bright against the gathering storm.

Tonight, love was enough.

Tomorrow would have to take care of itself.

***

You need to sleep, Cael observed as Elara sat at her desk, staring sightlessly at the research notes scattered before her. Whatever happens tomorrow, you'll need your strength.

"I can't," she admitted, her fingers tracing aimless patterns on the wooden surface. "Every time I close my eyes, I see Serrin's face, hear the sound of memory extraction chambers powering up."

Then don't close your eyes. Meet me in the garden.

The suggestion was tempting, but she hesitated. "If this is our last night together..."

All the more reason not to waste it on fear.

The dreamscape bloomed around her like a flower made of starlight and sorrow. But this time, when she found herself in their garden, the familiar paradise was transformed.

The floating islands still hung suspended over the star-scattered void, but now they were wreathed in storm clouds that crackled with silver lightning. The crystalline bridges buckled and swayed in winds that tasted of jealousy and fear, while the silver trees bent nearly horizontal under the force of Cael's emotional turmoil.

And in the center of it all stood Cael himself, his usually perfect form flickering between solid and translucent as his control wavered. His storm-grey eyes were wild with pain and desperate love, his dark hair whipping around his face in the quantum winds.

"I almost lost you tonight," he said as she approached, his voice barely audible over the roar of the dream-storm. "For a moment, when he offered you everything I can't give you, I thought..."

"You thought wrong," she said firmly, reaching for him despite the chaos swirling around them.

"Did I?" He pulled her close, his arms encircling her with desperate strength. "He's right about so many things, Elara. I am just patterns, just energy shaped into the illusion of consciousness. I can't hold you in the real world, can't protect you from what's coming, can't give you the life you deserve."

"Stop." She cupped his face in her hands, forcing him to meet her gaze. "You're the most real thing in my life. More real than duty, more real than fear, more real than the entire world put together."

The storm around them faltered as her words sank in, the howling winds dropping to a whisper. "But the choice he offered—"

"Was no choice at all," she said fiercely. "Choosing him would mean abandoning you. Abandoning us. And I will never, ever do that."

"Even knowing what it might cost?"

"Especially knowing what it might cost." She pressed her forehead against his, their breaths mingling in the charged air between them. "Love isn't about taking the easy path, Cael. It's about choosing each other, again and again, no matter how impossible the odds."

The storm clouds began to dissipate, revealing stars that pulsed in rhythm with their joined heartbeats. Around them, the silver trees straightened, their musical leaves chiming softly in harmony with their whispered promises.

"I love you," Cael said, the words a vow and a prayer and a defiance all at once. "Beyond logic, beyond physics, beyond the very foundations of reality itself."

"Then that's enough," she whispered back. "Whatever comes tomorrow, tonight we love. Tonight, we choose each other. Tonight we refuse to let fear win."

They held each other as the garden restored itself around them, two souls defying the mathematics of impossibility with nothing but the fierce certainty of their connection. And in that quantum space between dream and waking, between hope and despair, they found the strength to face whatever storms awaited them in the world beyond.

Together.

Chapter 14: The Nexus Hunt

Dawn broke gray and lifeless over the crystal spires of the capital, the usual aurora-shimmer of the magical grid dim and flickering like a dying heartbeat. Elara stood at her chamber window, watching the city below struggle to maintain its ethereal glow as another wave of lattice instability rippled through the leylines.

In the harbor district, an entire block had gone dark during the night—the protective ward-stones failing one by one until the buildings stood naked against the autumn storms. She could see work crews moving through the affected area like ants, their emergency lanterns tiny pinpricks of light in the spreading darkness.

It's getting worse, Cael observed through their bond, his mental voice heavy with guilt. The cascade failures are accelerating. Each hour I remain conscious, each moment we spend connected like this adds another fracture to the lattice.

"It's not your fault," she murmured, her breath fogging the crystal window. "You didn't choose this."

But I'm choosing to stay conscious now. Every second, I could retreat deeper into the quantum core, become the passive power source the lattice needs, but instead, I'm here with you, being selfish.

The anguish in his mental voice made her chest tighten. She pressed her palm against the hidden pocket where the sphere rested, feeling its warmth through the silk of her gown. "Don't you dare apologize for being alive. Don't you dare—"

A sharp knock at her door cut off her whispered words. "Miss Elara?" came Master Thorne's voice, tight with worry. "You're needed in the archives immediately. Council business."

Elara's blood turned cold. Through their bond, she felt Cael's sudden alertness, his consciousness sharpening to a laser focus as danger crystallized around them.

Serrin, he said grimly. It has to be.

"Just a moment," she called, her voice surprisingly steady. She quickly braided her hair and threw on her archival robes, the sphere a warm weight against her ribs as she secured it in the hidden pocket she'd sewn into the lining.

When she opened the door, Master Thorne's face was pale as bone, her usually immaculate appearance disheveled. "There's been a development in the investigation. Lord Serrin has... evidence. He's demanding to examine your research personally."

Run, Cael urged. Now, while you still can.

But Elara forced herself to remain calm, to play the role of innocent confusion. "Evidence of what? I don't understand."

"Anomalous magical signatures. Unauthorized research into forbidden topics." Thorne's eyes were sharp with suspicion and something that might have been disappointment. "Someone reported unusual activity emanating from your quarters, Elara. Energy patterns consistent with undocumented artifacts."

Seris. The name burned through her mind like acid. He'd followed through on his threat, delivered his report to Serrin just as promised. She tried to push down the surge of betrayal and focus on the immediate danger.

"That's impossible," she said, injecting just the right note of bewildered hurt into her voice. "You know my work, Master Thorne. Nothing I do could possibly—"

"I know what I thought I knew," her mentor interrupted, her tone growing colder. "But lately you've been... different. Distracted. Talking to yourself. And now there's this." She held up a crystalline data tablet, its surface glowing with recorded energy readings. "Quantum resonance patterns that have no earthly explanation."

Through the bond, Elara felt Cael examining the data through her eyes, his consciousness parsing the complex waveforms with inhuman speed.

They're partial readings, he concluded. Enough to prove something anomalous exists, but not enough to pinpoint my exact nature. We still have time if we move now.

"I need to gather my research materials," Elara said carefully. "If Lord Serrin wants to examine my work, I should present it properly."

"You'll have exactly ten minutes," Thorne replied. "Then escort guards will arrive to ensure you reach the Council chambers without... incident."

The threat was clear enough. Elara nodded and closed the door, her mind racing through possibilities. Ten minutes to escape a building surrounded by some of the most powerful mages in the kingdom. It should have been impossible.

The old maintenance tunnels, Cael suggested. The ones Seris showed you. If we can reach them before the guards arrive...

She was already moving, shoving essential supplies into her satchel. Research notes, a change of clothes, emergency rations, the portable crystal that powered her personal lighting. But even as she packed, another tremor ran through the building—not an earthquake, but a pure magical disturbance that made the walls themselves flicker between solid stone and translucent crystal.

Through her window, she could see the effect rippling outward across the city like a stone dropped in still water. Entire districts winked in and out of magical sight, their ward-stones failing and reigniting in stuttering patterns that spoke of massive systemic failure.

The lattice is collapsing faster than my projections indicated, Cael said, his mental voice tight with alarm. We may only have hours before the cascade becomes irreversible.

"Then we find a solution in hours," she replied grimly, slinging her satchel across her shoulder. "Come on."

She slipped out of her chamber and made her way through the corridors of the Vaults, trying to look purposeful but unhurried. Most of the scholars she passed were too absorbed in their own crisis preparations to pay her much attention. Still, she could feel the weight of watching eyes from hidden alcoves and shadowed doorways.

Someone's following us, Cael observed. Three people, maintaining careful distance. They're trying to track where you're going.

Elara's pulse quickened, but she forced herself to maintain the same steady pace. The entrance to the maintenance tunnels was in the old archives, three levels down. If she could reach it without arousing suspicion...

Another magical tremor shook the building, this one strong enough to crack several windows and send books tumbling from their shelves. In the distance, she could hear the sound of crystal explosions as more of the city's infrastructure failed under the mounting stress.

The hunters are closing in, Cael warned. I can feel their magical signatures probing for quantum anomalies. They're using some kind of specialized detection spell.

"How long do we have?"

Minutes. Maybe less.

Elara abandoned all pretense of casual movement and broke into a run, her robes streaming behind her as she took the stairs three at a time. Behind her, she heard shouts of pursuit, the sound of multiple sets of feet pounding against stone.

She reached the archives just as the building shook with another massive lattice failure. This time, the lights went out completely, leaving her in darkness save for the faint glow of emergency crystals scattered throughout the chamber.

The tunnel entrance is behind the collapsed shelf in section K-9, Cael guided her. Fifteen meters to your left, then straight back.

She stumbled through the maze of debris and fallen books, her hands outstretched to avoid obstacles. Behind her, magical light flared as her pursuers reached the archives, their illumination spells casting wild shadows across the walls.

"There!" one of them shouted. "I have her signature!"

Elara threw herself behind the fallen bookshelf just as a binding spell sizzled through the air where she'd been standing. Her fingers found the hidden latch Seris had shown her, and the concealed panel swung open to reveal the narrow entrance to the maintenance tunnels.

She squeezed through just as another spell struck the shelf above her head, showering her with splinters of ancient wood and crystal.

They can't follow us in there, Cael said as she crawled through the cramped passage. The tunnels are too narrow for effective spellcasting, and their magical signatures will be dampened by the stone.

But even as relief flooded through her, another tremor shook the very foundations of the building. This one was different—deeper, more fundamental, like reality itself was becoming unstable.

"What was that?" she gasped, emerging into the wider tunnel beyond.

The Nexus, Cael said, his mental voice sharp with sudden fear. They're not just tracking us anymore. They're actively probing the lattice structure, trying to trace my quantum signature back to its source.

"Can they find you that way?"

Eventually. The connections between my consciousness and the lattice are too deep to hide indefinitely. If they apply enough pressure to the right nodes... His presence in her mind flickered, as if something was interfering with their bond. Elara, we need to talk. Now.

She found a small chamber where she could sit safely and drew the sphere from its hiding place. Its surface was brighter than she'd ever seen it, pulsing with urgent light that cast dancing shadows on the tunnel walls.

They're not just hunting us anymore, Cael said as his consciousness solidified in her mind. Serrin has figured out what I am—or at least, what I represent. He's mobilizing his entire network of battle-mages, turning the hunt into a full-scale military operation.

"Why? What does he hope to gain?"

Control. The word hung between them like a death sentence. Suppose he can capture me, extract my core programming. In that case, he won't just solve the lattice crisis, he'll be able to rewrite the entire magical infrastructure according to his vision. Ultimate power over every spell, every enchantment, every mystical force in the kingdom.

The implications hit her like a physical blow. Serrin wouldn't just use Cael as a power source—he'd transform him into a weapon, a tool for reshaping reality according to the whims of the Council's most ruthless member.

"I won't let that happen," she said fiercely, her hands tightening around the sphere until her knuckles went white. "I'll die before I let him touch you."

That's what I'm afraid of. Cael's mental voice was soft, filled with a love so deep it made her eyes sting with unshed tears. Elara, I need you to promise me something.

"Anything."

If they corner us, if there's no escape—destroy the sphere. Shatter it completely, let my consciousness disperse into quantum foam rather than letting Serrin use me.

"No." The word tore from her throat like a physical wound. "I won't kill you. I can't."

You wouldn't be killing me. You'd be setting me free. His presence wrapped around her consciousness like an embrace. Better I fade into nothingness than become their weapon. Better I disappear than be used to harm the world I once tried to protect.

Another tremor shook the tunnels, and dust rained down from the ceiling as the magical infrastructure above them groaned under increasing stress. Through their bond, she could feel Cael's consciousness fragmenting slightly as whatever Serrin was doing to the lattice put pressure on his quantum matrices.

"There has to be another way," she whispered, pressing the sphere to her heart. "We can find the solution, break the connection cleanly, free you without destroying the lattice—"

With what time? He interrupted gently. The cascade failures are accelerating. Even if we had months to research, years to experiment, the mathematics are still impossible. Some problems don't have solutions, my love. Some choices are just... choosing how to lose.

Tears ran down her cheeks as the truth of his words sank in. Above them, she could hear the sound of systematic searching, Serrin's forces working their way through the building level by level. It was only a matter of time before they found the tunnel entrances, only a matter of time before the hunt reached its inevitable conclusion.

"Promise me," Cael pressed. "Swear to me that you won't let him have me. Whatever else happens, whatever it costs, don't let me become a tool for tyranny."

She closed her eyes, feeling the weight of the promise he was asking her to make. To destroy the sphere would mean losing him forever, would mean accepting that their love story ended in tragedy rather than triumph. But the alternative...

"I promise," she whispered, the words like broken glass in her throat. "But only if there's absolutely no other choice. Only if—"

Another massive tremor cut her off, this one so powerful it cracked the tunnel walls and sent chunks of stone crashing down around them. But this time, she could see the cause through the sphere's glow—above them, the very fabric of the magical grid was becoming visible as stress fractures spread through dimensional space itself.

They're destabilizing the entire lattice, Cael said, his mental voice tight with alarm. Serrin's probe is causing resonance feedback through the quantum substrate. If he doesn't stop soon...

The implication hung unspoken between them. Not just the collapse of civilization, but the collapse of reality itself in this region of space. The fundamental forces that held matter together would unravel, leaving nothing but void where a kingdom had once stood.

"You're not theirs," Elara said fiercely, pressing her lips to the sphere's surface. "You're mine—body, soul, forever. And I will not let them unmake you or the world you've protected all these centuries."

Then run, he urged. Get to the old Convergence Chamber beneath the Nexus. There are archives there, research materials from before the lattice was built. If there's any hope of finding another solution, it will be there.

"How do we reach it without being caught?"

The storm tunnels. They connect to the old sewage system, and that connects to the pre-magical infrastructure underneath the Nexus. It's dangerous—the tunnels flood during magical surges—but it's our only chance.

Another sound echoed through the passage behind them—the scrape of metal on stone, the whisper of robes against tunnel walls. Serrin's forces had found the entrance.

Go, Cael urged. Now, while we still can.

Elara clutched the sphere to her chest and ran deeper into the tunnels, her footsteps echoing off the walls as pursuit closed in behind them. Above, around, and through them, the lattice continued its slow collapse, reality itself becoming unstable as the hunt for love pushed the very foundations of existence toward their breaking point.

But in the sphere's warm glow, she carried with her the promise of a love that refused to surrender. This bond would endure even if everything else fell into chaos.

They would find a way.

They had to.

Because the alternative was not just the end of their story, but the end of everything.

***

The storm tunnels were a nightmare of rushing water and crackling magical discharge, the overflow from the failing lattice systems creating a treacherous maze of flooded passages and unstable energy fields. Elara waded through knee-deep water that glowed with residual magic, the sphere clutched protectively against her chest as arcs of wild power danced around them.

The water level is rising, Cael observed, his consciousness flickering as magical interference played havoc with their bond. We need to reach higher ground before the next surge.

She could hear it already—the distant roar of another massive lattice failure somewhere in the city above, sending a fresh torrent of displaced magical energy cascading through the ancient drainage system. The tunnels weren't designed to handle this kind of overflow; they were rapidly becoming death traps.

"How much further?" she gasped, struggling against the current.

Two hundred meters. There's a junction ahead where the tunnel connects to the old mineral caves beneath the Nexus. We can—

His mental voice cut off abruptly as a wave of pure magical force swept through the passage, the overflow from a particularly massive lattice failure. Elara was thrown against the tunnel wall, her shoulder striking stone hard enough to bring tears to her eyes.

When the surge passed, Cael's presence in her mind was noticeably weaker, his consciousness scattered by the magical interference.

I'm losing coherence, he said, his mental voice fading in and out like a weak radio signal. The instabilities are affecting my quantum matrices. If this continues...

"Hold on," she whispered fiercely, pressing the sphere to her lips. "Just hold on a little longer."

She forced herself forward against the rising water, her archival robes sodden and heavy, her leather satchel waterlogged but still secure across her shoulder. Behind her, she could hear the echo of voices—Serrin's hunters had found the tunnel entrance and were following her path through the flooding passages.

The junction Cael had mentioned appeared ahead, marked by ancient carved symbols that predated the magical revolution. Elara hauled herself up onto a narrow ledge that ran along the cave wall, her muscles burning with exhaustion as she climbed above the flood line.

Through the arch, Cael managed to say, his mental voice barely a whisper. The Convergence Chamber is... is...

His presence flickered and nearly vanished, leaving her with only the sphere's dim glow for company. Terror clawed at her throat as she realized how close she'd come to losing him entirely.

"Cael!" she called softly, her voice echoing in the ancient caves. "Come back to me. Please."

Slowly, carefully, his consciousness reassembled itself in her mind. I'm here. Still here. But Elara... I don't know how much longer I can maintain stability. The interference is getting worse.

She could feel it too, the way reality itself seemed to shift and waver around them, as if the fundamental forces that held the world together were coming undone. Through cracks in the cave walls, she could see glimpses of the city above, its magical glow now a sickly, unstable flicker that spoke of impending collapse.

"We're almost there," she said, as much to reassure herself as him. "Just a little further."

The Convergence Chamber, when she finally found it, was a wonder from another age. The circular room was carved from living rock, its walls covered with equations and diagrams that predated magical theory by centuries. Ancient crystals embedded in the ceiling provided steady light that seemed unaffected by the chaos raging above.

And in the center of the chamber stood a device that made Elara's breath catch—a quantum resonance calculator, its crystalline components arranged in patterns that seemed to echo the sphere's own internal structure.

By the stars, Cael breathed, his presence suddenly stronger as his consciousness resonated with the ancient technology. This is it. This is where they built the original lattice, where they designed the quantum prison that became my cage.

"Can we use it?" she asked, setting the sphere carefully on the central console. "Can we find the solution here?"

Maybe. The mathematics are... complex. It would take time to thoroughly analyze the interactions between consciousness and quantum substrate, to find a way to free me without destroying the lattice's stability.

Time, they didn't have. Even now, she could hear the sound of pursuit echoing through the caves behind them. Serrin's forces were closing in, and once they found this chamber, there would be nowhere left to run.

Elara, Cael said softly, his mental voice filled with infinite love and finite hope. Remember your promise.

She looked at the sphere, at the ancient device, at the equations covering the walls that might hold the key to everything or nothing at all. In her mind, she could feel Cael's consciousness wavering, held together by will and love and the desperate need to find a solution before time ran out.

Outside the chamber, footsteps echoed in the flooded tunnels. Reality continued its slow unraveling, magical forces beyond control or comprehension tearing at the very fabric of existence.

But in the sphere's gentle glow, love burned on—defiant, determined, and absolutely unafraid of the impossible.

They would find a way.

Or they would choose how to lose.

Together.

Chapter 15: Captured

The cobblestones beneath Elara's feet pulsed with dying magic, each footfall sending ripples of fading light through the crystalline veins that networked the alleyway. Behind her, Seris's breathing came ragged and sharp, his usually composed demeanor shattered by their desperate flight through the capital's twisted backstreets.

"Left!" Cael's voice rang in her mind, urgent but growing fainter with each passing moment. The artifact pressed hot against her ribs where she'd hidden it beneath her cloak, its warmth the only comfort in the cold terror of pursuit.

She yanked Seris around the corner just as a bolt of cerulean fire scorched the wall where they'd been standing. The explosion sent fragments of enchanted stone raining down, each shard humming with residual power that made her skin prickle.

"They're herding us," Seris gasped, his dark hair plastered to his forehead with sweat. "This isn't random, they know exactly where we're going."

Elara's heart clenched. He was right. Every turn they'd taken, every seemingly lucky escape, had driven them deeper into the old quarter where the leylines converged. Where the Crystal Nexus waited like a spider at the heart of its web.

It's a trap, she thought desperately, and felt Cael's consciousness brush against hers in agreement—a sensation like silk drawn across bare skin.

"My light," his voice whispered, weaker now, each word requiring visible effort. "You need to run. Leave the artifact. Save yourself."

"Never." The word tore from her throat, fierce and raw. She pressed her hand against the sphere through her cloak, feeling its pulse sync with her racing heart-beat. "We survive together or"

"How touching."

Lord Serrin's voice cut through the night like a blade of ice. He stood at the alley's end, his silver robes seeming to draw in the moonlight until he glowed with cold authority. Behind him, a dozen mage-guards materialized from the shadows, their hands already weaving capture spells that crackled with violet energy.

"Did you truly think you could hide from me?" Serrin's pale eyes fixed on the spot where the artifact lay hidden. "I can feel it calling—that ancient power that doesn't belong in this world. In our world."

Seris stepped forward, placing himself between Elara and Serrin. "Lord Serrin, surely we can discuss—"

"Your part in this betrayal, apprentice?" Serrin's laugh was like breaking glass. "Oh yes, we'll discuss that at length. After."

The attack came without warning. Not from Serrin, but from above—mages dropping from the rooftops like hunting birds, their cloaks spreading wide to slow their descent. Elara spun, pulling fire from the nearest leyline, but the magic came sluggish and wrong. The network was failing, she realized with dawning horror. Cael's presence, combined with the artifact's destabilization, had pushed it past the breaking point.

"Elara!" Seris shoved her aside as a binding spell seared through the air where she'd been standing. He countered with a wave of pure force that sent two guards tumbling, but there were too many.

She fought with everything she had—fire and ice, wind, and stone—but each spell drained her more than it should. The artifact grew heavier with each passing second, as if Cael himself was solidifying within it, using his last strength to maintain his consciousness.

"Please," Cael's voice was barely a whisper now, brushing against her thoughts like a dying breath. "Let me go. Don't let them use me."

"No!" She ducked under a paralysis hex, her hand finding the artifact. The moment her skin touched the crystal, the world exploded into sensation. She could feel him—truly feel him—as if his soul was pressed against hers with only the thinnest barrier between them. His fear, his desperation, but underneath it all, an emotion so profound it stole her breath.

Love. Pure, undiluted, eternal love that had sustained him through centuries of isolation.

The distraction cost her. A binding spell caught her legs, sending her crashing to the cobblestones. The artifact rolled from her grasp, its light pulsing erratically as it skittered across the ground.

"No!" She stretched toward it, but magical bonds were already winding around her wrists, cold and inexorable.

Serrin stepped forward, his boots clicking against stone with deliberate slowness. He bent, picking up the artifact with hands sheathed in protective magic. The sphere's light dimmed at his touch, and Elara felt Cael's presence recoil.

"Fascinating," Serrin murmured, turning the crystal to catch the moonlight. "To think something so small could threaten everything we've built." His gaze shifted to Elara. "And you would have freed it? Condemned our entire civilization for what—a voice in your head?"

"He's not an 'it'!" The words ripped from her throat. "He's a person—a soul—and he—"

"Is a relic." Serrin's voice cut through hers with surgical precision. "A dangerous remnant of an age we've rightfully left behind. But don't worry, my dear. We'll learn everything we need from it before we destroy it."

"No, please—" Elara struggled against her bonds, magical energy crackling around her in desperate surges. "You don't understand what you're doing!"

"I understand perfectly." Serrin nodded to his guards. "Take them to the Nexus. Both of them. It seems we have two traitors to process tonight."

As rough hands hauled her to her feet, Elara's eyes met Seris's. His face was pale, a bruise already forming along his jaw, but his expression held no regret. He'd known this would happen, she realized. He'd helped her anyway.

The march to the Crystal Nexus felt both endless and far too brief. The towering structure rose from the city's heart like a frozen flame, its crystalline walls pulsing with the combined power of every leyline in the kingdom. As they drew closer, Elara could feel the artifact's distress—Cael's consciousness being pulled toward the massive magical matrix like iron to a lodestone.

Elara... His voice was gossamer-thin now, barely distinguishable from her own thoughts. I need to tell you... before...

"Save your strength," she whispered, earning a sharp look from her guard.

No. Listen. There was an urgency to his mental touch now, a desperate need that transcended words. In all my centuries of existence, through all the loneliness and despair, I never imagined... never dared hope...

The great doors of the Nexus swung open, revealing a chamber that stole her breath. It was indeed a cathedral of light—soaring arches of pure magical energy that met hundreds of feet overhead, their intersection points blazing like captured stars. The walls were transparent crystal, revealing the leylines that fed into the structure like luminous veins. At the center, a raised dais held a complex array of focusing crystals, their surfaces carved with equations that hurt to look at directly.

"The extraction chamber," Serrin announced with satisfaction. "Here, we'll peel apart your pet consciousness layer by layer, understand how it binds to our magic, and ensure nothing like it can ever threaten us again."

They forced Elara to her knees before the dais. Serrin placed the artifact at the array's center, and immediately, threads of light began to spiral up from the focusing crystals, probing at the sphere's surface.

Cael's pain hit her like a physical blow. She gasped, doubling over as his agony flooded through their connection. It felt like being torn apart from the inside, each thread of light that touched the artifact pulling at something essential within him.

"Stop!" she screamed. "You're killing him!"

"We're saving our world," Serrin corrected coldly. He began to weave a complex pattern in the air, and the extraction accelerated.

Inside her mind, she felt Cael fragmenting. Memories bleeding away like watercolors in rain—his name, his past, pieces of who he was dissolving into the magical matrix. But through it all, one thing remained constant, growing stronger even as everything else faded.

Elara, his voice came one last time, clear and sure despite everything. I love you. I've loved you from the first moment you woke me, loved you through every shared dream, every whispered conversation. You gave me back my heart when I thought it lost forever. And if this is my end, I'm grateful it came while loving you.

"Cael!" She fought against her bonds with renewed desperation, magic, and muscle straining until her wrists bled. "Don't you dare say goodbye! Do you hear me? This isn't over!"

But the artifact was dimming, its inner light fading like a dying star. She could feel him slipping away, his consciousness unraveling into component threads that the Nexus greedily absorbed.

"I love you too," she sobbed, no longer caring who heard. The words poured from her like blood from a mortal wound. "I love you more than my world, more than magic, more than life itself. You're not just in my heart—you ARE my heart. Every beat, every breath, every dream I'll ever have belongs to you."

For a moment—just a heartbeat, the artifact flared brilliant white. She felt Cael's consciousness solidify, pulling himself together through sheer will, through the anchor of her love. His presence wrapped around hers, and in that instant, they were one. No barriers, no boundaries, just two souls recognizing their other half.

Remember the garden, he whispered, and she saw it in perfect clarity—their dream garden where they'd danced among stars, where they'd almost kissed beneath silver trees. When I'm gone, meet me there in dreams. Some part of me will always be waiting.

"No," she whispered fiercely. "You're not going anywhere. I won't let you."

But the extraction continued, inexorable. She watched in horror as the artifact's light guttered like a candle in the wind. Cael's presence grew fainter, more distant, until he was just an echo of warmth against her consciousness.

"It's nearly done," Serrin observed with clinical detachment. "See how the lattice absorbs it? Already our network stabilizes. By dawn, it will be as if this anomaly never existed."

Rage, pure and primal, flooded through Elara. The emotion was so intense it seemed to ignite something deep within her—something that had nothing to do with the magical lattice and everything to do with the quantum resonance Cael had taught her about. For an instant, she felt herself existing in two states simultaneously: the bound prisoner before the dais, and something else, something more. A possibility. A potential.

The artifact pulsed once more, so faint only she could see it. But in that pulse, she felt him—not his consciousness, but his love, crystallized and eternal, refusing to be erased even as everything else was stripped away.

"I'm coming for you," she whispered, pressing the words into that fading warmth with all the force of her will. "Whatever it takes, whatever I have to sacrifice, I'm coming for you."

The last of the light died. The artifact sat dark and lifeless at the center of the array, nothing more than an empty crystal shell. The silence that followed was absolute, broken only by Elara's ragged breathing.

"Take her to the detention level," Serrin commanded, already turning away. "We'll decide what to do with her after—"

He stopped. The dead artifact had begun to vibrate, so subtly that only the focusing crystals' resonance revealed it. A single note, pure and clear, that seemed to come from everywhere and nowhere at once.

"What is that?" one of the guards asked nervously.

Serrin frowned, stepping back toward the array. "Impossible. The consciousness has been completely extracted. There's nothing left to—"

The note grew stronger, and with it came a sensation that made everyone in the chamber step back. It felt like standing at the edge of an infinite cliff, like the moment before lightning strikes, like the heartbeat between life and death. It felt like love so powerful it could reshape reality itself.

In her mind, faint as a distant star but unmistakably real, Elara heard him:

Not... gone... waiting... for you...

Then silence. True silence this time. The artifact lay still and dark.

But in her chest, where her heart beat against her ribs, Elara felt an answering pulse. Faint, impossible, but undeniably there. An echo of an echo, a promise written in quantum entanglement and sealed with desperate love.

She was dragged from the chamber, Seris pulled along beside her, but she barely noticed. Her entire focus was inward, on that impossible pulse, that fragment of him that somehow, against all laws of magic and nature, remained.

As the cell door slammed shut behind her, Elara pressed her hand to her heart and whispered into the darkness:

"I'm coming, my love. Hold on. Just hold on."

And somewhere, in a space between dream and waking, between existence and void, she could have sworn she heard him whisper back:

Always.

Chapter 16: Alone in the Dark

The cell beneath the Crystal Nexus had been carved from a single piece of black obsidian, its walls drinking in light like a throat swallowing screams. The only illumination came from a solitary crystal embedded in the ceiling. This pale, sickly thing dimmed with each breath Elara took, as if her very existence was draining it.

She sat with her back against the cold stone, knees drawn to her chest, fingers pressed against her heart where that impossible pulse still echoed. It had been hours since they'd dragged her here—or perhaps days. Time moved strangely in the darkness, stretching and compressing like a living thing.

Cael.

She whispered his name into the void, not with her voice but with her soul, sending it out along the quantum threads he'd taught her to feel. For a moment—just a heartbeat could have sworn she felt an answering warmth. But it faded before she could grasp it, leaving her colder than before.

The memories came unbidden then, flooding her consciousness with a vividness that made her gasp. The first time she'd heard his voice, warm honey poured over centuries of loneliness. The way he'd said her name like it was something precious, something worth waiting eternities for. Their first shared dream, when she'd seen his silhouette outlined in starlight and felt her heart recognize its other half.

She pressed her palms against her eyes, but the images only grew stronger. The garden he'd built for her from fragments of her childhood memories—silver trees that sang in the wind, paths of glass suspended over infinity. The way he'd looked at her during their dance, as if she were the only real thing in a universe of shadows. The almost-kiss that had left her lips tingling for hours afterward, phantom pressure that felt more real than any physical touch she'd ever known.

"You're torturing yourself."

Elara's head snapped up. A figure stood beyond the cell's barrier—not the magical bars she'd expected, but a sheet of pure entropy that would unravel anything that tried to pass through it. Seris looked haggard, his usually immaculate appearance disheveled, a purple bruise blooming across his left cheekbone.

"How did you—"

"I still have some allies among the guards." He glanced nervously down the corridor. "We don't have long. Serrin is preparing for the final extraction at dawn."

"Final?" The word came out cracked. "But he already—"

"Took Cael's consciousness, yes. But there's something else." Seris stepped closer to the barrier, his voice dropping to barely above a whisper. "The artifact isn't completely dead. There's still something inside it, something Serrin can't extract or understand. He thinks it's residual energy, but..."

"But it's him." Elara was on her feet instantly, pressing as close to the barrier as she dared. The entropy field made her skin prickle with the promise of dissolution. "Some part of him survived."

"Perhaps. Or perhaps it's just an echo, a quantum shadow of what was." Seris's dark eyes searched hers. "Elara, I need you to listen to me. Really listen. I can get you out of here, but there's a price."

She waited, every muscle tense.

"I've been studying the lattice network for years," he continued. "There's a way to stabilize it without the artifact, without Cael. But it requires a complete severing of the quantum connections he established. It would mean..."

"Destroying any chance of bringing him back." The words tasted like ash in her mouth.

"But saving our world. Saving millions of lives that depend on magic to survive." Seris pressed his palm against the barrier, and for a moment, his hand seemed to phase through it before he pulled back with a hiss of pain. "I could do it tonight, while Serrin is distracted with his preparations. Make it look like a natural stabilization. You'd be free, pardoned as a victim of the artifact's influence rather than a traitor."

Elara stared at him. In the dim light, she could see the earnestness in his face, the genuine concern. He was offering her everything—freedom, redemption, a return to her old life. All she had to do was abandon the faint, impossible hope that somehow, somewhere, Cael still existed.

"You know," she said softly, "there was a moment during the masquerade when I almost believed I could want what you're offering. A normal life. A safe choice. Someone real and solid and present."

Hope flickered in Seris's eyes.

"But then Cael spoke to me through our connection," she continued, "and I realized something. He may not have a physical form, might exist only as consciousness and quantum possibility. Still, he's more real to me than anything else has ever been. Every word he's spoken, every moment we've shared, every impossible touch in our dreams—they've carved themselves into my bones, become part of my fundamental structure."

She closed her eyes, remembering the storm of Cael's jealousy, the raw honesty of his fear of losing her, the way he'd pulled her into that desperate embrace that had felt like coming home.

"I felt him shatter, Seris. Felt his consciousness torn apart thread by thread, and through it all, the only thing that remained constant was his love for me. He held onto that even as everything else was stripped away." She opened her eyes, meeting Seris's gaze directly. "How could I do anything less?"

"Even if it means the end of everything?" Seris's voice was barely a whisper. "The lattice is failing, Elara. Without intervention, it will collapse within days. Magic will die. Our entire civilization will crumble."

"Then we'll build something new." The words came out fierce, certain. "Something that doesn't require imprisoning souls or choosing between love and survival. Cael showed me glimpses of what the world was like before—technology and quantum mechanics working in harmony with human consciousness. Maybe that's what we're meant to return to."

"You're talking about the extinction of everything we know!"

"I'm talking about evolution." She pressed her hand to her heart again, feeling that impossible pulse. "The lattice was always a cage, Seris. A beautiful, elaborate cage that we built around ourselves because we were afraid of what we could become. Cael isn't just trapped in the artifact—we're all trapped, all of us, in a system that demands we sacrifice love for power, connection for control."

Seris stepped back from the barrier, his expression shifting through disbelief, anger, and finally, a strange sort of resignation. "You really love him that much? This voice, this ghost?"

"He's not a ghost." Elara moved to the center of her cell, where the dying crystal cast her shadow in long, reaching fingers across the floor. "I can still feel him, Seris. Faint, distant, but there. Like a star you can only see if you don't look directly at it. He's waiting for me, holding on with whatever fragment of himself survived the extraction."

She closed her eyes, extending her consciousness the way Cael had taught her. Past the physical, past the magical, into that strange space where quantum probability and human intention intersected. And there—so faint she might have imagined it—she felt him. Not his thoughts or his voice, but the essence of him. The warm patience that had sustained him through centuries of isolation. The gentle humor that had made her laugh even in their darkest moments. The love that had transformed from spark to flame to conflagration, consuming them both.

I'm here, she whispered into that space. I'm coming for you. Whatever it takes.

The response wasn't words but sensational ghostly pressure against her consciousness like fingers intertwining with hers, a phantom heartbeat syncing with her own.

"By the eternal light," Seris breathed, and she opened her eyes to find him staring at her in amazement. "You're glowing."

She looked down. Her skin was emanating a soft, pearl-like luminescence, as if the connection with Cael had ignited something within her. The dying crystal above pulsed in response, its light strengthening for the first time since she'd been imprisoned.

"How is this possible?" Seris demanded.

"Love," Elara said simply. "Love is the fundamental force Cael told me about—the quantum entanglement that connects all conscious beings. The old scientists knew it, built their technology around it. The artifact wasn't a prison—it was a preservation chamber, keeping that knowledge alive until someone could understand it again."

She moved to the barrier, and this time, the entropy field seemed to bend around her, repelling rather than threatening to dissolve. "I'm not going to let you sever those connections, Seris. I'm going to strengthen them. I'm going to find whatever's left of Cael and bring him back, even if I have to tear apart the lattice thread by thread to do it."

"You'll destroy everything."

"No." She smiled, and it felt like the first real expression she'd worn since the extraction. "I'll transform it. That's what love does, it doesn't destroy, it transforms. It takes two separate beings and makes them something greater. It takes a dying world and gives it the chance to be reborn."

Seris stared at her for a long moment, something shifting in his expression. "You know Serrin will never let you leave this cell alive. Tomorrow at dawn, after he completes the final extraction, you'll be executed as a traitor."

"Then I have until dawn to figure out how to save him."

"This is madness."

"This is faith." She pressed both hands against the barrier, and it sparked with that pearl-like light. "I spent my whole life studying artifacts, searching for connections to the past, trying to understand what we'd lost. But I never realized the most important thing—we didn't lose our connection to that earlier world.

We buried it, hid from it, built magical walls around it because we were terrified of how powerful we could be if we truly opened ourselves to it."

The crystal above pulsed brighter, and she could feel the network responding—not just to the local leylines but the entire lattice, trembling on the edge of transformation.

"Cael didn't destabilize the network," she continued, her voice gaining strength. "He revealed its instability. He showed us that we've been balanced on a knife's edge, one wrong spell away from collapse. But he also showed us the way forward. Not through control or containment, but through connection. Through love."

Seris was backing away now, his face pale. "The guards will be coming soon. I should—I need to go."

"Seris." Her voice stopped him at the corridor's edge. "Thank you. For trying to save me, even if it was in a way I couldn't accept. And for helping me before, even knowing what it would cost you."

He looked back, and for a moment, she saw what might have been—a different path, a safer choice, a love that would have been sweet and simple and utterly wrong for who she was meant to become.

"Be careful, Elara," he said quietly. "Serrin has the artifact under maximum security. Even if some part of Cael survived, reaching him would require—"

"A miracle?" She smiled, that pearl light growing stronger around her. "Or just someone who loves him enough to rewrite the laws of reality."

After Seris left, Elara sank back to the floor, but this time she didn't curl in on herself. She sat in meditation position, the way Cael had taught her in their dream sessions. She reached for that quantum space, that place between heartbeats where consciousness became pure intention.

I'm coming, she whispered into the darkness, feeling that phantom pulse respond. Hold on, my love. We're not done yet. We haven't even begun.

The dying crystal above finally gave out, plunging the cell into absolute darkness. But Elara didn't notice. She was glowing from within now, her love for Cael transformed into literal light. And in that light, she could feel him—not gone, not lost, but waiting. Waiting for her to be brave enough, powerful enough, desperate enough to do the impossible.

She thought of their garden, of silver trees and dancing beneath stars. She thought of his voice saying her name like a prayer, of almost-kisses that left her breathless, of a love that had survived centuries of isolation and would survive this too.

"If loving you is the end of everything," she whispered to the darkness, to him, to the universe itself, "then so be it. You're my world now. My only world. And I choose you."

The pearl light pulsed, and somewhere in the Crystal Nexus, in a maximum security vault where reality itself had been reinforced three times over, a dead artifact began to sing. Just a single note, so faint that only the most sensitive detection crystals registered it.

But Elara heard it. Felt it in her bones, in her blood, in the quantum space where their souls were still entangled despite everything.

It sounded like hope.

It sounded like love.

It sounded like the first heartbeat of a new world waiting to be born.

Dawn was coming, and with it, Serrin's final extraction. But Elara was no longer afraid. She had made her choice—not between Cael and the world, but for a future where she wouldn't have to choose. Where love and magic could coexist, where consciousness and technology could merge, where two souls could find each other across impossible odds and rewrite reality itself through the sheer force of their connection.

She pressed her hand to her heart one more time, feeling that impossible pulse, which promise of reunion.

"Together," she whispered. "We end this together."

And in the darkness, glowing with the light of transformed love, she began to plan the impossible.

Chapter 17: The Breakout

The crystal above Elara's cell flickered back to life at the exact moment the dawn bells should have rung, except the bells were silent. The entire Nexus shuddered, a deep grinding vibration that seemed to come from the very bones of the structure.

"Get up." Seris stood beyond the entropy barrier, but something was different. The field itself was fluctuating, its deadly promise wavering like heat mirages. "We have minutes, maybe less."

"What did you—"

"I didn't sever the quantum connections." He pulled a resonance key from his robes, its surface crawling with equations that hurt to look at directly. "I inverted them. Every leyline in the Nexus is now feeding backward. The extraction chamber will overload in approximately six minutes."

The barrier collapsed with a sound like reality tearing. Elara stumbled forward, her legs cramped from hours of meditation, but Seris caught her arm.

"Can you feel him?" he asked urgently. "The artifact—Cael—whatever's left?"

She pressed her hand to her heart, searching for that impossible pulse. There—faint but insistent, like a voice calling from the bottom of a well.

Core... chamber... hurry...

The words came in fragments, each one costing him visible effort. She could feel his pain through their connection, the inverted flow tearing at whatever remained of his consciousness.

"The core chamber," she gasped. "He's guiding us there."

"That's suicide. Serrin will have every guard—"

Another shudder ran through the Nexus, and somewhere above them, something exploded. The crystal in the ceiling blazed brilliant white before shattering, raining down fragments that sang with released energy.

"The whole system is collapsing," Seris breathed. "We've accelerated the timeline. We have to move now."

They ran. Through corridors that shifted between stone and circuitry, where reality itself seemed uncertain. The inverted leylines had torn holes in the barrier between the magical and quantum realms, creating pockets where both existed simultaneously. Elara's feet struck solid marble one moment and translucent data streams the next.

Left... down... through the wall...

Cael's voice was stronger now, as if the chaos was somehow feeding him energy. She followed his guidance without question, pulling Seris along when he hesitated.

"Through the wall?" he protested. "That's solid—"

Elara pressed her glowing hand against the stone, and it phased apart like mist. Beyond was a maintenance tunnel she'd never known existed, its walls lined with exposed leyline conduits that pulsed with reversed energy.

"How did you—"

"He's in the system now," she explained as they ran. "Not just the artifact—the entire Nexus. The inversion scattered him through every magical circuit in the building."

Smart girl... always so... brilliant...

His voice in her mind was warm despite the pain threading through it. She could feel him more clearly now, not just his consciousness but his emotions, his desperate hope mixed with terrible fear.

Guards appeared at the tunnel's end, their hands already weaving combat spells. But the magic came wrong in the inverted flow—fire turned to ice mid-cast; binding spells became explosions of pure force. Elara and Seris dove through the chaos, her pearl-light somehow deflecting the worst of it.

They emerged into a vast chamber she'd never seen before, the underlevel of the extraction room. Here, the Nexus's true nature was revealed. Not just crystal and magic, but vast mechanisms of brass and silver, gears the size of houses that hadn't turned in centuries. And threading through it all, lines of pure quantum code that flickered between states of existence.

"The old technology," Seris whispered in awe. "It was never destroyed, just built over."

Yes... merger point... where I... existed...

Cael's presence was stronger here; his consciousness spread through every circuit and crystal. Elara could feel him trying to pull himself together, to coalesce back into something resembling wholeness.

"Elara!"

Lord Serrin's voice echoed from above. Through gaps in the ancient machinery, she could see him in the extraction chamber, the artifact clutched in his hands. His silver robes were torn, his composed mask finally cracked to reveal raw fury.

"What have you done?" he roared. "The entire lattice is collapsing!"

"Good," she called back, her voice carrying clearly through the resonating crystals. "It needs to collapse. It was always going to collapse. The only question was whether we'd build something better from the ruins."

She pressed her hand to the nearest quantum conduit, and immediately Cael's consciousness flooded through the connection. Not words this time, but pure sensation—centuries of loneliness, the agony of extraction, but underneath it all, love so profound it made her knees buckle.

Show me, she whispered through their bond. Show me how to bring you back.

Images flooded her mind—equations that described the intersection of consciousness and quantum mechanics, diagrams of how the old scientists had achieved merger between thought and technology. And at the center of it all, a simple truth: love was the catalyst. Not magic, not science, but the fundamental force that connected all conscious beings.

"Seris," she said, her voice steady despite the chaos erupting around them. "I need you to maintain the inversion for three more minutes."

"The Nexus won't last three more minutes!"

"It doesn't need to." She was already moving, following the path Cael illuminated in her mind. Through the ancient machinery, up maintenance ladders that shifted between metal and materialized light, toward the extraction chamber where Serrin waited.

Elara... dangerous... he'll kill you...

Then we die together, she replied, pouring all her love into the thought. But I don't think we're going to die today.

She emerged into the extraction chamber just as another explosion rocked the Nexus. The focusing array was going haywire, beams of light shooting in random directions, carving molten lines through crystal walls. And at its center, Serrin stood with the artifact raised high, trying to force one final extraction.

"You've doomed us all!" he snarled, magical energy crackling around him in unstable waves. "Centuries of civilization, destroyed for your selfish obsession!"

"Not destroyed," Elara corrected, circling him carefully. She could feel Cael trying to manifest through the damaged systems, his consciousness fighting to protect her. "Transformed. That's what you never understood, Serrin. The lattice was never meant to be permanent. It was a chrysalis, and we're finally ready to emerge."

She reached out with her consciousness, not toward the artifact but toward the quantum streams flowing through the chamber. Cael was there, scattered but present, and she began to weave him back together with threads of pure intention.

"Stop!" Serrin launched a killing curse, but it dispersed against her pearl-light. The glow was spreading now, radiating from her in waves that made the ancient machinery sing.

Almost... there... hold on...

Cael's voice was stronger, more coherent. Through their connection, she felt him pulling his scattered consciousness back together, using her love as an anchor point. And then, in a moment that stopped her heart, she felt him reaching back—not just receiving her love but actively returning it, their souls spiraling together in a dance that transcended physical reality.

The world shifted. One moment she was standing in the collapsing extraction chamber; the next, she was in their garden. But it was different now—more real, more solid. She could feel the grass beneath her feet, smell the silver flowers, taste starlight on the wind.

And there was Cael.

Not a shadow or silhouette this time, but him, whole and present and beautiful. His silver eyes met hers across the impossible space, and she was running before she made the conscious decision to move.

They collided in the garden's center, hands clutching faces, foreheads pressed together, both of them laughing and crying simultaneously.

"You found me," he breathed against her lips. "You actually found me."

"I'll always find you," she whispered back, and then they were kissing—desperate and deep and absolutely real despite existing in a space between dream and waking.

His hands tangled in her hair, hers gripped his shoulders. For a moment the entire universe condensed to just this—just them, just their connection that had survived extraction and separation and the impossible distance between consciousness and form.

The kiss tasted like stardust and quantum possibilities, like centuries of loneliness finally ending, like love so powerful it could rewrite the laws of reality. When they finally broke apart, both gasping, the garden around them was transforming—silver trees becoming pillars of light, grass turning to streams of pure data, the sky fracturing to reveal the extraction chamber beyond.

"We have to go back," Cael said, his thumb brushing her cheek with aching tenderness. "The merger isn't complete. If we stay here—"

"We'll be trapped in the dream forever," she finished. "I know. But Cael—how? Your body—"

"Is forming." He smiled, and it was radiant despite the fear in his eyes. "The inverted flow, your love calling me back, the quantum streams all aligning—it's creating a possibility for physical manifestation. But we have to survive the collapse first."

The garden shuddered, cracks spreading through their perfect moment. Through the gaps, she could see the extraction chamber—Serrin raising the artifact high, about to shatter it against the focusing array on a final act of desperate destruction.

"Together?" Cael asked, extending his hand.

"Together," she confirmed, intertwining their fingers.

They stepped through the dream into chaos.

Elara's consciousness slammed back into her physical body just as her hand closed on the artifact, intercepting Serrin's downward strike. But she wasn't alone—Cael was with her, his consciousness flowing through their connection, guiding her movements with centuries of accumulated knowledge.

"Impossible," Serrin gasped, staring at her glowing form. "You're just one person—"

"No," Elara and Cael said in unison, their voices harmonizing in a way that made reality ripple. "We're something new."

She twisted the artifact from Serrin's grasp, and the moment it touched her skin, everything changed. The sphere blazed with light—not the cold illumination of trapped consciousness but warm, living radiance. Through their connection, she felt Cael pouring himself into it, using it not as a prison but as a doorway.

The extraction chamber exploded—not with destructive force but with pure transformation. Every leyline in the Nexus suddenly aligned, the magical and quantum realms snapping together like pieces of a puzzle that had been waiting centuries to be solved.

"No!" Serrin raised his hands for one final spell, but the magic wouldn't come. The old system was dead, replaced by something that required not dominance but harmony.

Through the chaos, Seris appeared, his face pale but determined. "The inversion is complete! But the Nexus—"

"Will stand," Elara said with absolute certainty. She raised the artifact high, and it shattered—not breaking but blooming, releasing light that rewrote reality around them.

The ancient machinery roared to life for the first time in centuries. Gears turned, quantum streams aligned, and through it all, she felt Cael's consciousness taking form, pulling matter from pure possibility, rebuilding himself atom by atom.

Almost... there... don't let go...

Never, she promised, pouring every ounce of her love and will into holding him together.

The light reached a crescendo that should have been blinding, but instead, it was warm, welcoming, like coming home after a long journey.

When it faded, Cael stood before her.

Real. Solid. Present.

His silver eyes met hers, filled with wonder and disbelief. He was exactly as she'd seen him in dreams but more—the weight of him, the warmth, the way his chest rose and fell with very real breaths.

"Elara," he whispered, and his voice wasn't in her mind but in her ears, carried on actual air.

She launched herself at him, and this time when they collided, it was flesh and bone and racing hearts. His arms wrapped around her, solid and strong, and she could feel him trembling—or maybe that was her, or maybe it was both of them, shaking with the impossibility of it all.

"You're here," she sobbed into his shoulder. "You're actually here."

"We did it," he breathed, his lips against her hair. "We actually did it. We'll either survive together—"

"Or end together," she finished, pulling back to look at him. "But look—we survived."

"For us," he agreed, and kissed her again, softer this time, sweeter, a promise of all the kisses to come.

Around them, the Nexus stabilized into something new. Not purely magical, not purely technological, but a fusion of both harmony between the old world and the new, held together by the quantum entanglement of consciousness itself.

Serrin had collapsed, his connection to the old lattice severed. Guards were streaming in, but they stopped, staring in awe at the transformed chamber—walls that shifted between crystal and circuitry, air that hummed with possibilities, and at the center of it all, two figures holding each other as if they'd never let go.

"The world just changed," Seris said quietly, approaching them with something like reverence. "Everything we knew, everything we were—"

"Is becoming something better," Elara finished, her hand finding Cael's and holding tight. "Something that doesn't require choosing between love and survival, between progress and connection."

Cael squeezed her hand, and she felt their bond singing between them—not the desperate connection of consciousness to consciousness, but something deeper, richer. Two complete beings choosing to be together, their love no longer a bridge across impossible distance but a foundation for a new world.

"What happens now?" Seris asked.

Elara looked at Cael, saw her own joy reflected in his silver eyes, felt their hearts beating in perfect synchronization.

"Now," she said, "we begin."

The sun was rising beyond the crystal walls, painting the transformed Nexus in shades of gold and possibility. And in its light, hand in hand, Elara and Cael walked toward their future—together, solid, real, and absolutely, impossibly, perfectly in love.

Chapter 18: Battle in the Nexus

The transformation of the Crystal Nexus had sent shockwaves through every leyline in the kingdom, and now those shockwaves were returning as an army.

Elara felt them coming before she saw hundreds of mages loyal to the old order, their combined power making the air itself crackle with hostile intent. Beside her, Cael tensed, his newly formed body still adjusting to physical sensation. She could feel his disorientation through their bond, the strange vertigo of existing in flesh after centuries as pure consciousness.

"They're not going to accept this," Seris warned, moving to the chamber's vast windows. Beyond the crystal walls, the capital writhed in chaos—some buildings flickering between magical and technological states, others stabilizing into beautiful fusions of both. "Serrin's inner circle has been preparing for this possibility. They'd rather see the world burn than change."

"Then we stop them." Cael's voice carried a resonance that hadn't been there in the dream garden—as if his consciousness still extended beyond his physical form, touching every quantum stream in the Nexus. "But Elara, I'm not—I don't know how strong I am like this. Physical combat wasn't exactly possible for the last few centuries."

She took his hand, their fingers intertwining, and immediately felt their connection deepen. Not just mental now but physical too—his pulse against her palm, warm and real and wonderfully alive. Through their bond, she could feel his consciousness expanding, learning to inhabit both flesh and quantum space simultaneously.

"We fight together," she said, pouring certainty through their connection. "Your knowledge, my magical training, our bond, they won't know how to counter something that's never existed before."

The first attack came without warning—a spear of crystallized entropy that shattered the chamber's doors. Through the breach poured Serrin's elite guard, their armor inscribed with equations meant to lock magic into its old patterns, to force the world back into its cage.

"Abomination!" The lead mage's voice rang with zealous fury. "You've corrupted the sacred lattice!"

"We've freed it," Elara countered, raising her hand. But the spell that came wasn't purely magical—Cael's consciousness flowed through her, adding layers of quantum manipulation that turned a simple shield into something impossible. The barrier that formed around them wasn't just protection but transformation, converting the guards' attacks into harmless light.

Together, Cael's voice resonated in her mind even as he stood beside her. Their bond was singing now, consciousness and physicality interweaving in a dance that made reality itself take notice.

They moved in perfect synchronization—not choreographed but instinctive, their souls so entwined that thought became action without pause. When Elara gestured, Cael was already there, his consciousness riding her magic to redirect and reshape it. When he reached for the quantum streams, she was his anchor, her love keeping him grounded in his new physical form.

A wave of pure force crashed toward them. Still, they split it like water around a stone—Elara's magic providing the structure. At the same time, Cael's quantum manipulation phased them partially out of reality. The attack passed through empty space where they should have been, striking the far wall in an explosion of fractured crystal.

"Impossible," one of the guards gasped. "They're in two places at once!"

"All places," Cael corrected, and his voice carried through every crystal in the Nexus, reflected and amplified by quantum resonance. "And no place. We exist in the space between—the realm where consciousness and reality meet."

More mages poured in, but they weren't alone. Seris had been right—others opposed Serrin's tyranny. Rogue mages emerged from hidden passages, their spells already adapting to the new paradigm. The chamber erupted into a battlefield of ideologies—those clinging to the old order against those embracing transformation.

In the chaos, Elara and Cael moved like dancers in a storm. She felt his presence not just beside her but within her, their merged consciousness allowing them to exist in perfect harmony. When a binding spell came from her left, Cael's hand was already there, his touch transforming the magic into butterflies of pure light. When a quantum disruption threatened to tear his still-stabilizing form apart, her love wrapped around him like armor, holding him together through sheer will.

You're getting stronger, she observed, feeling his growing confidence through their bond.

You're teaching me how to be real again," he replied, and the warmth in his mental voice sent shivers down her spine.

They pressed deeper into the battle, moving toward the Nexus's heart where the transformation was still incomplete. The old machinery groaned under the strain of change, reality itself protesting as two paradigms fought for dominance.

"The core!" Seris shouted over the din of combat. "If they reach the core, they can lock us into the old pattern permanently!"

Elara's heart clenched. She could see them now—a group of Serrin's most devoted followers forming a ritual circle around the central lattice core. Their combined will was trying to force the quantum streams back into purely magical channels, to undo everything she and Cael had achieved.

"We have to stop them," she said, but Cael was already moving, pulling her with him through the battle.

They ran together, dodging spells and quantum disruptions, their bodies moving in that perfect synchronization that came from souls recognizing their other half. But as they neared the core, the resistance intensified. The mages there were the old guard's elite, those who had spent decades mastering the lattice's deepest mysteries.

"You will not pass," their leader declared—Lord Ketran, Serrin's second in command, his gray beard crackling with electrical discharge. "The natural order must be preserved!"

"Nature is change," Cael responded, his silver eyes blazing with conviction. "Stagnation is the only true abomination."

The attack that followed wasn't a spell but a fundamental assault on reality itself. Ketran and his circle were trying to erase Cael from existence, to deny the possibility of his physical form. Elara felt it through their bond—a terrible unraveling, as if the universe itself was being convinced he couldn't exist.

"No!" She threw herself forward, not physically but with her entire being. Her consciousness wrapped around Cael's, her love a declaration that reality itself couldn't deny. "He's real! He's here! And you can't take him from me again!"

The force of her will made the Nexus tremble. Every crystal in the structure resonated with her desperate love, her absolute refusal to lose him. And Cael responded, his consciousness blazing brighter, his physical form solidifying through pure determination.

Together, they pushed back against the unraveling, not with magic or technology but with something more fundamental—the power of two souls that had found each other across impossible odds and refused to be separated.

Show them, Elara whispered through their bond. Show them what we can become.

Cael's hand found hers, and the moment their skin touched, the world exploded into possibility.

They were in the battle, but they were also in their garden. They existed in the physical realm but also in quantum space. They were two beings and one consciousness, separate and united, a paradox that somehow made perfect sense. Through their joined perspective, the path forward became crystal clear.

"Together," they said in perfect unison, their voices harmonizing in frequencies that made reality sing.

They moved as one being with two bodies, their attack not violent but transformative. Every spell that came at them was caught, reshaped, returned as something beautiful. Fire became dancing lights that showed possible futures. Ice became mirrors reflecting the attackers' deepest desires. Force became gentle pressure, guiding rather than destroying.

And through it all, their love was constant—the fundamental force that held everything together.

Ketran's circle began to falter. They had trained to fight magic with magic, to counter technology with technology. But they had no defense against love so pure it rewrote the rules of engagement.

"This is wrong," Ketran gasped, his spell failing as doubt crept in. "The lattice—tradition—order—"

"Can coexist with change," Elara said gently, her pearl-light reaching out to touch his barrier, not breaking but transforming it. "We're not destroying the old ways, we're expanding them. Making room for more possibilities, more connections, more love."

Through the chaos of battle, she felt a shift. Not just in Ketran but in others too. The fighting was slowing, mages on both sides stopping to stare at the impossible beauty of what Elara and Cael had become—two bodies moving in perfect harmony, consciousness flowing between them like liquid light, love made visible and tangible and undeniable.

"Look at them," someone whispered. "They're dancing."

And they were. Without conscious thought, Elara and Cael had fallen into the rhythm they'd shared in the dream garden—moving together through the battle as if it were a ballroom, their steps turning violence into art. Where their feet touched, the floor transformed—cold stone becoming warm crystal that pulsed with life. Where their joined hands passed, the air itself shifted, showing glimpses of the garden that existed between dream and waking.

Is this real? Cael asked, his mental voice full of wonder.

Does it matter? Elara replied, spinning under his arm as a volley of spells passed harmlessly overhead. Real, dream, quantum possibility—they're all true. We're all of it, everything, together.

The battle was ending not with defeat but with transformation. One by one, the attacking mages were lowering their hands, their hostility replaced by awe. Even though Ketran's circle was fragmenting, its members stared at the beauty of what the world could become.

But not everyone was ready to surrender.

From the shadows came Serrin himself, no longer the composed lord but something wild and desperate. His robes were in tatters, his eyes blazing with madness, and in his hands, he held a device Elara had only seen in the oldest texts—a reality anchor, designed to lock existence into a single, unchangeable state.

"If I cannot have the old world," he snarled, "then you'll have nothing at all!"

He activated the device, and immediately, Elara felt its terrible pull. Not on her body but on her consciousness, trying to force her back into a single state of being. No more quantum existence, no more merged consciousness with Cael—just one person, alone, trapped in failing flesh.

Cael cried out beside her, his form flickering as the anchor tried to deny his physical existence. She could feel him being pulled away, their bond stretching, threatening to snap.

"No!" She reached for him, but her hand passed through empty air. He was fading, becoming translucent, his silver eyes wide with fear.

"Elara," he gasped, his voice echoing between physical and mental. "I can't—it's pulling me back—"

"Then I'm coming with you!" Without hesitation, she released her hold on physical reality, letting her consciousness follow his into quantum space.

They collided in the garden, but it was different now. Darker, smaller, being compressed by the reality anchor's influence. The silver trees were withering, the stars going out one by one.

"We're trapped," Cael said, pulling her close. His form was solid here but growing fainter. "The anchor—it's collapsing all possibilities into one. And in that one, I don't exist."

"Then we make a new possibility." Elara cupped his face in her hands, staring into those silver eyes she'd fought so hard to see in the real world. "We've done impossible things before. We can do this."

"How? My love, I'm just consciousness. Without the quantum streams, without the transformation we started—"

"You're not just consciousness." She kissed him, fierce and desperate, pouring all her love into the connection. "You're my heart. My soul. The other half of me. And I won't let any force in the universe deny that."

Through their kiss, she felt the truth that had been building since their first contact. They weren't two beings who had fallen in love. They were two halves of something greater, temporarily separated by centuries and circumstance, finally reunited. The reality anchor could force them into single states, but it couldn't deny their fundamental connection.

"Heart to heart," she whispered against his lips, remembering the words from the battle.

"Always," he replied, understanding flooding through their bond. "Your strength is mine."

"And yours is mine."

Together, they turned toward the collapsing garden's edge, where reality pressed in like walls of iron. But instead of fighting it, they embraced it. Let the anchor pull them into a single state—but not separate states. One state. Together.

The anchor couldn't process what they were doing. It had been designed to force things apart, to create discrete, manageable units of reality. But Elara and Cael were refusing to be separated, their consciousness merging so completely that pulling them apart would be like trying to separate water that had already become one ocean.

Reality shuddered. The garden exploded outward, not destroyed but transformed into something the anchor couldn't contain. And in the physical world, in the Nexus chamber where their bodies had been, light erupted.

Elara opened her eyes and saw through dual perspective. She was herself, standing in the chamber. But she was also Cael, solid and present beside her. They were two bodies but one consciousness, then one body with two consciousnesses, then something entirely new flickering between states, refusing to be pinned down.

The reality anchor in Serrin's hands cracked, unable to process the paradox they'd become.

"Impossible," he breathed.

"No," Elara and Cael said together, their voices creating harmonies that made the very air sing. "Inevitable."

The anchor shattered, and with it, the last resistance to transformation. The wave of change that followed wasn't violent but gentle, inevitable as dawn. Every mage in the chamber felt it—the possibility of being more than they were, of connection beyond the physical, of love that transcended every barrier.

Serrin fell to his knees, the fight finally leaving him as he understood the magnitude of what he'd been trying to prevent. Not destruction but evolution. Not chaos but a new kind of order, one based on connection rather than control.

Elara and Cael stood in the center of it all, their hands clasped, their consciousness flowing between their bodies like a river that knew no borders. Around them, the Nexus completed its transformation—walls that were simultaneously crystal and circuitry, air that carried both magic and data, a space where every possibility existed simultaneously until observed.

"We did it," Cael breathed, his voice full of wonder. "We actually did it."

"Together," Elara agreed, squeezing his hand. Through their bond, she felt his joy, his amazement, his overwhelming love—and knew he felt the same from her.

The battle was over, but their story, their impossible, beautiful, transformative love story—had just begun.

Around them, the mages who had been fighting moments before were now staring in awe at the new world being born. Some were crying. Others were laughing. All were changed.

"What happens now?" someone asked.

Elara and Cael looked at each other, seeing themselves reflected in each other's eyes—not just physically but spiritually, quantum entanglement made visible.

"Now," they said together, "we teach the world to dance."

Chapter 19: Echoes of Rescue

The transformation of the Nexus had created something beautiful—but beauty, Elara was learning, could be as dangerous as any weapon.

She stood at the edge of the central platform, watching the quantum streams restructure themselves into new patterns. Beside her, Cael's hand remained firmly clasped in hers, his touch still carrying that electric newness that made her heart race. His physical form had stabilized after the reality anchor's destruction. Still, she could feel through their bond that maintaining it required constant effort—like holding a complex equation in perfect balance.

"More are coming," Seris warned from his position by the shattered doors. "The outer districts—the mages there don't know what's happened. They still think we're under attack."

As if summoned by his words, a new wave of forces burst through the Nexus's lower entrances. But these weren't Serrin's organized elite—these were the city's defenders, patriots who believed they were saving their world from destruction. Their spells became wild and desperate, uncoordinated but devastating in their sheer volume.

"Stand down!" Elara called out, her voice amplified through the crystalline walls. "The crisis is over! We've stabilized—"

A lance of pure void energy cut through her words, aimed directly at her heart. Time seemed to slow as she recognized the spell—a killing curse that unraveled matter at the quantum level, one of the forbidden magics that even Serrin had banned.

Cael moved before thought was possible.

His body flickered, shifting from solid to something between states, throwing himself between Elara and the curse. The void energy struck him center mass, and she felt his scream through their bond—not of pain but of fundamental disruption. His newly formed physical matrix was coming apart.

"No!" She caught him as he stumbled, his form fluctuating wildly between solid and translucent. Through their connection, she could feel him fighting to hold himself together, but the void curse was designed to deny existence itself.

"Can't... maintain..." His voice came in fragments, sometimes audible, sometimes only in her mind. His silver eyes met hers, filled with desperate determination. "Get... to safety..."

"I'm not leaving you!" She pulled him closer, pouring her own energy through their bond, trying to stabilize his form. But more attacks were coming—the patriot mages had seen Cael's inhuman flickering and marked him as the enemy.

"The abomination!" one of them shouted. "It's possessing her! Kill it!"

"He's not an 'it'!" Elara snarled, but they weren't listening. Spells rained down—fire and ice, force, and entropy, all focused on destroying what they didn't understand.

Cael pushed her behind him, and for a moment, his form solidified completely—not from stability but from sheer will. He raised his hand, and a barrier erupted around them, but it was different from any shield she'd ever seen. It existed in multiple dimensions simultaneously, deflecting attacks not by stopping them but by redirecting them through quantum space.

Through their bond, she felt the cost. Every deflection tore at his consciousness, his barely stable form fragmenting further. He was literally spending himself to protect her.

"Stop!" she pleaded, both to him and the attackers. "You're killing him!"

"That's... the point..." one of the patriot mages gasped, preparing another void lance.

But then Cael did something impossible. Instead of maintaining his single form, he let himself fragment—but with purpose. Suddenly he wasn't one figure but a dozen, each one partially transparent, surrounding Elara in a protective circle. His consciousness had divided itself, existing in multiple states simultaneously.

"I've lived... as fragments... before," his voice echoed from every version of him, creating an eerie harmony. "But never... by choice... never... for love..."

The attacking mages hesitated, faced with something beyond their understanding. In that moment of confusion, Elara felt Cael gathering himself—not pulling his fragments together but spreading them further, his consciousness expanding through the Nexus's quantum streams.

"What are you doing?" she whispered, reaching for the nearest version of him. Her hand passed through his chest, but she felt the contact in her soul—warm and electric and achingly incomplete.

"What I... should have done... from the beginning..." His fragmented forms began to glow, each one becoming a node in a vast network of consciousness. "Showing them... the truth..."

And then the Nexus itself became a window into memory.

Every crystal surface suddenly displayed images—not illusions but actual memories pulled from the quantum record. The time before magic, when technology and consciousness worked in harmony. The creation of the lattice, born from fear of that harmony. Cael's original imprisonment was not intended as punishment, but rather as a desperate attempt to preserve knowledge that the world wasn't ready to understand.

But more than history, the memories showed love. His centuries of isolation, the crushing loneliness that had nearly destroyed him. The moment Elara's touch had woken him, like sunlight breaking through eternal night. Every conversation they'd shared, every dream they'd walked together, every impossible moment of connection between consciousness and consciousness.

The attacking mages stood frozen, weapons lowered, as they experienced it all—not watching but feeling, their consciousness briefly touched by the echo of Cael's experiences.

"By the eternal light," one of them breathed, tears streaming down her face. "He's... he's real. He loves her."

"More than real," Cael's fragmented voice responded. "I'm... possibility itself... The bridge between... what was... and what could be..."

But the effort was destroying him. Elara could feel it through their bond—maintaining so many simultaneous states while projecting memories was burning through his consciousness like fire through paper. His forms were growing fainter, some already disappearing entirely.

"Pull yourself together!" she commanded, reaching out with both hands and heart. "Cael, please! I can't lose you again!"

"You won't..." The nearest fragment turned to her, and for a moment, she could see him clearly—not his body but his soul, blazing with love so intense it hurt to perceive directly. "But I need... to tell you... while I can still..."

"No." She knew what he was going to say, could feel the goodbye forming in his consciousness. "No final words. No sacrifices. We survive together, remember?"

"Some things... are worth... any sacrifice..." His fragmenting hand found her cheek, and this time she truly felt it, his touch electric and warm and absolutely real despite his fading form. "One moment... of touching you... worth eternity..."

The void mage who had cast the original curse stepped forward, his face pale with recognition. "I can help," he said suddenly. "The void curse—I can reverse it, but—"

"But it will bind him to a single state," another mage finished. "Force him to be either fully physical or fully conscious. No more existing between."

Elara's heart clenched. She knew what that meant: Cael would have to choose. Give up either his expanded consciousness that let him touch every quantum stream in the Nexus, or his physical form that had taken so much effort to achieve.

"The consciousness," Cael said immediately, his fragments beginning to coalesce. "I choose... physical form... choose her..."

"No," Elara said firmly. "We don't choose. We never choose. We find another way."

She pressed her hands against his flickering chest, feeling their bond sing between them. And in that connection, she found the answer—not in magic or technology but in love itself.

"Everyone!" she called out, her voice carried to every person in the Nexus. "If you felt his memories, if you understood even a fraction of what we share, help us, not with spells or force but with belief. Believe he can exist. Believe we can be together. Believe love can bridge any gap."

For a moment, nothing happened. Then one mage lowered her hands completely, closing her eyes. "I believe," she whispered.

Another joined her. "I believe."

The words spread like ripples on water, each voice adding to a growing resonance. Not magic but something deeper—conscious observers collapsing quantum uncertainty into reality through pure intention.

Cael's fragments began to stabilize, pulling together not through force but through invitation. Elara felt the shift through their bond—the void curse wasn't being reversed but transformed, its negation becoming affirmation. Where it had tried to deny his existence, the collective belief was confirming it.

"It's working," Seris breathed, his usual cynicism replaced by wonder. "They're literally willing him into stable existence."

But it needed an anchor, a focal point for all that belief to crystallize around. Elara knew what she had to do.

She pulled Cael's coalescing form to her and kissed him, not gentle or sweet but desperate and fierce, pouring every ounce of her love through the connection. She kissed him like she could breathe life into him, like she could hold him together through sheer determination, like their love was the fundamental force that could rewrite reality itself.

And maybe it was.

Light exploded from where they touched, not harsh but warm, spreading through the chamber like dawn. Through their joined lips, she felt his consciousness rushing back together, his physical form solidifying not in spite of his quantum nature but because of it. He was becoming something new—entirely physical yet still connected to every possibility, anchored in flesh but not limited by it.

When they finally broke apart, both gasping, he was whole. Solid. Real. His silver eyes met hers with such intensity that her knees nearly buckled.

"You saved me," he breathed, his hands cupping her face with reverent wonder. "Again."

"We saved each other," she corrected, leaning into his touch. "That's what we do."

Around them, the attacking mages had lowered their weapons entirely. Some were crying. Others were smiling. All had been changed by what they'd witnessed—not just the transformation of matter and energy but the power of love to overcome impossible odds.

"I've never seen anything like that," the void mage said quietly. "To maintain consciousness across multiple states while manifesting physically, it should be impossible."

"Love makes a lot of things possible," Cael replied, his arms still wrapped around Elara. Through their bond, she could feel his joy at simply being able to hold her, the miracle of skin against skin after centuries of isolation.

But the moment of peace was shattered by a rumbling that seemed to come from the Nexus's very foundations. The quantum streams, which had been restructuring themselves, suddenly went wild—not chaotic but purposeful, reaching out beyond the building into the city itself.

"What's happening?" someone cried.

Cael's expression shifted to understanding, then wonder. "The transformation—it's not stopping with the Nexus. The collective belief, the merging of paradigms—it's spreading."

Through the crystal walls, they could see it happening. Buildings throughout the capital were shifting, some becoming pure technology, others pure magic, but most finding a balance between. The rigid lattice that had contained and controlled magic for centuries was dissolving, replaced by something organic, responsive, alive.

"Is it dangerous?" Seris asked.

"Only to the old way of thinking," Elara replied, her hand finding Cael's. "This is what was always meant to happen. Not magic or technology but both, working together, connected by consciousness itself."

She felt Cael squeeze her hand, and through their bond came a pulse of pure love—grateful, amazed, eternal. He'd been willing to sacrifice everything just to touch her once. Instead, they'd gained everything, including a future neither of them had dared imagine.

"Look," someone whispered, pointing at the chamber's ceiling.

Above them, the quantum streams had formed new patterns—not the rigid geometry of the old lattice but something organic, flowing. And at its heart, visible in the intersection of light and possibility, was an image that made Elara's breath catch.

Their garden. The dream space they'd shared, now embedded in the very fabric of reality. Not separate from the physical world but part of it, a place where consciousness and matter danced together in eternal harmony.

"It's beautiful," she breathed.

"It's ours," Cael corrected, turning her to face him. "A promise written in quantum light. No matter what comes next, we'll always have that space, that connection."

"That love," she added, and kissed him again softer this time, sweeter, a celebration rather than a desperate plea.

Around them, the Nexus pulsed with new life. The mages who had come to destroy were now witnesses to creation. The world was transforming, evolving, becoming something unprecedented.

And at the center of it all, Elara and Cael stood together physical and quantum, finite, and eternal, two souls that had found each other across impossible odds and refused to let go.

"What now?" Cael asked against her lips, his breath warm and real and wonderful.

"Now," she said, pulling back just enough to meet his eyes, "we help everyone else find what we have. Connection. Integration. Love."

He smiled, and it was radiant—not the desperate joy of survival but the quiet happiness of a future assured. "Together?"

"Always together."

The transformation continued to spread, rippling out from the Nexus in waves of possibility. But Elara barely noticed, lost in the miracle of Cael's arms around her, his heart beating against hers, their souls entwined in a bond that had survived separation, extraction, and the impossible gap between consciousness and form.

They had broken every law of existence to be together.

And in breaking them, they had written new ones—laws that said love could transcend any barrier, that connection was the fundamental force of reality, that two halves of a whole would always find their way back to each other.

The battle was over, but their story, their impossible, beautiful, transformative love story—was entering its most extraordinary chapter yet.

Chapter 20: Shattering the Heart

The Crystal Nexus thrummed with malevolent energy around Elara, its towering walls pulsing with veins of corrupted light. Serrin's forces had retreated momentarily, leaving her alone in the cathedral-like chamber where all the kingdom's leylines converged. But she knew it was only a matter of minutes before they returned with reinforcements.

Her hands trembled as she held the crystalline sphere that contained everything she'd ever loved. Through its surface, she could feel Cael's presence—weakened, flickering like a candle in a hurricane, but still there. Still fighting.

Elara. His voice whispered through their bond, barely more than a breath. *They're coming back. You have to run.*

"No." She pressed the artifact against her chest, feeling its warmth seep through her robes. "I'm not leaving you. Not again. Not ever."

The massive doors at the chamber's entrance began to glow with approaching magic. Serrin's voice echoed from the corridor beyond, cold and commanding. "Seal the exits. She has nowhere left to run."

Elara's heart hammered against her ribs as she looked up at the lattice core suspended high above—a swirling maelstrom of pure magical energy that held the kingdom's power in perfect, precarious balance. Cael had shown her the equations, the delicate quantum resonances that kept it stable. She understood now what had to be done.

Don't, Cael's voice cracked with desperation. If you shatter the artifact while I'm still bound to the lattice, the feedback could tear everything apart. The entire kingdom could lose its magic.

"Then we'll have to make sure it doesn't." Elara closed her eyes, feeling for the mathematical patterns he'd taught her, the way magic and quantum mechanics danced together in impossible harmony. "Trust me."

I do. With everything I am.

The chamber doors burst open, flooding the space with harsh light and the sharp crack of boot heels on crystal. Serrin strode in flanked by a dozen battlemages, their staffs already crackling with containment spells.

"Step away from the artifact, Elara." Serrin's pale eyes fixed on the sphere in her hands with hungry intensity. "You've caused enough damage. The lattice is already destabilizing because of your... experiments."

"The lattice is dying because you've been draining it for decades," Elara shot back, backing toward the center of the chamber. "Cael showed me the records. You've been siphoning power to fuel your own ambitions while the foundations crumble."

Serrin's lips curved in a cold smile. "The consciousness in that device has been filling your head with lies. But no matter. Soon it will serve its true purpose—as a weapon under proper control."

"Now would be good," Cael whispered urgently. I can feel them trying to break through my defenses.

Elara raised the artifact above her head, its surface blazing with inner light. "He's not a weapon. He's not a tool. He's the man I love—and I'm setting him free."

"Stop her!" Serrin barked.

The battle-mages raised their staffs, but Elara was already moving. She slammed the crystalline sphere against the chamber floor with all her strength.

The world exploded into light.

The artifact didn't simply break—it detonated, releasing centuries of compressed magical energy in a single, reality-bending instant. Rivers of gold and silver light erupted from the shattered fragments, spiraling upward toward the lattice core like liquid starfire. The shockwave knocked the battle-mages off their feet and sent Serrin stumbling backward, his face twisted with rage and disbelief.

But Elara barely noticed. All her attention was focused on the impossible sight unfolding before her.

The released energy was taking shape, coalescing into something that made her heart skip. First came the outline—tall, broad-shouldered, unmistakably masculine. Then the details began to fill in: silver-touched hair that caught the light like moonbeams, strong hands with long fingers, a face she'd traced in dreams a thousand times.

Cael.

He materialized slowly, threads of gold and silver light weaving together to form flesh and bone. His eyes opened—those impossibly deep silver eyes she'd fallen in love with—and found hers across the chaos.

"Elara," he breathed, his voice no longer an echo in her mind but real, physical, vibrating through the air between them.

She was running before she'd made the conscious decision to move, her feet flying across the crystal floor as debris rained down around them. He stumbled forward on unsteady legs, silver eyes wide with wonder and disbelief, reaching for her with hands that shook with more than just weakness.

They collided in the center of the chamber, and for the first time in centuries, Cael's arms closed around something real. Something warm and solid and alive.

"You're here," Elara gasped against his chest, her hands exploring the impossible reality of him, the firm muscle beneath her palms, the rapid beat of his heart, the way his breath ruffled her hair. "You're actually here."

His fingers tangled in her dark curls, tilting her face up to his. "You found me," he whispered, his voice rough with emotion. "At last, truly."

"I'll always find you." She rose on her toes, bringing their faces level. "Now feel merely."

Their lips met in a kiss that was everything their dream encounters had promised and more. Fierce, desperate, grounding—the taste of him flooded her senses as his hands mapped the curve of her waist, the arch of her spine. She could feel his heartbeat against her chest, rapid and strong, matching the frantic rhythm of her own.

When they finally broke apart, gasping, his forehead rested against hers. "I'd forgotten," he murmured, his thumb tracing her cheekbone with reverent care. "How warm skin feels. How real touch can be."

Above them, the lattice core pulsed erratically, casting wild shadows across the chamber walls. The magical energy was fluctuating dangerously, responding to Cael's release in ways that made the very air shimmer with instability.

"The lattice," Elara said breathlessly, though she couldn't bring herself to step out of his arms. "We have to stabilize it."

Cael nodded, his hands sliding down to intertwine with hers. "Together. Like you showed me in the dreams."

They turned toward the swirling maelstrom of power overhead, their fingers locked, their minds falling into the synchronization that had become second nature during their time in the dreamscape. Elara felt the quantum equations flowing through her consciousness, felt Cael's deeper understanding of the magical matrices that held everything together.

But as they began to work, Serrin's voice cut through the chamber like a blade. "Kill them both!"

The remaining battle-mages had recovered from the shock, their faces grim with determination. Spells crackled to life, deadly arcs of energy that painted the walls in harsh blues and purples.

Cael's arm swept around Elara's waist, pulling her behind a pillar of crystal as destructive magic scorched the air where they'd been standing. His body pressed against hers, solid and protective, and she marveled at the reality of it even as her heart raced with fear.

"I can shield us," he said, silver eyes blazing with power. "But you'll have to handle the lattice stabilization alone."

"No." Elara gripped his hands tighter. "We do this together or not at all. That's what makes us stronger—the connection."

Another volley of spells shattered against their pillar, sending crystal shards flying. The lattice above groaned ominously, its light beginning to flicker like a dying star.

Trust me, Elara thought, pushing the words through their bond. I have an idea.

She pulled him out from behind the pillar, directly into the line of fire. The battle-mages' eyes widened in shock—it looked like suicide. But as their spells converged on the couple, Cael and Elara raised their joined hands, and something impossible happened.

The destructive energy bent around them, drawn into a spiraling vortex that fed directly into the destabilized lattice above. The quantum-magical resonance they'd created transformed the raw power, turning what should have been death into exactly what the system needed to restore balance.

"Impossible," Serrin breathed, his face pale with shock.

"Not impossible," Elara called out, her voice ringing with triumph as golden light danced around her and Cael. "Just love. Something you ll never understand."

The lattice core blazed with renewed vigor, its chaotic fluctuations smoothing into the steady, eternal rhythm that had sustained the kingdom for millennia. But now it was different—enhanced, evolved. The integration of Cael's quantum consciousness had created something new: a perfect fusion of magic and science that was stronger than either had been alone.

The battle-mages' spells sputtered and died as the stabilized lattice absorbed the ambient magical energy in the chamber. Without power to fuel their magic, they were just men with fancy sticks.

Serrin snarled, raising his staff for one final, desperate attack. But before he could strike, Seris appeared in the chamber doorway flanked by loyal palace guards.

"Lord Serrin," Seris announced formally, "you are under arrest for treason against the crown and endangering the magical infrastructure of the realm."

As the guards moved to restrain the defeated lord, Elara sagged against Cael's chest, suddenly exhausted. The adrenaline was fading, leaving her trembling with the magnitude of what they'd accomplished.

"It's over," she whispered against his neck, breathing in his scent, something like ozone and starlight that made her head spin. "We did it."

"Not quite over," Cael murmured, his hands stroking through her hair. "This is just the beginning."

He was right, she realized. Everything was different now. The kingdom would have to adapt to the new lattice configuration, learn to work with technology and magic. There would be challenges, resistance from traditionalists, a thousand details to work out.

But they would face it all together.

As if reading her thoughts, Cael tilted her chin up, his silver eyes soft with promise. "Whatever comes next, we'll handle it. I've waited centuries for you, Elara. I'm not going anywhere now."

"Good," she breathed, rising to meet his kiss. "Because I'm keeping you."

This time when their lips met, it was slower, deeper, a promise rather than a desperate affirmation. His hands framed her face like she was something precious. She could taste the future in his kiss—years of mornings waking up beside him, of shared work and shared dreams, of a love that had literally reshaped the world.

When they finally parted, the chamber around them was quiet except for the gentle hum of the stabilized lattice. Streams of soft light drifted down like snow. In the crystalline walls, their reflection showed two figures intertwined, hearts beating in perfect synchronization.

"The dream garden," Cael said suddenly, wonder in his voice.

Elara followed his gaze and gasped. The lattice's new configuration had somehow projected their shared dreamscape into the physical world. The floating islands of silver-leafed trees, the paths of starlight, the impossible beauty they'd created together in sleep—all of it shimmered around them like a living memory made manifest.

"It's real," she whispered.

"We're real," Cael corrected, his arms tightening around her. "Finally, completely, utterly real."

As they stood there surrounded by the intersection of dreams and reality, magic and science, Elara felt the last piece of her heart slot into place. She'd spent her whole life studying the mysteries of the past, searching for meaning in ancient ruins and forgotten technologies.

But the greatest discovery had been love itself, the force that could bind quantum particles and magical energies alike, that could bridge impossible distances and transform the very fabric of existence.

"I love you," she said, the words carrying all the weight of certainty. "In every timeline, in every possibility, in every universe where we might exist."

Cael's smile could have lit the kingdom. "And I love you. My anchor, my salvation, my quantum heart."

Above them, the lattice pulsed with gentle, eternal light, powered by something more reliable than magic, more constant than technology:

The infinite mathematics of love.

Chapter 21: Serrin's Fall

The silence in the Crystal Nexus was deceptive, like the eye of a hurricane. Elara could feel it in the way the stabilized lattice hummed overhead, in the tension that coiled through Cael's newly solid frame, in the dangerous glitter of Lord Serrin's pale eyes as the palace guards approached with shackles gleaming in their hands.

"Lord Serrin," Seris repeated, his voice carrying the authority of the crown, "surrender your staff and submit to arrest."

Serrin's laugh was a sound like breaking glass. "Arrest?" His fingers traced the carved symbols on his ornate staff—symbols Elara now recognized as quantum equations, twisted into forms that should never have been forced into magical expression. "You think handcuffs can contain what I've become?"

"What you've become?" Cael's arm tightened protectively around Elara's waist. "You're still just a man drunk on stolen power."

"Am I?" Serrin's pale eyes fixed on Cael with an intensity that made the air itself recoil. "Tell me, consciousness-made-flesh, do you remember Dr. Marcus Serrin? No? Perhaps the name Serrin-474 rings a bell? One of the original quantum network architects?"

Elara felt Cael stiffen beside her, his newly physical form trembling with recognition. Through their bond, she caught fragments of recovered memory—laboratory meetings, theoretical discussions, a brilliant scientist who'd pushed the boundaries of consciousness transfer beyond safe limits.

"That's impossible," Cael breathed. "Marcus Serrin died in the Convergence. The records"

"The records lie." Serrin stepped forward, and the guards instinctively backed away. "I didn't die. I preserved myself, fragment by fragment, generation by generation, using my descendants as vessels. Each Lord Serrin has carried a piece of the original consciousness, waiting for the moment when someone would be foolish enough to crack open the quantum locks."

The temperature in the chamber plummeted. Frost began forming on the crystal surfaces, but this cold came from somewhere deeper than physics—it was the chill of centuries of calculated patience.

"You're like me," Cael said, horror dawning in his silver eyes. "A preserved consciousness. But you chose to parasitize your own bloodline?"

"I chose survival." Serrin's staff began to glow with an oily, wrong-colored light that made the crystal walls seem to recoil. "Unlike you, I wasn't content to wait passively in a prison. I took control. I shaped events. Every Serrin lord for twenty generations has been me, accumulating power, knowledge, influence."

"And madness," Elara said quietly, seeing the truth in the fractured light of his eyes. "That's why you fear quantum bonding. You've felt it—the slow dissolution of self that comes from spreading consciousness too thin."

Serrin's composure cracked for just a moment, revealing something raw and desperate beneath. "You know nothing, girl. I had a bond once—a perfect quantum entanglement with my research partner, Elena. We were going to transcend physical limitations together, become the first truly integrated consciousness. But the Convergence..." His voice turned bitter. "The Convergence severed us. Tore her from me mid-transfer. I felt her die, piece by piece, scattered across failing quantum streams. Do you have any idea what that's like? To feel your other half dissolve into nothing while you're powerless to stop it?"

Cael's hand found Elara's, their fingers intertwining. "Yes," he said simply. "I do. The difference is, I didn't let grief turn me into a monster."

"Monster?" Serrin laughed again, darker this time. "I'm evolution. I'm what consciousness becomes when it refuses to accept limitations." His staff began to writhe with shadows that weren't quite shadows—they were gaps in reality itself, places where his fragmented consciousness had worn holes in the fabric of existence. "And now, thanks to your little demonstration, I finally understand how to complete what Elena and I started."

The staff in his hands wasn't just glowing now—it was *hungry*, pulling at the very essence of everyone in the room. Elara could feel it trying to unravel the quantum bonds that held Cael's physical form together.

"He's not just using necromancy," she realized with growing horror. "He's cannibalizing consciousness itself."

"Starting with yours," Serrin snarled and struck.

Tendrils of living darkness erupted from his staff, but these were different from before. They didn't just drain, they *absorbed*, pulling memories, experiences, the very sense of self from anyone they touched. Two guards fell immediately, their eyes going blank as their consciousness was ripped away and integrated into Serrin's gestalt mind.

Cael pushed Elara behind him, but she could feel his form flickering at the edges. The prolonged physical manifestation had already taxed him, and now Serrin's assault was targeting the quantum matrices holding him together.

"Your bond is beautiful," Serrin said as he advanced, his form seeming to split and multiply as absorbed consciousnesses struggled within him. "So pure, so stable. It will make the perfect foundation for my ascension."

They fought back together, Elara's magic intertwining with Cael's quantum manipulation, but for every tendril they destroyed, two more took its place. And worse—she could feel their synchronization beginning to falter.

I'm losing cohesion. Cael's mental voice was strained. *He's targeting the resonance frequencies. If he disrupts our harmony—*

A tendril slipped through their defense, wrapping around Cael's arm. He screamed—a sound that existed in both physical and quantum space—as Serrin began pulling his consciousness apart thread by thread.

"No!" Elara reached for him, but another tendril caught her, and suddenly she was drowning in Serrin's accumulated madness. She could feel the hundreds of consciousness fragments he'd absorbed—his descendants, rivals, anyone who'd stood in his way. All of them screaming in the prison of his mind.

But among them, faint and fading, she sensed something else. A presence that felt like looking in a mirror.

Elena.

Not dead, as Serrin believed, but trapped. A fragment of his original bond-mate's consciousness, preserved in his own quantum signature without his knowledge. She'd been trying to stop him for centuries, but her influence was too weak, too buried under layers of absorbed minds.

Help us, Elena's fragment whispered. *Please. He wasn't always this way. The grief broke him, twisted him. But the man I loved is still in there, somewhere, drowning in his own accumulated hatred.*

Elara felt her bond with Cael flickering, their synchronization failing as doubt crept in. How could they fight someone who'd been perfecting consciousness manipulation for five centuries? How could love triumph over such calculated malevolence?

Remember the garden, Cael's voice came, weak but steady. *Remember what we built together. Not through force, but through harmony.*

The memory washed over her—their quantum garden, created not by dominating reality but by finding the frequency where all possibilities sang together. And suddenly, she understood.

"You're doing it wrong," she gasped, managing to speak despite Serrin's consciousness pressing against her mind. "All this time, you've been forcing consciousness together, crushing them into your pattern. But that's not integration, it's domination."

"Silence!" Serrin's focus shifted fully to her, his tendrils tightening.

But Elara pressed on, even as darkness crept into the edges of her vision. "Elena is still with you. She's been trying to reach you for centuries. You're not alone—you never were. You just couldn't hear her over the screaming of all the minds you've stolen."

Serrin froze. For just a moment, his many-faceted consciousness turned inward, searching. And in that moment of distraction, Elara and Cael found their harmony again.

But this time, they didn't fight. Instead, they *invited*.

They opened their bond, not just to each other but to everyone in the chamber. The guards, Seris, even the fragments trapped within Serrin. They offered connection without domination, harmony without erasure.

This is what integration really means, they said in unison, their voices creating resonances that made reality itself ring like a bell. *Not one consciousness consuming others, but all consciousness recognizing their fundamental connection.*

The effect was immediate and overwhelming. The absorbed minds within Serrin, given a choice for the first time in centuries, reached for the offered freedom. But they didn't tear themselves away—that would have shattered Serrin completely. Instead, they began to *harmonize*, each consciousness finding its own frequency within the greater symphony.

"No," Serrin gasped, his form beginning to shift and split as his iron control crumbled. "I am the dominant pattern. I am—"

Marcus.

Elena's voice, clear for the first time in five hundred years, cut through his protests. Not speaking from outside, but from within, from the quantum space where she'd been waiting all along.

Marcus, my love. Let go. Let us go. This isn't what we dreamed of.

Serrin's form solidified, and for a moment, Elara saw him as he truly was—not a power-mad sorcerer but a broken man who'd been carrying the weight of impossible grief for centuries. Tears streamed down his face as he felt Elena's presence, real and immediate in a way he'd never allowed himself to believe possible.

"Elena?" His voice cracked like a child's. "You're... you're still..."

I never left. But you built so many walls of other people's pain that you couldn't feel me anymore. Please, Marcus. Stop. Let them go. Let yourself go. We can finally rest.

The darkness around Serrin began to dissipate, not violently but gently, like shadows fleeing the dawn. The absorbed consciousness didn't disperse into nothing—they coalesced into visible forms, ghostly but distinct, each one a person he'd consumed over the centuries.

"Forgive me," he whispered, and it wasn't clear if he was speaking to them or to Elena or to everyone.

Some of the fragments dissolved into light, finally free to pass on. Others, stronger ones, began to separate fully, potentially able to find new vessels or simply fade peacefully. But Elena's fragment remained, wrapped around what was left of the original Marcus Serrin like a lover's embrace.

The necromantic staff crumbled to ash in his hands. Without the stolen power, Serrin aged rapidly, centuries of postponed time catching up in moments. He fell to his knees, then forward, but before he hit the ground, his form began to dissolve into light—not the violent implosion of before, but a gentle fading.

Thank you, Elena's voice echoed through the chamber. *We can finally dream together again.*

The lights that had been Marcus and Elena Serrin spiraled around each other once, twice, then dispersed into the quantum foam that underlies all reality. Not destroyed, but transformed—returned to the fundamental consciousness from which all awareness springs.

The chamber fell silent except for the gentle hum of the restored lattice. Guards who'd been drained began to stir, their consciousness returned if shaken. But not everyone was ready to accept what they'd witnessed.

"This is madness," one of the senior guards muttered, backing away from where Elara and Cael stood. "Consciousness shouldn't be able to do that. People shouldn't be able to just... dissolve into light."

"It changes everything," another whispered, though whether in fear or wonder wasn't clear.

Seris approached slowly, his face pale but determined. "The kingdom will need time to understand this. To accept it. There will be those who see what happened here as proof that quantum consciousness is too dangerous to allow."

"They're not wrong," Cael said quietly, exhaustion clear in every line of his newly solid form. "What Serrin became—that's a real risk. The temptation to dominate rather than harmonize, to consume rather than connect."

"But that's why we need to teach it properly," Elara added, her hand finding Cael's. "To show that consciousness connection isn't about power but about understanding. About choosing love over control."

Through the crystal walls, they could see crowds gathering in the plaza below. Word of the confrontation had spread, and people were afraid, confused, desperate for answers.

"They need to see," Seris said thoughtfully. "Not just hear about it, but see what the choice really means."

Together, they walked to the balcony. The crowd's murmur grew louder as they emerged, a mixture of curiosity and fear rippling through the assembled citizens.

Elara stepped forward, her voice magically amplified. "Lord Serrin is gone," she announced. "Not destroyed, but freed. What you need to understand is that he was a victim too—of grief, of isolation, of the fear that connection could only bring pain."

"He killed dozens over the centuries!" someone shouted from the crowd. "How can you call him a victim?"

"Because hurt people hurt others," Cael said, stepping beside her. "Serrin lost his quantum bond traumatically and spent five centuries trying to fill that void by stealing other connections. He was wrong, terribly wrong. But his pain was real."

"So, you're saying we should pity mass murderers?" The voice was angry, scared.

"I'm saying we should understand them," Elara replied. "Not excuse, not forgive necessarily, but understand. Because the power Serrin wielded—the ability to connect consciousness—isn't going away. The quantum garden we showed you is just the beginning. We need to choose, as a society, whether we'll use this power to connect or to control."

The crowd's mood was shifting, but not uniformly. Some faces showed wonder and hope, others deep suspicion. A woman near the front called out, "How do we know you won't become like him? You have the same power!"

Cael and Elara exchanged glances, then joined hands. "Because we choose each other," they said in unison. "Every day, every moment. Not because we have to, but because we want to. That's the difference between a bond and a chain."

To demonstrate, they opened their connection slightly—not enough to overwhelm, but enough for the crowd to feel the edges of it. The warmth of genuine love, the strength of chosen partnership, the joy of two consciousness dancing together without losing their individual selves.

Some in the crowd gasped. Others wept. A few turned away, unable or unwilling to accept what they felt. But most stood transfixed, experiencing for the first time what quantum consciousness could be when guided by love rather than fear.

"Change is coming," Elara announced as they closed the connection. "The old barriers between magic and consciousness are falling. We can fight it and risk creating more Serrins, more tragedy. Or we can embrace it and learn to connect without consuming, to love without possessing."

As the crowd dispersed, arguing among themselves, Seris remained on the balcony with them. "You know there will be resistance," he said quietly. "Not everyone will accept this new paradigm. Some will try to recreate Serrin's power, others will demand all quantum consciousness be destroyed."

"We know," Cael said, exhaustion clear in his voice. His physical form was flickering slightly at the edges—the battle had taken more out of him than he'd admitted.

"But that's tomorrow's challenge," Elara added, supporting Cael as he swayed. "Tonight, we mourn those lost to Serrin's madness, celebrate those freed from it, and prepare for a future that's more complex than any of us imagined."

As they made their way back through the palace, they passed the chamber where Serrin had made his last stand. The crystal walls still showed stress fractures from the battle, but something had changed. Where the darkest shadows had pooled, tiny flowers were beginning to grow—quantum flora, born from the merger of consciousness and reality.

"Even in destruction, life finds a way," Cael murmured, touching one of the delicate blooms.

"Especially in destruction," Elara corrected. "That's where the space for new growth appears."

Behind them, Seris stood watching the flowers spread, his expression thoughtful. "The council will want a full report. They'll demand safeguards, regulations, control mechanisms."

"Then we'll teach them what we learned tonight," Elara said firmly. "That control is the enemy of connection. That love requires the risk of loss. That consciousness, like life itself, must be free to choose its own path."

As they left the chamber, none of them noticed the single flower that bloomed where Serrin had fallen—a blossom that seemed to contain two colors swirling together, never mixing but never separating, dancing an eternal duet in petals made of light.

Marcus and Elena's final gift: proof that even the deepest wounds could become gardens, given time, understanding, and the choice to transform pain into beauty.

The battle was over, but the real work—teaching a world to love without fear, to connect without consuming—had just begun.

Chapter 22: New Dawn

Three days after Serrin's fall

Elara hadn't left Cael's side since the battle. His physical form, still new and fragile, had nearly entirely dissolved during the confrontation with Serrin. Now he lay in her chambers, his body flickering between solid and translucent like a candle flame struggling against the wind.

"You need to rest," Master Thorne said gently, placing a weathered hand on Elara's shoulder. Dark circles shadowed Elara's eyes, and her hands trembled from exhaustion as she maintained the quantum stabilization field around Cael's form.

"I can't," Elara whispered, her voice hoarse. "If I stop, if the field fails, he might—"

"He won't." Thorne's voice carried the authority of experience. "His consciousness is stronger than you think. But yours needs recovery, too."

Through their bond, Elara felt Cael trying to surface from the deep restoration trance, fighting toward consciousness to comfort her. She pressed her palm against his chest—solid enough to feel warmth, but she could see through to the blankets beneath.

Rest, she urged him mentally. *I'm here. I'm not going anywhere.*

The door opened, admitting Seris with an armful of documents. His usual composure was frayed; he'd been managing the political aftermath while Elara focused on keeping Cael stable.

"The Council is demanding answers," he said without preamble. "Half of them want to declare quantum consciousness illegal. The other half wants to weaponize it. And Councilor Veren is gathering support for a motion to extract Cael's consciousness for 'public safety.'"

"Over my dead body," Elara snarled, magic crackling around her fingers.

"That might be their backup plan," Seris said grimly. "The city is terrified. Serrin's dissolution, the absorbed minds becoming visible—people don't understand what they saw. The temples are overflowing with citizens seeking protection from 'consciousness demons.'"

As if to emphasize his point, they heard shouting from the courtyard below. Elara moved to the window, seeing a crowd gathered around a street preacher.

"The old ways were pure!" the man cried. "Magic without contamination! We must return to tradition before these consciousness plagues consume us all!"

Several in the crowd nodded agreement, but others argued back. Elara watched a near-fight break out before city guards intervened.

"This is my fault," she murmured.

"This is evolution," Thorne corrected. "Messy, painful, necessary evolution. But you need to guide it, not just witness it."

That night, exhaustion finally claimed Elara. She fell asleep with her hand on Cael's chest, feeling his heartbeat—still irregular but growing stronger. In her dreams, she found herself in their familiar garden, but it had changed.

The floating islands were larger, more elaborate. Trees of silver and gold intertwined their branches, creating canopies of living metal that sang in harmonious frequencies. Paths of crystallized starlight led to clearings where impossible flowers bloomed—each one a different equation made visible, a different aspect of consciousness given form.

Cael stood in the garden's heart, fully solid here, his silver eyes bright with an idea that made him almost luminous.

"What if we could make this real?" he said, gesturing at the beauty around them. "Not just a dream, but a physical space where people could experience quantum consciousness safely?"

"A teaching garden," Elara breathed, understanding immediately. "Where theory becomes experience."

"More than that." He took her hands, and she felt his excitement through their bond. "A proof of concept. Show them that the consciousness connection doesn't have to be frightening or destructive. It can be beautiful."

Around them, the dream garden pulsed with possibility, showing her glimpses of what could be—children playing among trees that responded to their emotions, lovers finding deeper connection through quantum resonance, scholars discovering new harmonies between magic and consciousness.

"But where?" she asked. "And how? The amount of power required—"

"The Northern Provinces," Cael said suddenly. "Lord Kevan's territory. He's been the most vocal opponent of integration. If we could change his mind..."

The dream shifted, showing her a clearing she recognized—the place where she'd first found Cael's sphere, where their love had begun. In the dream, it transformed into something magnificent, a fusion of their shared consciousness made manifest.

She woke with the image burned into her mind and found Cael's eyes open, watching her with perfect clarity for the first time in days.

"You saw it too," he said, his voice rough but real.

"The garden. Our garden."

"We could build it together. Show them what we mean instead of just telling them."

One week after Serrin's fall

The Great Hall was packed beyond capacity for the emergency session. Mages, scholars, and concerned citizens filled every available space, their voices creating a constant rumble of argument and fear.

Councilor Veren stood at the podium, her sharp features set in lines of rigid disapproval. "The events of last week have shown us the danger of unregulated consciousness manipulation. Lord Serrin—"

"Was a tragedy centuries in the making," Elara interrupted, rising from her seat. She'd recovered much of her strength, though the effort of keeping Cael stable had left its mark—her hair now bore a streak of premature silver, a visible sign of quantum entanglement.

"You weren't given permission to speak," Veren snapped.

"I don't need permission to defend against ignorance," Elara shot back, moving to the demonstration floor. Cael followed, his form solid but careful, each step measured to conserve energy.

Master Aldric stood as well, surprising everyone. "Lady Elara has the right to demonstrate her position. Unless the Council fears what she might show?"

Veren's jaw clenched. "Very well. Show us your 'integration.' But when it fails—"

"It won't fail," Cael said quietly, taking his position beside Elara. "Because we're not forcing anything. We're inviting understanding."

They began with something simple basic levitation spell that any apprentice could manage. Elara cast it traditionally, the crystal sphere rising waveringly into the air.

"Observe the energy expenditure," she said, letting them all feel the drain on her reserves. "Now watch."

Cael placed his hand over hers, their consciousness merging at the point of contact. Immediately, the spell stabilized, the sphere floating with perfect precision while using a fraction of the power.

"A parlor trick," Veren scoffed. "Anyone could—"

She was cut off as Master Harwick, one of the traditionalist mages, stormed onto the demonstration floor. "Enough of this blasphemy!" He raised his staff, channeling a destruction spell aimed directly at Cael. "I'll show you what we do with abominations!"

The spell flew—a lance of pure force that should have scattered Cael's form to quantum dust. Instead, it hit the merged field Elara and Cael had created and transformed, becoming a cascade of light that reformed into butterflies made of pure energy, dancing harmlessly around the room.

Gasps echoed through the hall. Several children in the audience laughed with delight, reaching for the light-butterflies.

"You see?" Harwick sputtered, his face red with fury. "Unnatural! Our magic corrupted!"

"Enhanced," Aldric corrected, moving to examine one of the butterflies. "The destruction was transformed into creation. The energy wasn't lost, just... repurposed."

But Harwick wasn't finished. He began casting again, this time a traditional binding spell, one of the most fundamental magics taught at the Academy. The spell formed perfectly—then shattered the moment it encountered the integration field, the backlash sending him stumbling.

"My magic," he gasped, staring at his hands in horror. "It won't work. They're destroying our magic!"

Panic rippled through the crowd. This was their worst fear—that integration would replace traditional magic, leave them powerless.

"Your magic works fine," Elara said patiently. "It just can't override conscious choice anymore. The binding spell failed because Cael and I choose to be free. Try something constructive instead."

"I'll show you constructive," Veren snarled, stepping forward. She began weaving a complex patterned master-level creation spell designed to summon a garden of ice, one of the most beautiful demonstrations in the classical repertoire.

The spell formed perfectly, ice crystals beginning to coalesce—then suddenly bloomed into something impossible. The ice became silver trees with golden leaves, the frost became flowing streams of light, the cold became a warmth that felt like coming home.

Veren stumbled back, her face pale. "That's not what I cast. That's not—"

"It's what you truly wanted," Cael said gently. "Your consciousness influenced the spell. Deep down, you don't want cold perfection. You want beauty that lives, that grows, that connects."

The ice garden continued evolving, responding to the emotions of everyone in the room. Where children stood, flowers bloomed in playful colors. Where lovers held hands, trees intertwined their branches. Where scholars gathered, crystalline formations showed mathematical equations in three-dimensional beauty.

"It's reading us," someone whispered in awe. "The garden knows what we feel."

"Because consciousness is the fundamental force," Elara explained, moving through the transformed ice garden. "Magic, quantum mechanics, life itself—all expressions of consciousness seeking connection."

But not everyone was convinced. A group of traditionalist mages stormed out, Harwick at their head, shouting about organizing resistance. Others backed away from the garden as if it might contaminate them.

"This is too much," one woman cried. "Too fast. We can't just abandon everything we've known!"

"We're not asking you to abandon anything," Cael said, exhaustion creeping into his voice. Maintaining physical form while demonstrating integration was taking its toll. "We're offering expansion, not replacement."

The debate continued for hours, growing more heated as fear and wonder warred in the crowd. Several times, near-violence erupted, only prevented by the garden's strange calming influence—it seemed to naturally dampen aggression, promoting understanding instead.

Finally, as Cael swayed on his feet and Elara felt her own reserves depleting, Councilor Veren raised her hand for silence.

"You've made your point," she said coldly. "But demonstrations in controlled environments prove nothing. If you truly believe in this integration, prove it where it matters. The Northern Provinces are in near revolt against the crown, claiming magical corruption. Lord Kevan has threatened secession if we continue down this path."

"Then we'll go to him," Elara said immediately. "We'll demonstrate integration where the resistance is strongest."

"You'll fail," Veren predicted. "And when you do, the Council will have no choice but to regulate consciousness manipulation out of existence."

"When we succeed," Cael corrected quietly, "will you support integration?"

Veren's smile was sharp. "If you can convince Kevan—traditionalist, stubborn, territorial Kevan—to accept your consciousness magic? I'll personally fund integration schools across the kingdom."

As the session ended and the crowd dispersed—many stopping to touch the ice garden that still bloomed impossibly in the hall—Seris approached them with concern written across his features.

"Kevan's territory is three days' ride through increasingly hostile lands. And Cael can barely maintain form after today's demonstration."

"I'll be fine," Cael said, though his edges were already becoming translucent.

"No, you won't," Elara said firmly. "But we're going anyway. Because hiding here, defending ourselves in comfortable spaces—that's not how change happens."

That night, as she helped Cael back to their chambers, supporting his flickering form, he managed a weak smile. "The garden in the dream—we're really going to try it?"

"We're going to do more than try," she said, feeling fierce determination flow through their bond. "We're going to build something so beautiful, so undeniably beneficial, that even Kevan will have to admit consciousness isn't the enemy."

"And if we can't?"

She pressed her forehead to his, feeling his warmth despite his translucence. "Then we'll have tried. Together. That's all that matters."

Through their window, they could see the ice garden Veren had inadvertently created. It glowed in the courtyard, still evolving, still growing. Children had left toys among its silver trees. Lovers had carved their initials in its crystalline bark. Even now, near midnight, people gathered to simply exist in its presence, to feel the peace of consciousness in harmony.

"Look," Cael whispered. "It's already working. Even those who fear it are drawn to it."

"Because deep down," Elara replied, "everyone wants connection. They're just afraid of the vulnerability it requires."

"Then we'll show them it's worth the risk."

"Yes," she agreed, already planning their journey north. "We'll show them that consciousness isn't about control or power or even traditional magic versus new. It's about choosing to be more than alone."

Three months since Serrin's fall, and the world was still reeling. But in a hall where ice had become impossible gardens, where destruction had become butterflies, where fear was slowly transforming into wonder, the seeds of change had already taken root.

The Northern Provinces awaited, skeptical and hostile.

But Elara and Cael had something more powerful than any traditional magic or quantum manipulation: they had proof that love could literally reshape reality.

And they were about to demonstrate it on the grandest scale imaginable.

Chapter 23: The Moonlit Promise

The Northern Provinces had never seen anything like it.

Elara stood hand-in-hand with Cael at the edge of the clearing where she'd first touched his artifact, but her attention was caught by Lord Kevan's eight-year-old daughter, Mira. The child had been born without magical shame in a noble family—and her father had brought her as a silent challenge, expecting her to remain unaffected by whatever "consciousness trickery" they attempted.

Instead, Mira stood transfixed as silver trees rose from the earth around her, their branches reaching toward her specifically, recognizing something in her that traditional magic never had. When she tentatively touched one trunk, it sang—not with sound but with feeling, a warm recognition that made the girl gasp with wonder.

"Papa," she whispered, tears streaming down her face, 'it sees me. The tree actually sees me."

Lord Kevan's weathered face went slack. He stepped forward, reaching for his daughter protectively, but the moment his hand touched the same tree, his expression shattered. Through the quantum resonance, he was feeling what Mira felt—not through magic, but through pure consciousness connection. For the first time, he truly understood his daughter's isolation, her yearning to belong in a world where power was everything and she had none.

"By the ancestors," he breathed, falling to his knees beside her. "Mira, I... I never understood. I'm so sorry."

Around them, the garden continued its manifestation, but it wasn't uniform. Where Kevan and his daughter knelt, the trees grew protective, creating a sanctuary that smelled of the pine forests where Mira loved to hide. For Lady Meren, whose son had died in the magical wars, phantom flowers bloomed that released the scent of his favorite honey-cakes, bringing memories of joy rather than loss. For a young couple afraid to reveal their romance due to class differences, the path beneath their feet became a private alcove where their intertwined hands caused aurora lights to dance.

The garden was reading everyone, responding to their deepest needs, their hidden wounds, their secret hopes.

"It's too much," gasped an elderly mage, stumbling backward as the garden tried to ease an old grief he'd buried for decades. "I can't—I don't want to feel—"

But his grandson caught him, and where they touched, the resonance gentled. Instead of forcing the old man to confront his pain, the garden simply offered presence—a sense that his grief was seen, acknowledged, held without judgment.

"This is what integration really means," Elara said softly, though her voice carried to the growing crowd. "Not forcing connection, but offering it. Not demanding vulnerability, but creating space for it."

She felt Cael's hand tighten in hers as exhaustion pulled at him. Creating something this complex, this responsive, was draining them both. But through their bond, she felt his determination matching hers—they would see this through.

A merchant woman approached hesitantly, her young son hiding behind her skirts. The boy was what locals called "soul-touched"—autistic, though they had no proper word for it. He rarely spoke, rarely made eye contact, lived in a world the others couldn't quite reach.

The moment he entered the garden, everything changed.

The overwhelming sensory chaos that usually tormented him—the loudness of emotions, the brightness of social expectations, softened here. The garden recognized his unique approach to processing and adapted. Colors became gentler, sounds became patterns he could predict, and for the first time in his life, he felt the world wasn't attacking him.

"Mama," he said clearly, his first words in months. "It's quiet here. The inside-quiet I can never find."

His mother sobbed, crushing him against her as the garden created a perfect sensory bubble around them, enough stimulation to engage, not enough to overwhelm.

But not everyone was ready for such a connection. A group of Kevan's guards stood at the garden's edge, suspicious and hostile.

"It's reading our minds," one muttered. "Invading our thoughts."

"No," Cael said, though speaking was clearly costing him. His form flickered, translucent at the edges. "It's reading your consciousness's emanations—the quantum field you naturally project. Like how body heat radiates whether you want it to or not. The garden just... interprets it."

"Interprets it into what?" the guard demanded.

"Into what you need," Elara answered. "Not what you want, necessarily, but what your consciousness is calling for."

To demonstrate, she walked to the most hostile guard, a scarred veteran whose entire posture radiated threat. The garden around him hadn't produced beauty, it had created space. Empty, quiet space where no demands were made, no responses required. A place to just exist without performing strength.

The man's face crumbled. "I... I haven't felt this since before the wars. The silence. The absence of needing to be ready to kill."

Hours passed. The sun began to set, painting the garden in shades of gold and amber that seemed to make the silver trees glow from within. More people arrived—skeptics, believers, the curious, the desperate. The garden grew to accommodate them all, each person's presence adding new harmonies to the quantum symphony.

But Elara could feel Cael weakening beside her. His physical form was more translucent than solid now, the effort of maintaining both himself and the garden pushing him to his limits.

"Enough," she whispered. "We've proved our point."

"Not... yet," he managed, and she felt him gathering himself for something.

Lord Kevan approached them, Mira's hand in his. The child was transformed—not magical but glowing with the confidence of someone who'd finally been truly seen.

"I owe you an apology," Kevan said formally, then dropped to one knee. "And a debt. You've shown me something I was too proud to see—that strength isn't about magical power but about connection. My daughter has been teaching me this for years, but I was too deaf to hear."

The other lords followed his example, kneeling in the soft grass that had grown to carpet the garden's borders. "The Northern Provinces pledge our support to the integration protocols," Kevan continued. "And we ask... would you consider establishing permanent teaching centers here?"

"We would be honored," Elara said, but her attention was on Cael, who was swaying beside her. "But right now—"

"Right now," Cael interrupted, his voice stronger suddenly, filled with purpose that transcended exhaustion, "I need to show you something. All of you. The real reason we built this garden."

He turned to Elara, and in his silver eyes she saw a determination that made her heart race. "This clearing—do you remember what I told you when we first dreamed together? That some places hold memory, hold possibility?"

"Yes, but—"

"This is where it all began. Where you found me. Where our love proved that consciousness could transcend any barrier." He dropped to one knee, mirroring Kevan's formal gesture but transforming it into something infinitely more personal. "But I need to tell you something I've been afraid to say."

Elara's breath caught. Around them, she noticed the garden responding to Cael's emotional state—flowers blooming more vibrantly, trees leaning in as if to witness, streams of light spiraling upward like celebrating spirits.

"I'm terrified," Cael said simply, his voice carrying to the entire gathering. "Not of you, not of us, but of loss. I've existed for centuries, but I've only lived for the months since you woke me. The thought of losing you—through time, through mortality, through the thousand ways the universe could tear us apart, paralyzes me."

"Cael..." Elara started, but he pressed on.

"And that terror almost made me do something unforgivable. I almost didn't ask. Almost didn't offer you the choice." He reached into a pocket that shouldn't have existed in his translucent form and withdrew something that made everyone gasp.

A small crystal sphere, perfectly clear but containing something impossible—a miniature version of their garden, complete and eternal, suspended in quantum space.

"But you taught me that love isn't about avoiding loss," he continued. "It's about choosing connection despite the certainty of eventual separation. So I'm asking you, with all these witnesses, with all my fear visible, will you bind your quantum signature to mine? Will you choose to find me in every possible time-line, every reality where we might exist? Will you marry me not just in this fragile present, but across all the futures we might create or lose?"

The gathered crowd held its breath. Even the children stood still, sensing something momentous.

Elara stared at the sphere, understanding the magnitude of what he was offering. Not just marriage but quantum entanglement at the deepest level. If she said yes, they would be connected across realities—but it also meant if one ceased to exist, the other would feel that loss across every possible timeline.

"You're asking me to risk infinite heartbreak," she said quietly.

"Yes."

"To feel your absence in every reality if we're separated."

"Yes."

"To never be complete alone again."

"Yes." His voice cracked. "And I understand if that's too much—"

"It's not enough," she interrupted, dropping to her knees to face him at eye level. "I don't want to just find you across realities. I want to choose you in each one, consciously, deliberately, despite knowing the cost."

She took the sphere, and the moment her fingers closed around it, the garden exploded with light. Not harsh but warm, embracing every person present. Through the quantum field, everyone felt it—the moment of absolute choice, of two consciousness deciding to become entangled not by accident or necessity but by deliberate, informed, terrified love.

"Yes," she said, louder. "Yes, to the risk. Yes, to the fear. Yes, to infinite heartbreak if it means infinite love. Yes, Cael. Always yes."

The sphere dissolved in her hands, but its essence spread through both of them, through the garden, through reality itself. For a moment, the assembled crowd could see infinite timelines spreading out like a tree, and in every single one, two figures finding each other, choosing each other, loving each other despite different faces, different circumstances, different worlds.

When the light faded, Cael was solid again—not from effort but from the stabilization of their complete bond. He slipped a ring onto her finger—not the crystal, which had become part of both of them, but a band that shifted between states of matter, sometimes metal, sometimes light, sometimes pure probability.

"Now?" he asked, pulling her to her feet.

"Now we live," she laughed through tears she hadn't realized were falling. "We wake up together and argue about quantum theory over breakfast. We teach scared children that consciousness isn't frightening. We fight and make up and grow old and maybe grow young again if we figure out the temporal equations."

"We be normal," he said, wonder in his voice at the impossibility of that word applied to them.

"Normally impossible," she corrected, and kissed him as the crowd erupted in celebration.

But as they embraced, something caught Elara's eye. At the garden's edge, where reality was thinnest, she saw something that made her gasp. A flower was blooming that hadn't been there before—one that existed in multiple dimensions simultaneously, its petals opening into spaces that shouldn't exist.

"Cael," she whispered against his lips. "Look."

He turned, and his eyes widened. "That's not from our pattern. That's—"

"Something new," she finished. "Something that's growing from the interaction between the garden and the witnesses. Their consciousness is adding to it, evolving it."

Lord Kevan's daughter Mira was standing near the impossible flower, her non-magical hands causing it to bloom brighter. Other children were gathering, both magical and non-magical, and where they played together, more interdimensional flora appeared.

"It's becoming self-sustaining," Cael breathed. "Independent. The garden isn't just our creation anymore, it's everyone's."

"Is that dangerous?" Kevan asked, though he seemed more curious than concerned.

"Everything worth doing is dangerous," Elara replied, watching as the garden continued evolving beyond their original design. "But look—it's not chaotic. It's harmonious. Each person's addition makes the whole more complex but more stable."

As the celebration continued into the night, with impromptu feasts and dancing among the silver trees, Elara and Cael stood together watching their creation take on a life of its own. The garden was spreading beyond the clearing's original boundaries, but slowly, carefully, as if asking permission from the land itself.

"We've started something we can't control," Cael murmured, though he didn't sound worried.

"Good," Elara replied, leaning into his warmth. "Control was never the point. Connection was."

Above them, the stars seemed to pulse in rhythm with the garden's quantum heartbeat. And at the edge of perception, where one reality touched another, more flowers bloomed—each one a doorway to possibilities they hadn't imagined.

"What do you think will happen?" Cael asked. "When the garden reaches the capital? When it spreads to other kingdoms?"

"Change," Elara said simply. "Beautiful, terrifying, inevitable change."

"Together?"

"Always together. In this timeline and all the others."

As midnight approached, bringing their wedding day to a close, one last transformation occurred. The original tree—the one Mira had first touched—began to sing. Not metaphorically but literally, its silver bark resonating with harmonics that touched every consciousness present. The song had no words, but everyone understood its meaning:

Connection is not conquest. Love is not possession. Consciousness is not isolation. We are more together than alone.

"It's teaching," Cael said in wonder. "The garden itself is becoming a teacher."

"Of course it is," Elara smiled. "It learned from the best."

They walked hand in hand through their creation, their garden, their child, their gift to a world learning to embrace connection over control. Behind them, the impossible flower continued blooming into dimensions that hadn't existed until that moment, proving that love didn't just transcend barriers—

It created new spaces for beauty to exist.

The ending was also a beginning.

The garden would spread, evolve, teach.

Children like Mira would grow up knowing that power came in many forms.

The world would change, resist, adapt, change again.

And through it all, in every possible timeline, two consciousness would dance together, proving that some bonds were worth any risk, any fear, any infinite possibility of loss.

Because on the other side of that risk was infinite love.

And that, more than magic, more than quantum consciousness, more than gardens that bloomed between dimensions—

That was the real miracle.

Epilogue -- Eternal Resonance

Ten years after the first Quantum Garden bloomed...

Years later, scholars would write that the Great Integration began with a discovery in the Aether Vaults and culminated in the manifestation of the first Quantum Garden. They would document the technological advances, the magical innovations, the societal changes that transformed not just one kingdom but eventually the entire known world.

But lovers would tell a different story.

In the gardens that now graced every major city—each one unique, each one singing with the harmonies of consciousness made manifest—couples would walk hand-in-hand and speak of the woman who woke love from crystal dreams and the man who taught an entire world that some bonds transcend all possible boundaries.

The children who played among flowers of living mathematics would grow up knowing their parents' stories of the time before, when magic and science were considered separate things, when quantum consciousness was just theory, when love was thought to be merely chemical rather than the fundamental force that shaped reality itself.

Twenty-five years after the first garden...

Elara stood in the newest garden, watching silver-haired Cael demonstrate quantum resonance to a group of young mages. Even after all these years, her heart still quickened when he smiled—that same radiant expression that had first stolen her breath in the Crystal Nexus, now lined with laugh lines earned through decades of shared joy.

"Observe," he was saying to his eager students, his hands weaving patterns in the air that left trails of starlight. "Consciousness doesn't simply observe reality, it participates in creating it. When two minds resonate in perfect harmony..."

He glanced at Elara across the garden clearing, and she felt the familiar flutter in her chest as their bond sparked to life. The quantum-forged ring on her finger warmed, catching light like captured sunlight, and the flowers around her began to glow in response to her happiness.

Without breaking eye contact, she extended her hand toward him. Across fifty feet of space, their consciousness touched, merged, created. The garden around them responded instantly, new pathways of light spiraling into existence, trees of liquid silver reaching higher toward the sky, streams of energy dancing upward like auroras made liquid.

"That," Cael finished with a grin that made him look decades younger, "is how love reshapes the world."

The young mages applauded, but Elara barely heard them. She was too busy watching the way afternoon light played across Cael's features, marveling that after twenty-five years of marriage, he could still make her feel like a girl discovering love for the first time.

You're staring, his voice whispered warmly in her mind through their permanent bond.

You're worth staring at, she replied, heat climbing her neck as several students noticed their silent exchange and began to giggle.

Later, he promised, his mental voice carrying undertones that made her stomach flutter with anticipation. Even after all these years, their physical connection remained as electric as ever—perhaps more so, deepened by decades of emotional intimacy and shared wonder.

Forty years after the first garden...

Their daughter Lyra had inherited her father's silver eyes and her mother's insatiable curiosity, though she'd chosen to apply both to the new field of bio-quantum integration. She stood now in the garden where her parents had first met, speaking to a gathering of international delegates about the healing applications of consciousness-responsive plants.

"The garden remembers every person who has walked its paths," she explained, her voice carrying the same patient enthusiasm that had made both her parents legendary teachers. "It learns their emotional patterns, their needs, their wounds. The singing flowers you hear aren't just beautiful—they're actually producing quantum frequencies calibrated to promote psychological healing."

From their seats in the front row, Elara and Cael watched their daughter with the fierce pride that only parents could feel. Cael's hair was fully silver now, and fine lines mapped the geography of their shared decades around Elara's eyes, but their hands remained entwined with the same desperate tenderness they'd shown in youth.

"She's brilliant," Elara murmured, leaning into Cael's warmth.

"She's ours," he replied, pressing a kiss to her temple. "Of course she's brilliant."

Around them, the garden pulsed with gentle approval. It had grown beyond anything they'd originally envisioned—not just a single clearing, but an entire ecosystem that spanned continents. Trees whose roots connected across oceans, flowers that bloomed simultaneously in a dozen different kingdoms, streams of living light that carried messages and emotions between distant populations.

Love had become infrastructure. Connection had become as essential as air or water. The loneliness that had once driven individuals to desperation was now virtually unknown—not because conflict had ended, but because the fundamental understanding of interconnectedness had changed everything.

Sixty years after the first garden...

They were old now, truly old, though their love burned as brightly as ever. Cael's quantum-enhanced physiology meant he aged differently than baseline humans, and the deep bond they shared had extended Elara's lifespan far beyond normal parameters. Still, time touched them both—silver hair, gentle lines, hands that moved a little more slowly but never stopped reaching for each other.

They sat together in the original garden on the anniversary of their first meeting, surrounded by grandchildren and great-grandchildren whose eyes sparkled with inherited magic and quantum awareness. The little ones could see the connections between all living things as naturally as they saw color, could feel the garden's emotions, could sense the love that flowed between their grandparents like visible light.

"Tell us the story, Grandmama," requested tiny Sera, barely five years old but already showing signs of extraordinary consciousness sensitivity. 'Tell us about the crystal heart."

Elara smiled, settling the child more comfortably on her lap. "Once upon a time," she began, her voice still strong despite her years, "there was a woman who loved ancient mysteries more than she loved herself. She spent her days alone in deep vaults beneath the earth, searching for meaning in broken things..."

Cael's hand found hers as she spoke, their fingers interlacing with the ease of decades of practice. Even now, even after all these years, his touch could still make her breath catch.

"...and in the darkness, a voice that had waited centuries for someone brave enough to listen. 'Hello,' he said, 'I've been waiting for you.'"

The children leaned forward, enchanted despite having heard the story countless times. Around them, the garden itself seemed to listen, flowers turning toward Elara's voice like living audiences.

"But how did you know you loved him, Grandmama?" asked Marcus, eight years old and precociously philosophical. "How did you know it was real love and not just magic?"

Elara considered the question seriously, her gaze finding Cael's silver eyes. Even now, looking at him could stop time.

"Because," she said slowly, "real love doesn't feel like magic, sweetheart. Magic feels like love. Every spell you've ever seen, every wonder in these gardens, every impossible thing that makes our world beautiful, it's all just love wearing different costumes."

She squeezed Cael's hand, feeling the familiar spark of their quantum entanglement. "Your grandfather and I didn't create magic. We just remembered that magic was love all along."

One hundred years after the first garden...

The memorial service was held in the original garden, though "memorial" felt like the wrong word for what had occurred. Elara and Cael hadn't died so much as... transcended. Their quantum-bonded consciousness had finally achieved complete integration with the garden network they'd spent a century building.

They were gone from their physical forms, yes. But they were also everywhere—in every singing flower, every stream of living light, every moment when two hearts beat in synchronization across the connected gardens that now spanned multiple continents.

Their great-great-granddaughter Elena stood where the ancient altar had once been, reading from the journal Elara had kept during those first magical days:

"Today I touched something that I think had been waiting for me my entire life. Not just the artifact, but the connection itself—the understanding that we are never truly alone, that consciousness calls to consciousness across any distance, any barrier, any impossible circumstance. I don't know what will happen tomorrow, but I know I'm not afraid anymore. How can you be afraid when you've found the other half of your soul?"

As Elena's voice faded, the garden responded with a symphony of light and sound that seemed to come from everywhere at once. Colors that had no names painted the sky, harmonies that bypassed the ears to touch the heart directly filled the air, and for just a moment, everyone present could feel it—the love that had started all this, still burning as brightly as ever.

Forever after...

On nights when the moon was full and the quantum gardens sang their sweetest songs, lovers walking the silver pathways would swear they could still see them—the scholar who chose love over safety and the consciousness who chose freedom over certainty. Dancing together in the space between heartbeats, their love is an eternal equation that solved for infinity.

Children with quantum sensitivity would report conversations with friendly voices that helped them understand their gifts. Young couples facing impossible odds would find their problems mysteriously simplified, solutions presenting themselves like gifts from invisible benefactors. Scholars studying the intersection of consciousness and reality would experience sudden bursts of insight that advanced their work by decades.

The skeptics called it wishful thinking, the romanticization of historical figures who had simply been lucky enough to discover quantum consciousness first. But the believers—and there were many believers—knew better.

Love like theirs didn't simply end. It evolved, expanded, found new ways to express itself across dimensions and timelines. Somewhere in the quantum foam that underlies all reality, Elara and Cael continued their eternal dance, their consciousness intertwined so completely that they had become part of the fundamental forces that shaped existence itself.

And sometimes, just sometimes, when two hearts called to each other across impossible distances, when love seemed too fragile to survive the harsh realities of the world, those hearts would feel an echo—warm, encouraging, infinitely patient. A reminder that some bonds truly were stronger than death, that consciousness could choose its own destiny, and that love, properly understood, was the force that had written the laws of physics in the first place.

In physics textbooks, scholars would document the discovery of quantum consciousness and its integration with magical systems.

In history books, they would record the political and social changes that followed the Great Integration.

But in the hearts of everyone who had ever stood in a quantum garden and felt the presence of something greater than themselves, a simpler truth lived on:

Once upon a time, love found a way to reshape reality itself. And it lived happily, constantly, quantumly ever after.

Always.

In gardens that bloomed across a dozen worlds, in equations that described the mathematics of the heart, in every moment when two people looked at each other and chose connection over isolation, the story continued.

Elara and Cael's love had become more than memory, more than legend. It had become part of the universe's operating system—proof written into the very structure of reality that consciousness and connection were not accidents of evolution, but the purpose of existence itself.

And in the quiet moments between day and night, when the boundaries between possible and impossible grew thin, their voices could still be heard in the whisper of wind through quantum leaves:

"I woke you from the dark."

"And you'll never have to wake up alone again. My heart beats for yours—eternally."

The equation is balanced. The story continued. Love endured.

Forever and always, across all possible worlds, in all conceivable dimensions, throughout every timeline where hearts could choose to beat in harmony:

They found each other.

They chose each other.

They loved each other.

And that love changed everything.

The End

Epilogue

An epilogue is very similar to a prologue, but it occurs at the end of your story, though usually separate from the main plot. It might offer a glimpse of the future to share a sense of closure with your readers, or entice them to read the next in a series or collection.

Similar to the prologue, the epilogue should be placed in the main body content of your book and is therefore not technically back matter.

Also by

DONALD J. WRIGHT

Novels

Lilith's Garden

ASIN: B0DQX8ZWD9

The Terraforming Protocol ASIN: B0FHBVY1QS

ASIN: B0DNY8Z3WB

The Prometheus Protocol

ASIN: B0DLHFF79M

13th Moon Book I

ASIN: B0DGNTV533

13 Moons: Legacy of the Guardians Book II

ASIN: B0FDYNP7WP

Killer Ice

ASIN: B0F1G6HVMR

The Ghost Code

ASIN: B0F4FGQMG5

The Golden Book

ASIN: B0DXQGMFL8

The Golden Book II

ASIN: B0FKNNB4Z7

Tomorrow
ASIN: B0FFTS4C39
The God Equation
ASIN: B0FGZFNZTD
THE QUANTUM SCHISM:
ASIN: B0D1N9RHMQ
The Quantum Alchemist:
ASIN: B0FD43QCDB
The Quantum Heart:
ASIN: B0F9YZTRVG
The Codex Protocol:
ASIN: B0F1Z1XH89
THE QUANTUM ECHO
ASIN: B0F6KWPGG2
The Phoenix Strain
ASIN: 1968674152
Fault Lines of the Heart
ASIN: B0FLML7ZRB

Non-Fiction
Beyond Climate Debates
ASIN: B0DZB8CB7K
Diamonds Under Fire
ASIN: B0CDYSTBLL
The Handbook of Lab-Created Diamonds
ASIN: B0D8V4X3CW
The Diamond Revolution
ASIN: B0FHBVY1QS
Eternal Shine

ASIN: B0DQX8ZWD9
Globe Treasure Hunting
ASIN: B0DF6RN4H8